MARKED ANGEL

KEEPERS OF THE LIGHT 3

TAMAR SLOAN

V P ALLASANDER

KEEPER
CHRONICLES

CONTENTS

I

COLT

G ray fog rolls over the floor of Colt's black-walled cell, the bare skin of his back feeling the wetness and cold that permanently seeps from this hellish prison. He suppresses a groan as he cracks his eyes open, rolling his desiccated tongue around his even drier mouth. When was the last time he ate? Drank? He has no idea how long he's been down in this dungeon.

He shifts his weight, his bones aching at the slight movement. Even the faint pain has him reliving the agony-filled torture his master's demons had inflicted on him with relish. It reinforces what Colt learned within days of being thrown in here—the echoes of agony remain in the mind far longer than the physical pain itself.

But he suspects Belphegor knows this.

Colt ignores the groaning of his bones as he rubs his jaw, more pain-stained memories rising in his mind. The archdemon's furious face pressed close as he held Colt's jaw in a punishing grip, screaming that he would make him pay for betraying him. The lashes of fire and whips of ice along his back as the torture continued. The way the agony took his breath away. He couldn't scream even if he wanted to.

Colt pushes to his feet, as if he can escape the memories. His breathing reverberates around the small cell, his only companion

The black room is empty, no bed, no chair, not even a window. He never thought he'd miss the sulfuric scent of Hell or the blazing heat that felt like it burns the very air, but right now, even that's preferable to this.

And the promise of what is to come.

Belphegor was clear. He'd sentenced Colt to eternal imprisonment. A forever filled with nothing but torture.

All because of a single mistake.

Days ago, Belphegor suspected that one of the other Kings of Hell, Asmodeus, was trying to take over one of his castles. He'd needed someone to find out the truth, and if so, which castle. Colt had willingly obeyed his wishes. He'd served his King for centuries, it was what he did. How he proved his honor. He'd snuck into Asmodeus' castle and found a demon willing to spill the details.

Returning to Belphegor, he'd shared everything he'd learned, proud to have pleased his sovereign.

Belphegor had prepared his castle in the third circle of Hell, ready for an attack.

Except Asmodeus attacked the one in the second. Colt's information had been wrong. He'd inadvertently lied to his King.

And now, he's in prison, paying for his error.

Stumbling to the bars that line the only wall not built of stone, Colt resists the urge to shake them. To scream. To do what he's always done when he's trapped or cornered—fight his way out.

Not when the bars will inflict as much pain as Belphegor himself. Within the first day of his imprisonment, Colt had realized they were his only way out. He'd dislocated his shoulder, the pain little more than an ache compared to what he'd just endured, and tried to slip between the iron bars.

The burning pain had been instantaneous. He'd leapt back, hissing as the smell of scorched flesh stung his nostrils. The fresh wave of agony had accompanied an equally painful realization.

There was no escape.

No way out. No one who would try to save him.

He was trapped here for as long as Belphegor's wrath raged, and Colt knew that could be centuries. The archdemon didn't become one of the Kings of Hell by being merciful or forgiving.

Colt staggers backward, fighting the weight of hopelessness. He promised himself Belphegor may break his body, but he'd never fracture his mind. But even now, as his body heals from the latest round of torture, he's not sure he can keep that promise. The thought of doing this, day after day, year after year, decade after decade, century after century...

A soft creaking sound has him straightening, his heart already pounding. Surely Belphegor or his sadistic minions are not back already. They'd need their rest after the pummeling they inflicted only hours ago.

But there's no one on the other side of the bars. In fact, it's the bars themselves that grab Colt's attention.

They're moving. Bending. Arching as if invisible hands are flexing them apart.

Colt watches in amazement, wondering if his mind has, indeed, snapped. What demon would be fool enough to challenge Belphegor by doing this? Any use of magic would have tripped the alarms of the castle, bringing in the guards and their ruthless hellhounds. Colt remains where he is, the cold of the wall behind him prickling his skin.

But no one comes. No guards ready to beat him for somehow tapping into his magic. No red-eyed dogs baying for his blood.

The bars continue to stretch, the high-pitched creaking noise crawling over Colt's nerves. Suddenly, they snap with a resounding crack. He flinches. If the magic doesn't bring the guards down on him, the noise will. Colt wonders if he should fight them when they storm in, or just take the beating. He clenches his fist. Does it really matter? They won't believe that he didn't do this. The punishment will be inevitable.

Yet, the dungeon remains eerily quiet. All that's changed is there's now a man-sized hole in the bars. Colt glances around, but then jolts into action before he can change his mind. There's no time to question how this has happened. He needs to make the most of the fact it has.

He slips through the hole, his shoulders brushing the edges of the bars and singing his flesh. He ignores the burning pain and acrid tendrils of smoke as he breaks into a run down the black corridor. Although his footsteps are silent, his heart is a bass drum in his chest and his breathing rasps over his ears. His body cries out at the sudden use of bruised muscles and barely-healed bones. But Colt doesn't slow down. The slim possibility of freedom infuses him with energy he didn't know he had.

He weaves his way through the maze of dungeons and caverns, his demon sight allowing him to see in this place of perpetual night. He knows his way well seeing as he grew up here. These hellholes were his playground, time alone from the misery above. It's probably why he doesn't come across any guards. He doubts anyone knows of the secret route he's taking apart from Belphegor himself, the man who molded this labyrinth with his own magic. In fact, if they did, the archdemon would make sure it was wiped from their memories.

The trust his King placed in him is Colt's one chance at escape. It was that trust that also fueled Belphegor's fury. The betrayal from his most faithful demon had cut deep, whether it was intentional or not.

As Colt progressively ascends, the air warms and the walls dry out, although it's still stale and sour. No one has been this way in a very long time. It doesn't take long for Colt's muscles to tire, but he ignores it. His time in the dungeon taught him exactly how much pain he can endure, even if it was a lesson he never wanted to learn. He runs for minutes that feel like hours, but he finally reaches the door he's seeking.

Little more than a side entrance that leads to one of the many wastelands of Hell, it's the last hurdle before freedom. Once out there,

Colt can hide in any of the circles of Hell. He'll spend the rest of his life running, but that's preferable to remaining down here.

He waves his hand, glad to see the muting of his magic doesn't work up here like it did in the dungeon, and the door swings toward him. Digging his feet into the cold stone floor, he prepares to run the fastest he has in all his years of existence.

Only to freeze.

A hellhound is crouched on the other side of the door, red eyes flashing and yellowed teeth bared. It launches forward, only to be yanked back by an invisible chain. Something is holding it back. Or someone. Either way, there's no way Colt can pass.

He curses. Of course Belphegor would place hellhounds at each exit. The absence of guards was aimed at lulling him into a false sense of security. Of freedom. It's possible this was nothing but a trick. Another excuse to rain fury on Colt as he has no choice but to endure it.

He takes a cautious step backward, wondering how long he can survive in the labyrinth of darkness. Although the rabid hellhound doesn't move, its growls grow louder as gelatinous saliva drips from its jowls. It thirsts to do what it does best—kill.

"Heel," growls a voice somewhere behind it.

The beast instantly drops to its haunches, its teeth disappearing as its head drops to rest between its paws.

Colt frowns. The voice isn't Belphegor's, but just as powerful. The air is practically rippling with energy. Another archdemon is controlling the hellhound.

A figure appears, a three-pronged crown on his forehead, a large ruby adorning its center.

"Asmodeus," Colt gasps.

COLT'S EYES fly open as he gasps once again. He blinks, even though his surroundings are just as dark as sleep. Was that red ruby why he remembered this now? It was so similar to the gem that someone swapped, stopping the Tear from being closed. Or is the memory assaulting him because once again, he's been imprisoned unjustly by those he allowed himself to care for?

He growls deep in his throat. In the same way Belphegor had believed him guilty of betrayal, so has Gabby. All because he was framed by that video.

Colt struggles against the cold stone containing him. He needs to get to Gabby and explain. He needs to find out who would want to fracture their relationship. He has to tell her that, despite it all, he didn't betray her.

But just like all the other times he's struggled, just like the time he tried to find a way out of Belphegor's prison, it's useless. The stone is hard and unforgiving, forged by the power of betrayal. His body can barely move and he's already rubbed himself raw trying to find a nonexistent weakness. If he screams, the sound batters his eardrums and he doubts it gets beyond the shell holding him immobile.

Weariness overcomes him.

What if he can't get out?

What if he does and Gabby doesn't believe him?

What if she hates him...

Memories of Hell try to crowd in again but Colt fights them off, even as he wonders how long he'll have the energy to do that. Gabby wouldn't know that being trapped with them is the ultimate torture she could inflict on him.

He's stuck in his very own Hell.

He hadn't realized exactly how much Gabby replaced those memories with something far lighter. Something infinitely beautiful.

There's a *crack* so soft that Colt wonders if he imagines it. Except there's a second. Then a third.

A pinprick of light pierces the stone skin wrapping around him, making him squint. His heart stutters into overdrive. Gabby's back! She's releasing him.

A fracture zig-zags across the cold rock covering his face and Colt doesn't waste any time. He headbutts it, excited when it crumbles away. Next, he shakes his shoulders and flexes his arms, freeing his chest. He rips away the chunks around his waist, hips, legs. Within seconds, he's free. Cool air fills his lungs as he adjusts to the light. He twists and turns, looking for Gabby, wanting to tell her. He has the chance to make this right.

But it's not Gabby in the room with him.

"No," he gasps in disbelief.

Asmodeus stares down his aquiline nose, his long goatee brushing his chest. "As a King of Hell, you're the one supposed to be serving *me*, Colt. And yet, here I am, once more saving your demon backside."

Colt stands frozen, the remnants of his stone cage scattered around him. Asmodeus is the last person he expected to free him, and he's not sure what it means.

Surely he's not going to owe another archdemon a favor… And Asmodeus might have a reputation as being more reasonable than Belphegor, but he's also known to be calculated and cold in his dealings. And punishments.

"What do you want from me?" he asks, noting the closed window and door. Neither will stop him if he has to run.

"No need to look like a caged hellhound, Colt," Asmodeus says, adjusting the cuffs on his suit. "If I were angry with you, why would I have freed you from the prison that angel girl trapped you in?"

Colt doesn't have an answer to that question, or any of the others whirling in his mind. "What do you want?" he repeats.

"The same as you," Asmodeus purrs. "The mortal world safe from the weapons coming out of Hell. You know, freeing humanity from drowning in a sea of chaos, death and destruction." He waves a casual hand. "Etcetera, etcetera, etcetera."

"And you expect me to believe that?"

The Kings of Hell don't come to Earth to save anything but their own interests.

"You're smart not to trust me, Colt." Asmodeus lifts his chin, a smile dancing within his carefully manicured beard. "But can you trust Belphegor? What did he tell you? That he wants all the demons here on Earth, living peacefully among humans? And to save them from their blind faith in the angels?"

Colt doesn't answer, even though that's exactly what Belphegor said.

Asmodeus snorts. "Belphegor wants nothing but chaos on earth, my dear demon. He wants the human world to burn to the ground. Why else would he be bringing demon weapons into this world? He knows we will have to fight the angels, ending in war. Of course, that will only lead to one thing—the apocalypse." He takes a step closer, rubble crunching under his leather loafer. "Do you really want that, Colt?"

Right now, all he wants is to make things right with Gabby, but he's not saying that. "And what do you want?" Colt asks, not backing down.

A tight smile spreads across Asmodeus's smooth face. "Smart question, demon. One I've answered before. What happens in the mortal world is none of my concern."

Colt knows exactly what the archdemon is referring to. Sometime in the tenth century, the mortal world witnessed a disturbing religious military conflict in the Middle East. Looking back now, he wonders if it was because of the influence of the obsidian. Hell experienced an influx of tormented human souls dragged into the dark bowels by the reapers. Colt had asked Asmodeus then whether they should do something about it. Asmodeus had used the same dismissive words. "What happens in the mortal world is none of my concern."

Which doesn't explain why the archdemon is here.

"I'm only concerned with the events in our home," Asmodeus continues. "And what's happening there isn't good for anybody, let alone the demons. After Belphegor came out into this world through the Tear, the realms of Hell descended into chaos. Outright battles between the demonic factions broke out. It's become a dangerous place to be Colt, and you know what that means."

"More demons on Earth."

"Exactly. Earth is looking far more palatable to our kind right now. If this continues, only more will come." Asmodeus tugs on his long goatee. "Belphegor doesn't mean well for humankind. I suspect he's trying to find a way to get every demon in Hell out. Once that occurs, the war between angels and demons will be inevitable."

"And humans will be collateral damage," Colt finishes, his gut churning. Yet, Belphegor is a King of Hell, just like Asmodeus. He has as much interest in humans. Something isn't adding up.

"Belphegor wouldn't want that," Colt says. "He likes his demons around him in Hell. How do I know you're not the one lying?"

Asmodeus sighs, almost looking bored. "I'm telling the truth. I want the Tear closed, and I want the demonic weapons that were stolen returned. It's the only way this world will be free of Hell's danger. And I need your help to do that."

Although that's also what Colt wants, he doesn't answer. He has no intention of entering an agreement with Asmodeus. He still has Belphegor to deal with. Aligning himself with another archdemon would be downright foolish. That means he has to think of a way out of here. He doubts Asmodeus is just going to let him go after going to the effort of releasing him.

The demon king sighs again, this time far louder and longer. "Okay, I'll make you a deal," he snaps. "Help me get the weapons back and the Tear closed, and in return, I'll help you find the object that your doppelgänger stole." He lifts his hand as Colt goes to reject the offer. "And when I return to Hell, I'll take Belphegor with me."

Colt would be free of his debt. There would be nothing standing between him and Gabby.

That is, if she's ever going to trust him again.

Although Asmodeus is extending the one way Colt can do that. Closing the Tear will prove to her that's what he was trying to do all along. Being free of Belphegor means no more promises to betray her.

Even if it means working with another King of Hell. One he trusts as much as the first one he was beholden to.

Colt nods sharply. "Very well. I'll do it."

A slow smile spreads across Asmodeus's face as his eyes flare red. "Excellent. I look forward to working together."

Colt keeps his lips tightly shut seeing as he can't say the same thing.

Asmodeus tugs at his sleeves again, gold cufflinks glinting in the low light. "Now, we need to—"

"I have something I need to do first. I'll be in contact."

Colt stalks around Asmodeus, not caring what the archdemon thinks. Tear or no Tear, Belphegor or no Belphegor, something else takes priority.

He needs to speak to Gabby.

2

GABBY

Gabby's hand hesitates on the doorknob of her childhood home. She should be feeling good. No, great.

The Grigori have been imprisoned. As far as she knows, they're all tucked up in a cell somewhere in the Pearl City. Their zealous quest for the obsidian has ended.

And she put them there. Just like the prophecy predicted.

But there's no happy dance inside her. In fact, she's not sure there's anything inside of her. It's as if she's hollow. Empty. Nothing but a vacuum.

Probably because the Tear is still open.

Then there's the secret organization headed by Malcolm who have been hungering for the obsidian for centuries.

And Colt—

Gabby stops herself, although the painful shudder in her chest still takes her breath away. She holds onto the doorknob for a few seconds, trying to find her equilibrium again. She can't think about *him* and what he did to her. It just hurts too much. If that means facing whatever's coming, feeling as if she's been excavated by a pitchfork, then so be it.

She turns the doorknob and enters her house. She'll deal with things one at a time. And first, is her mother.

Gabby stops after the first step. "Mom?" she calls frantically, her worry multiplying exponentially with each rapid beat of her pulse.

The house is in disarray. Shelves are half empty. Books are scattered on the floor. There's a pile of clothes by the door.

"Mom!"

She appears through the doorway to the kitchen, looking frantic. "Gabby!" she half-screams. "Are you okay?"

Gabby stops, confused. "I'm fine." She looks around, realizing there's some semblance of order to the chaos. "I thought we'd been broken into or something."

Her mom's shoulder's sag as her hand comes to rest on her chest. "Don't scare me like that." She wipes the edge of her strawberry apron across her forehead. "I thought we were being attacked again."

Guilt punches Gabby in the gut. The last thing she wants to do is scare her mom after what she's been through. "Sorry, it's just that..." She looks around again, registering the cardboard boxes that she'd missed. Three sit beside the half-empty shelves. Two more beside a toppled pile of books. "Ah, what's going on?"

Her mom straightens her spine. "We're moving, Gabrielle."

"What?"

"You heard me. We can't stay here. It's not safe."

Of all the things Gabby expected to walk into, this wasn't it. "Mom," she starts, her voice soft but guarded. "I know what happened at City Hall freaked you out—"

"Freaked me out?" her mother yelps. "Freaked me out?" This time, it's more of a screech. "I was terrified, Gabby!"

She takes a cautious step forward as if she's suddenly found herself surrounded by landmines. "It was terrifying. But it all worked out."

"It what?"

That time, it was definitely a screech. "We need to talk about it." Not move to Uzbekistan.

Her mother throws her hands in the air. "There's nothing to talk about. First, the ritualistic murders, now this! What if you were hurt, Gabby?" Her face crumples. "I couldn't live with that. You're all I have."

Gabby's heart wrenches painfully. "But I wasn't. And neither were you."

"There were..."

"Angels," she finishes for her. "They were angels."

Her mother takes a wobbly step and crumples onto the couch. "They're nothing like what we've been led to believe. They were so...angry. They wanted to hurt us." She blinks up at Gabby. "They wanted to hurt you."

Gabby rushes to sit next to her. "But they didn't."

Her mom's lower lip trembles. "Because you're also one of them."

"Yes, I am," says Gabby, watching her closely. A little part of her is hoping that the truth being out will be liberating. That her mom will finally understand.

"How?" her mom whispers. "I'm certainly no angel."

Gabby squeezes her hand. "You are in a way," she says warmly, trying to lighten the mood. "You'll do anything to protect those you love."

Her mother frowns. "Now isn't the time for jokes."

Sobering, Gabby suppresses a sigh. "Technically, I'm a half-angel."

"Your father..." her mom breathes. She pulls her hand away and Gabby tries not to frown, unsure what that means. "You've met him."

An uneasy feeling coils in Gabby's gut. "He showed himself to me when I learned the truth."

Her mom shifts until her back hits the armrest of the couch. "He's been close. Possibly for a while."

Gabby doesn't answer, knowing the question is rhetorical. The uneasiness is now churning up acid, making her feel ill. The devastation across her mother's face isn't easy to watch. She's realized the man she's refused to speak badly of for almost twenty years really is a bastard. He's visited Gabby, multiple times, in fact.

And never once stopped by to see the mother of his child.

Burning anger at her father's actions once more flashes through Gabby. The list of why she should resent him is progressively growing.

Her mother pushes to her feet, her hands tightly clasped. "All the more reason to get out of Mercy City," she says adamantly. "There's nothing for us here."

"No," says Gabby, trying to modulate her voice as she also stands. "I can't leave."

"There are plenty of other good colleges, Gabby. You can have a fresh start, away from here."

She's already shaking her head. "No. I don't want to go."

"Because your father is here?"

"Heck no. You're the one who was his personal cheerleader, not me." Her mother winces, and Gabby instantly regrets the words. "I can't go."

"Well you can't stay," her mom snaps right back. "It's too dangerous! You've been at the heart of all this trouble, haven't you?"

Gabby decides it's best not to answer that question.

Her mom huffs with frustration. "Exactly as I thought." But the anger is short-lived. She tucks her hands back in the pocket of her apron, wringing them with enough anxious energy to make it flutter. "Why can't you see this is important to me?"

This time, Gabby has no idea *what* to say. What's keeping her here? The Grigori are gone. There are others focused on protecting the Tear. And as long as the secret organization doesn't get their hands on the parchments, the obsidian should remain hidden. Certainly not—

She determinedly turns her mind away from *him* as she hides her wince.

"Because this is also important," she says quietly. Although this fight has already cost her heart, she can't turn her back on it.

"Why, Gabby? Why does it have to be you?"

Because no one seems to be able to do what she does—wield celestial fire. Oh, and infernal fire at the same time. But she can't tell her mom that. She's not coping with what she's learnt so far.

Gabby's shoulders droop on a sigh. "I want to stay here."

Her mother rears back as if she's been slapped. She strides over to the toppled stack of books and jams them in the box with short, sharp movements. "This conversation is over. We're leaving."

Wiping her hand down her face, Gabby has no idea what to do next. She can't leave Mercy City. But she can't lose her mom, too. She's barely holding herself together as it is.

The door opens behind her and it's with relief that she registers her aunt Sierra entering. Sierra pauses as she glances around, seeing the boxes, her sister packing them without acknowledging her entrance, then Gabby standing helplessly not far away. An it's-worse-than-I-thought expression settles on her face.

"Did I miss something, Shell?" she asks, stopping beside a box and nudging it with her toes.

Gabby's mother holds a book to her chest like a shield. "You knew, didn't you?" she accuses.

Sierra nods, looking both apologetic but stoic. "Yes, I suspected for a while. But it was all confirmed a few months ago."

"And you kept quiet about it? You should've told me!"

"And what would that have achieved?" Sierra asks gently. She glances around the partially packed room. "Leaving Mercy City sooner?"

"No! Yes!" Gabby's mom throws her hands up in exasperation. "I don't know! I would've protected her. We both know how reckless she can be."

Sierra takes a cautious step closer. "She's also saved a lot of lives."

But Gabby's mom is already shaking her head. "Why does it have to be her? Why can't someone else do it?"

"This is what she was born to do, Shell. She stopped the Grigori twice, and now they've been captured and taken to Heaven to serve prison time for the rest of eternity. You should be proud of her."

"Proud?" Gabby's mom demands, horrified. "Proud! She's not a soldier, Sierra. She's barely an adult. She should be studying, making friends, meeting boys. The worst I was hoping to deal with was a few too many parties."

Gabby bites her lip. Her mom just described the perfectly beautiful life she worked so hard to create, in part because that's what her mom wanted for her. She fought losing that, with disastrous consequences. And yes, living with the supernatural is infinitely harder, and admittedly far more dangerous, but as Sierra pointed out, Gabby's stepped up to this as if it's her destiny.

Because it is.

"She tried to be normal," says Sierra, echoing Gabby's

thoughts. "Do you remember those episodes? The one where she attacked a teacher and a student and was suspended?"

Gabby's mom nods warily, her gaze flicking to her daughter.

"That's what happens when Gabby denies her supernatural side," Sierra says, compassion softening her tone. "She denied it with such determination that her angel side would take over when things got dangerous. Now, she's helping save people, not hurting them."

"But Gabby is..." Tears stream down her mother's eyes.

Gabby wants to go to her and hug her, but she knows her mother wouldn't accept the gesture.

"Your daughter. I know. But she's also part angel." Sierra finally covers the distance between them, wrapping an arm around her sister. "And the world is better off because she is."

Gabby's mother's gaze falls on her and she holds her breath. Her aunt's always had a way with her mom. Often, she's the only person she'll listen to. And right now, Gabby really needs her mom to listen. So much has happened, and she can feel there's plenty more to come. If she can't have her blessing, she'd at least like to face it with her mother's understanding.

Her mom sighs. Then steps away from Sierra. And shakes her head. "No. I'm not okay with this. I won't be. You're my daughter. I would never choose for you to throw yourself so blatantly into danger."

Gabby's shoulders sag as her breath huffs out. Stalemate.

Sierra reaches out again. "Shell—"

"No!" she snaps, stepping further away. "Don't try and tell me I'm overreacting. What if it were Ari? Would you want this for her?"

"Want what for me?"

They spin around, three sets of eyes wide with surprise when they realize Arielle just stepped through the front door.

They were either too engrossed in the conversation or Sierra hadn't closed the door properly.

Arielle frowns as she registers the state of the house and the heavy silence. "What's going on?"

Sierra rushes to her daughter. "Ari, I didn't think you'd be home until later."

"Obviously," she says, sidestepping her mother. Her eyes widen as they shoot to Gabby. "What's going on?" she repeats, sounding even more worried.

Gabby's physically and emotionally exhausted brain has no idea how to respond to that question. Arielle doesn't know about the supernatural. And it's best it stays that way. She smiles a little. "It's nothing. We're just—"

"Keeping me in the dark," snaps Arielle, her blue eyes flashing. "What's new?"

"Ari," Gabby implores.

But she storms past, her face twisted with anger. "It's fine. Go back to the academy, Gabby. They're your new family, anyway."

Gabby watches as Arielle runs up the stairs, then winces as she slams the door shut.

Great.

It's not just her mom she's on the cusp of losing.

It's also the girl who's been like a sister to her.

3

GABBY

S ierra's face twists. "She's been missing you," she says, glancing in the direction of Arielle's bedroom door.

Gabby's mom crosses her arms. "Because you've been busy playing angels and demons."

Gabby's jaw hardens. None of this has been fun.

She's about to tell her mom exactly that when Sierra steps into her line of sight. "Why don't you go check on Ari?" she suggests, eyes full of don't-argue-with-me. She turns back to Gabby's mom. "I think we should make some muffins."

She narrows her eyes. "You're trying to distract me."

Sierra walks over and loops her arm through her sister's. "Or I really feel like some muffins."

Knowing that if she stays, she and her mom will just jump back on the pointless-argument horse and get nowhere, Gabby follows Sierra's suggestion. She wants to talk to Ari. The thought she's made her feel forgotten doesn't sit well with her.

Upstairs, Gabby knocks gently. "Ari? Can we talk?"

"Go away!"

Gabby's shoulders droop as she presses her hand against

the door. "Please? You know I don't like you being angry with me."

There's a shuffling sound and then the door cracks open. "Did your mom distract my mom?" she whispers

Blinking in surprise, Gabby nods. "They're making muffins," whispering back even though she's not sure why.

Arielle opens the door a little wider to confirm that Gabby is indeed alone, and then opens it completely. "Fine then," she says a little too loudly as she throws the words toward the stairs. "But don't think this means everything's okay."

She steps back and lets Gabby in, closing the door behind her, then sits on the bed, smiling smugly.

"It was all an act?" Gabby asks, relief rushing through her.

Arielle looks down and picks at a thread on the duvet. "Your mom needs a short circuit sometimes, or she just works herself up into a storm."

Gabby sits on the bed beside her, watching her cousin closely. Her aunt's words that Arielle's felt her absence are still hanging in her mind. "Yeah, she really can."

Arielle glances up, then quickly looks back down again. "What were you talking about?"

"She's worried that college is too much," says Gabby, desperately wishing she could tell Ari the truth. "It's been a tough semester."

"You've certainly been busy," she says, once more focused on the loose thread.

Gabby shuffles closer. "It was so much harder than I expected. I didn't know there'd be so much to...adjust to." She places her hand over Arielle's. "I'm sorry that I didn't reach out more often."

Arielle shrugs a single shoulder, the motion tellingly vulnerable. "Like you said, you had a lot going on."

"But nothing so urgent that I'd want you to think you're not important to me, Ari."

Her cousin's lashes flutter as her gaze meets Gabby. "I know," she says again, although the hurt in her eyes is unmistakable.

"You're more of a sister to me," Gabby says, glad she can be totally honest. "I feel awful that I made you feel like that."

Arielle gives her a tremulous smile. "I only felt like that a little bit. I exaggerated it for Aunt Shell's benefit."

And yet, Sierra, Ari's own mom, thought she was being genuine. Gabby engulfs her cousin in a hug. "Let's go shopping sometime soon. We'll splurge and get those triple-choc banana splits."

Arielle pulls back. "With hot caramel sauce," she adds with a giggle.

"Definitely." Gabby grins, enjoying the sensation. But then she grows serious again. "I really am sorry. No matter how tough college gets, I won't let this happen again."

Her cousin nods, the sadness chased from her eyes. She nudges Gabby with her shoulder, sliding her a glance. "I assumed it was a guy."

Gabby stills as she feels like she was just sucker punched in the gut. She considers denying it, but she's tired of the lying and the secrets. And if things had been different, Ari would've been one of the first people she would've told about Colt. "There was," she says, trying to keep the pain out of her voice. "But it's over now."

Arielle frowns. "What happened? You're not one for flings."

No, it seems Gabby's preference is to fall hard and fast for her sworn enemy. "He betrayed me."

"Oh, Gabby, I'm so sorry."

"And then had the gall to say he's been framed," she spits,

bitterness jostling for room in her chest alongside the overwhelming hurt.

Arielle angles her head. "Is that possible?"

"What?" Gabby asks, blinking. "Multiple people warned me I shouldn't trust him. They all saw this coming."

"Oh, okay." Arielle goes back to picking the thread. "Just checking. You sounded like you were really into him."

Damn her cousin for knowing her so well. "I was," she admits. "But not anymore."

The lie settles between them and Arielle doesn't move, obviously not intending on acknowledging it. She shrugs. "You've always been good at judging people, like a second sense or something. I'd just hate for you to throw something away because of how things looked."

It's Gabby's turn to frown. "I saw the footage with my own eyes."

Arielle smiles as she puts her hands up in surrender. "I'll drop it. And if I ever see him, I'll rip his face off and stomp on it."

Gabby shakes her head with a rueful smile even as she thinks that Ari would have to get past the stone holding Colt captive first. For the first time, guilt filters through the betrayal and pain. As does the knowledge that she acted in haste.

She shoots to her feet. "I'll get over him," she assures Arielle, even as she wonders if she's lying again. The pain feels like it's made a nest in her chest and has no intention of going anywhere. Ever.

Arielle also stands. "Cool. But I'm here if you need to talk."

Gabby clasps her in another hug, moisture stinging her eyes. She's essentially ignored her cousin for the best part of a semester, and here she is, offering unconditional support. "Love ya," she murmurs.

"Back at ya," Arielle says, giving her a squeeze. She withdraws herself. "Now, let's see if my mom has worked her magic."

She leads the way out of her bedroom as Gabby's struck by those words. Sierra's human, as is Arielle. Yet, they're working magic as they soothe the rips and tears of her life.

Downstairs, the familiar sounds and smells of baking rise from the kitchen. Arielle skips forward and through the doorway. "Ooh, banana choc chip?"

Sierra grins. "Yep. Wanna help?"

"I'd love to." Arielle moves over to the sink to wash her hands, glancing over her shoulder. "Go," she mouths.

Gabby hesitates, even though that's exactly what she needs to do. Sierra makes a surreptitious shooing motion over the bowl filled with batter. Both are obviously doing a wonderful job of creating a distraction.

Gabby clears her throat. "Anyway, I'd better get back before curfew."

"Sure thing," Sierra says cheerily. "Curfew waits for no muffin, even choc chip banana ones."

"I'll eat your muffin for you," Arielle teases.

Gabby rolls her eyes, playing along with the light atmosphere. This is what things used to be like before she went to college. "Thanks, you're such a team player."

"I'll see you later, Mom." Although Gabby means to say the words as a statement, they come out more as a question.

"I'll be here," her mom says primly, her gaze barely making it to Gabby and then sliding away, tightness framing her eyes and mouth.

Gabby sighs. It's probably the best she can hope for, considering the circumstances. Her anxious, risk-averse mother is going to need time to come to terms with her daughter being an angel.

One who everyone seems to want a piece of.

Gabby makes her way to the door, the sound of bowls clanging and Arielle's giggle tugging at her heart. As she leaves her house and the domestic scene that's so familiar, she wonders if she'll ever be a part of it again.

She needs to get back to the academy and her responsibilities as an angel.

Which right now, feel as if they've taken more than she's gained.

THE CRESCENT MOON has settled into the night sky as Gabby stands at the gates of Mercy Academy. She draws in a shaky breath, knowing she needs to pass through them and get inside.

But she can't.

Too many memories are crowding around her.

This is where she first met Colt. This is where they'd reconnected after he'd had to leave with little warning. And both times she'd been angry with him. The first she'd thought he was rude, although admittedly hot. The second she'd been upset because he'd left her with barely a goodbye thanks to some mysterious demon business. It had taken all of five seconds for her to melt into his husky awesomeness.

She tries to kindle that same anger. Colt betrayed her. He swapped the stones.

If it wasn't for him, the Tear would be closed. No more demons would be able to come out. That means no more angels too. They could have had a good life together. A normal life.

And yet he ruined it all.

But there's no heat sparking through Gabby's veins. No fury igniting. She feels...empty.

Colt's not here. Because she trapped him in stone. The same cold, hard material that her heart now feels made of.

Gabby wipes her cheeks, surprised, yet unsurprised to find them wet. Now that the anger has abandoned her, she acknowledges she just plain old hurt. Devastated. Shattered.

And that she may have lashed out as a result.

"Crapsticks," she mutters. She acted impulsively.

In fact, Colt had sworn he didn't do it. And she'd reacted, without even hearing his side of the story.

She spins on her heel, knowing why she can't enter Mercy Academy. Not without answers. Not without repairing what she's done.

But her foot never lifts off the ground. She freezes, her breath splinters. Her heart stutters.

Colt is only a few feet away, as glorious as always. The faint moonlight caresses his wine-colored hair, his broad shoulders. The intensity carving his face.

"I didn't do it, Gabby," he says, his voice wrapping around her heart. She's not sure if it's the honesty or the words themselves, but the fragments are instantly fused. Healed.

"How...how are you here?"

"I'll tell you everything," he says, taking a step forward. "Just give me a chance."

Which is what she should've done in the first place. Gabby presses her palms to her thighs, wanting to touch him more than anything. But she punished him without thought. She can't forgive him by doing the same thing. "How do I know you're not lying?" she asks hoarsely.

Colt seems to relax a little. "I'll do better than tell you. I'll show you that someone impersonated me."

Impersonated him. She wants to believe that so bad. "How?" she asks again, the single word all that her tight throat and frozen chest will allow.

He takes another step closer, his chocolate eyes warming. "Have you ever mind-melded before?"

Gabby hesitates. "It sounds dangerous." It sounds intimate. "Will you be able to see my memories, too?"

This could be the ultimate invasion of a demon into an angel's most secret space.

Colt acknowledges the question with a slight nod. "It's a two-way street, but I wouldn't see anything you didn't want me to see. I'd be totally focused on proving my innocence." He waits, silent and still, as she mulls over his words.

Trust is key.

That's what Donald said to her. How odd that his words would rise in her mind right now, but they're true. She didn't trust Colt when Maya showed her the video of him exchanging the gems. She owes him that now.

And she wants to know.

"Okay."

Colt's breath whooshes out as if he'd been holding it. "I'll need to move closer."

She nods, swallowing. Despite everything, she likes the sound of that. Craves it, if she's being totally honest with herself.

Colt moves with his usual stealthy grace, his dark gaze trapping hers. Snaring her breath. Arresting her pulse. He stops with their feet almost touching and raises his hands, his palms clasping her face.

Her eyes almost flutter closed at the sensation. Heaven. A world of tenderness and warmth and the feeling of coming home.

But Gabby holds herself still. Just because she wants Colt to be innocent, doesn't mean he is. If she was wrong to trap him in stone, then she'll own that. Guilt is already worming its way through her ribs. But she won't make another decision without more evidence.

Did Colt betray her?

His eyes flutter closed and Gabby locks her body as it wants to sway toward him. Words pour out of Colt in an ancient language, one her angelic self only seems to partially understand. She makes out that it's a version of Aramaic, but there are a few strains of Enochian mixed up in it.

Her eyes close as she feels his spell tugging at her. She begins to feel fuzzy as it drags her conscious mind into a foreign territory. When she opens her eyes, she finds herself standing in blackness, thousands, maybe more, orbs of light dancing around her.

"Where am I?" she asks, surprised when her voice echoes around her even though her lips didn't move

"In my mind, Gabby," Colt answers, materializing in front of her.

She looks around, trying to process exactly how many floating, flickering lights there are. When she was in her mind, there were a lot, but not this many. "These are your memories?" she asks, a little awed.

"I've been alive a long time," Colt says wryly.

Gabby nods mutely, a little overwhelmed. Yet, absolutely fascinated. She takes a step toward the nearest one, faint images of a large house that looks like it belongs in the Bridgerton series in the background, when Colt grabs her hand.

"This way," he says, sounding amused.

Realizing she's pouting, Gabby follows, also realizing she's holding his hand right back. She'd let go if it didn't feel so good. As if her world is spinning once more.

As she falls into step beside Colt, she angles her head. Did she just hear something? Like a soft thudding. If it wasn't so uneven and frantic, she'd assume it was Colt's heartbeat.

Release me!

Gabby glances at Colt, but he shows no sign of hearing the faint voice. One that's clearly not his.

Release who? And from what?

"This one," says Colt, standing before an orb flickering with color.

Gabby eyes it warily, suddenly realizing what she's about to do—step into Colt's memory of the time in the abandoned building. She doesn't think she's ever endured anything so painful.

But she needs to know.

She looks up at Colt. "Show me," she says, discovering her hand tightens around his.

He nods, his gaze steady even as a flash of his own pain echoes in the depths.

One step and they're inside the memory. Gabby finds herself back in the room that was the cult's headquarters where they found the gem. Or rather, the fake one. She sees herself opening the wall to reveal the gem, realizing she's watching this through Colt's eyes.

The Gabby of that fateful moment hovers her hands on either side of the floating gem. "My father suspected the spell may have been tied to an enchanted object. He had me learn a spell to break them. We're about to find out whether I was paying attention."

Suddenly, she's surrounded by emotion as she watches this unfold through Colt's eyes. She feels his indecision. The flash of dislike for her father because he gave her the tools to destroy the gem. The horror that he has to make this decision.

The hair blows back from clueless Gabby's face as her hands hover around the gem, and a new emotion buffets through the memory. No, several emotions. Attraction. Admiration. Adoration.

Memories bubble up within this memory.

Her words after they'd defeated the Grigori. "I really like you, too."

Their first kiss.

Every touch after that.

They're as much a part of him as they are her.

The knowledge that he can't betray her weaves through the memory. Defining it. Bringing with it a flush of relief so strong Gabby isn't sure if it's his or hers.

She turns to Colt. He chose not to betray her, despite the consequences. "This is your proof?" she asks, trying to reconcile it with what she saw in the video Maya showed her.

"A part of it," Colt says. "There's more."

The memory dissolves, another orb of light appearing before them. One step and they're inside it.

This time, Colt's still inside the cult's headquarters, the remains of his stone casing in pieces around him. What's more, there's another man with him.

"Who's that?" Gabby asks.

"Asmodeus. The archdemon who rescued me."

Great. Another archdemon from Hell.

Before Gabby can say anything, though, Colt points. "Watch."

Asmodeus lifts a cell phone to Colt's eyeline and presses play. Gabby squints as she realizes it's the same footage Maya showed her—the footage of Colt betraying her. It starts the same way. A cry of pain. A spray of blood. Something in the room moving too fast for her to be able to tell what it is.

Then silence.

Gabby braces herself, the betrayal already slicing through her.

In the moment that Colt's about to enter the frame, Asmodeus taps the screen. The footage slows, and although it's

Colt who appears, his image flickers, like a movie that's glitching. In that split-second, an apparition is visible.

Someone, or something, else.

Gabby steps back with a gasp, breaking the memory bubble. Sweet heavens, she was wrong. Colt was nothing but loyal to her.

Back beside the gates of the academy, she finds she can't move. Can barely breathe. She punished Colt for nothing. What sort of person is she?

Colt steps forward, the darkness around them dissolving as the mind-meld spell disappears. "I don't know what it was, but they took my form. I didn't sabotage the spell, Gabby."

She closes her eyes, trying to block out the pain. The reality of what she's done. "I'm so sorry," she whispers. Tears trickle down her cheek, scalding her skin. She's burning up with shame.

The gentle brush of a thumb, two warm palms cupping her face, sweet, heated breath brushing her mouth has her opening her eyes again. "You reacted so strongly because of what's grown between us, Gabby," Colt murmurs.

She blinks. It's true. If she didn't feel so strongly for Colt, she wouldn't have been sliced so deeply.

If she wasn't in love with him.

"But I..."

"I don't know what I would do if I thought everything I felt for you was a lie." Colt smiles, a sweet mix of tenderness and pain shifting in the depth of his gaze. "That you could throw it away so easily."

Gabby swallows, wondering what she did to deserve this amazing demon in her life. "I sure could use a kiss right now," she says huskily.

A smile flashes over his lips. "Me, too."

And then their lips are locked, tongues are mating, and

pulses are leaping. Gabby falls into Colt's arms, clinging to him. She begs his forgiveness with every stuttering breath, her hands roaming over his face, his shoulders, his back, trying to convey exactly how sorry she is.

But with each tightening of his hands, with each heated pass of his lips, Colt burns the apology away. His every touch sears her. Inflames the desire and feelings and hope.

Until there's nothing between them but *this*.

As Gabby gives herself over to the beauty, one thought still survives the inferno of their passion.

Who said love between an angel and a demon is impossible?

Because she's going to prove them wrong.

4

COLT

Colt shifts subtly, merging with the shadows of the forest more completely as he waits. It's been two days since Gabby saw he was telling the truth, and the band around his chest is almost gone. He draws in a deep breath, enjoying the sensation of it hitting the bottom of his lungs. As long as he and Gabby are together, he can breathe.

Freeing him to find the malaka who tried to tear them apart. A shape-shifter.

A vile creature that can transform into anyone it chooses. They're known as trouble-makers, but he's never heard of them being involved in something as large as what they're facing right now. Shape-shifters often destroy a family so they can sit back and enjoy the riches they stole from them, but this time, this shifter stole the gem that is keeping the Tear open. Is he or she working for the secret organization thirsting for the obsidian? Or the demons?

Colt's mouth twists. There's no way of knowing. Shape-shifters are abominations. Evil.

Just like the Shifter of Dunabar.

Resisting the urge to move restlessly, Colt tries to shy away from the memory. Those days in Hell are ones he's tried hard to forget. Back at a time when he was known in the demon world as Geryon.

But the images are soundly encased in a flickering orb in his mind, whether he likes it or not. And the memory overcomes him as completely as the ones he showed Gabby.

"You really thought I would let you languish in Belphegor's dungeons, did you?" Asmodeus asks. "You did me a great disservice, Geryon, by spying and then passing information onto Belphegor." The archdemon chuckles. "But you also helped me attain one of Belphegor's castles."

"You tricked me!" Geryon snarls. "You fed me lies."

"That was because I knew who you were the moment you stepped foot inside my castle. Do you think I wouldn't have wards like those to protect myself against Belphegor? But I let you spy for a while and report to your boss."

Something moves behind them, back at the opening to Belphegor's dungeons, putting Geryon on alert.

Asmodeus grunts. "We don't have much time. We need to get to Dunabar."

"Dunabar." Geryon scowls. Dunabar has a sinister reputation, even for Hell. Most demons fear going anywhere near its fortifications. Dark clouds hang over its spires throughout day and night. The castle is tainted by a dark power. "Why Dunabar?"

"You'll see when you get there," the archdemon answers.

Before Colt can object, even as he knows refusing means returning to Belphegor's endless tunnels, his surroundings disappear.

And then he's standing in a wide expanse of gray, broken by nothing but intermittent stretches of ash. Out of all of Hell, the land surrounding Dunabar is the hardest to imagine the stories of Hell being a paradise when it was first created, long before dark powers soiled the place with its evil taint.

Geryon's eyes scan the horizon where tall dark spires punch through thick, black clouds. He didn't like that he was about to do what demons avoided the most. And for what?

"Why have we come here?" he asks. Nobody ever visits Dunabar, and for good reason. "This place is a blight."

Asmodeus squints as he, too, stares at the foreboding castle. "And yet all the powers of Hell come from this place."

"You mean, all our darkness?"

The archdemon nods. "Many demons have yet to accept that a dark power turned our Paradise into Hell. "

"Because no one knows if it's fact or fiction," Geryon points out.

"Well, I know it's true." Asmodeus turns to Colt, his eyes glittering. "I want that dark power. And you're going to help me get it."

And there it is. The price for being freed. "Why?" Geryon asks. "This power is evil."

"Maybe, but it's what makes Hell, and it's the one power that can defeat Belphegor."

Geryon almost shakes his head. "So, this is about a war between the Kings of Hell?"

"It has always been, Geryon, you know that."

"And you believe you should be the one ruling Hell?" Geryon tries to keep the skepticism from his voice, the glance the archdemon flashes suggesting he failed.

"Lucifer governs Hell from his Cage, Geryon, and he made us kings so we could look after it. But Belphegor and Beelzebub have failed as custodians. Don't tell me you haven't noticed. Demons are becoming increasingly corrupted. We have become greedy, lustful, too proud of ourselves. Our thirst for vengeance translates to wrath. And we've become lazy, many of us are envious of what others possess. And we have also started to deplete our once abundant resources. We have become gluttons."

"The seven sins," he remarks, wondering at the link.

"Exactly. Belphegor and Beelzebub might be disregarding the corruption of our kind, but I am not. I intend to fight it with every-

thing I have, but for that, I need to take a hold of this power. And you're going to help me because you owe me, Geryon. I freed you from Belphegor's dungeons. And you will help me free the demons."

Before Geryon can reply, the sound of footsteps has them both spinning around. Adrenaline spikes through Geryon's veins. He doesn't want to help Asmodeus, but the thought of returning to Belphegor's dungeons is even more distasteful.

But it's not a guard or an army approaching them, weapons ready, but a female demon. Her hips sway provocatively, a riot of midnight curls brushing against them.

She stops a few feet away, her red eyes blazing as she scans Geryon as if he's edible. With a sultry curl of her lip, she turns to Asmodeus. "It's an interesting plan, my liege," she purrs. "But I fear the darkness of Dunabar is the least of your concerns. There's something strange going on inside the castle. Someone, I should say."

"Who are you?" Geryon demands.

"So silly of me not to introduce myself," she replies, her thick lashes fluttering. She sashays closer until her hot breath caresses his jaw as she speaks. "My name is Mazikeen. What's yours?"

A faint rustle behind Colt tells him Asmodeus is near. He shakes away the taint the memory always brings, extending his senses once more. If the archdemon is here, then the time must be drawing near.

Asmodeus stops beside him, eyes also scanning the road visible through the trees several yards away. "Just like old times, Colt," he chuckles amiably. "The last time we were together like this, we were near Dunabar."

A muscle twitches in Colt's jaw. "Yes, but hopefully, this won't be as deadly as Dunabar."

Asmodeus glances at him in his periphery. "No one could've predicted what happened to Mazikeen."

"No, they couldn't," Colt agrees, wishing for the wisdom of

hindsight, "but even she didn't intend for all those things to happen."

"Except what she did in Dunabar meant the persecution of an innocent demon."

Colt frowns. "She did?"

Asmodeus nods. "Do you remember the weak little demon, Ran? Mazikeen, in her insanity, involved her in a dangerous plan that resulted in Ran being the most wanted demon in Hell."

Colt's frown deepens. "What happened to Ran?"

"I don't know, but I don't believe she's dead. She's been missing ever since the Tear opened."

"You think she escaped?"

Asmodeus shrugs. "If she did, she'll need to be careful. If the demons get a whiff..."

Colt nods in understanding. Demons aren't the sort to forget and forgive. He hopes that wherever Ran is, she's safe. Even though she was the one who fed him misinformation on Asmodeus' behalf, he didn't wish her ill. She was doing what she thought was right.

Asmodeus leans forward, his eyes flashing crimson. "They're here."

The rumbling of the trucks reaches Colt a second before the sight does. Three trucks, each looking fresh from the factory, power up the hill Colt and Asmodeus are standing on. Five armored SUVs accompany the trucks on either end. To the average person, it would look like a military consignment, something no officer would question or intercept. But Colt knows differently.

"What's the plan?" he asks Asmodeus.

"I'm considering securing this consignment of demon weapons for ourselves," the archdemon muses. "I could return it to Hell once everything is accounted for."

Colt's gut clenches. If it becomes public knowledge that he helped Asmodeus steal the consignment, it would be equivalent to him siding with the archdemon and waging war upon Belphegor. He can't risk a war with Belphegor right now, not after he failed to sabotage Gabby's spell. It didn't matter that the gem was stolen by a shape-shifter and replaced with a fake.

"Keeping the weapons for yourself would be foolish," he says, keeping his voice level.

"You think you'd be alienating Belphegor." Asmodeus says slyly, although perceptively. He shakes his head. "Why are you so afraid, Colt? The Geryon I knew wasn't afraid of anyone."

"I'm not Geryon anymore," he snapped. "I don't want a war with anyone."

"But a war is coming, Colt. You can't just sit on the sidelines forever. Belphegor will stop at nothing to get what he wants. He's trying to use the Tear to bring demons into this world. Demons who don't belong here."

"I won't be seen helping you steal from Belphegor, Asmodeus. I don't want any kind of confrontation with the demon king."

The archdemon sighs dramatically. "Very well then, we'll do this to your liking." He smiles. "Luckily for you, I have a wonderful plan."

Colt frowns again, not liking the sound of that any more than he did the first plan. But before he can ask, the archdemon is gone. He curses and looks to the road again. The demonic consignment has turned around a bend and is now closing on them.

Suddenly, a series of loud screeches greet his ears. A dark smoke spears into the center of the road, hitting with enough force to create a jagged crater. The smoke swirls and shifts, quickly forming into the archdemon. Asmodeus stands tall, the crater behind him, raising his chin as he waits.

The trucks have come to a halt a few yards away, and men pour out of the armored SUVs, guns in hand.

"Meshugas," Colt mutters to himself.

Although he has to give them credit for their determination, even if it is foolish. They spread out, unwavering before one of the Kings of Hell. Colt breaks into a run, sensing the men's auras. Demons.

That doesn't surprise him. It's classic Belphegor.

Belphegor wouldn't trust humans. He'd use demons to ferry the consignments, just like the first two times they were robbed.

The possessed humans collectively aim their guns at Asmodeus, who openly laughs. He raises his hands and conjures two monstrous balls of infernal flame, crimson dancing over his fingers.

Colt runs ever faster. If he knows anything of Asmodeus, he'll slaughter these poor people so he can get the weapons. But Colt can't let the archdemon ruin everything. They need answers about the cult and its links to this mysterious organization.

Determined to save the demons, Colt leaps and lands in front of them, waving his hands to create a protective shield.

Asmodeus's demonic grin only grows, and without hesitation he throws the two balls of flame toward Colt. They collide with his shield, instantly burning a hole in it. The fires singe the skin of Colt's hands as the force throws him backward.

Colts tumbles over the asphalt, but as he comes to a stop, it's the burns that hurt the most. His skin looks and feels like it's been touched by one of the most potent weapons of Hell. Luckily, there's no time to dwell on the scorching pain. The possessed humans simultaneously fire at the archdemon, who unsurprisingly dodges each one as if children are throwing balls at him. Every dodge and twist is faster than the bullets coming aimed for him.

The moment the barrage stops as the demons run out of ammunition, Asmodeus moves. He morphs into black smoke and rushes at them so fast he's a blur. Colt launches too, determined to protect them, but Asmodeus darts toward him, a fist plowing into his ribs like a concrete battering ram. Once more, Colt's sent flying backward, this time arcing through the air and landing on one of the SUV's. The windshield cracks but doesn't stop his momentum. He skates over the bonnet and drops to the ground on the other side, a groan wrenched from him as he crashes to the ground. He scrambles to his feet as fast as he can, willing himself to heal faster.

Asmodeus can't kill every single demon. They need answers.

While the bruises and cuts from the crash disappear quickly, hot pain still surges through the burns. Colt ignores the agony, launching forward with a snarl, his focus solely on the archdemon. Asmodeus reaches another possessed human, never pausing as he strikes the man in the neck, instantly killing him. He twirls to face Colt, as if he knew he was coming, his eyes flashing crimson. Asmodeus bares his teeth as he twists his hands even before Colt can reach him.

This time, a scream claws up Colt's throat. The agony wrenches through his muscles, contorting sinew and tendons. His face merciless, Asmodeus kicks Colt in the chest, launching him hard and fast. Air whistles past Colt's ears as he flies, only stopping when he crashes into an old shed. The brittle walls collapse and wood splinters, the roof collapsing on him in a cloud of dust.

Refusing to give up, Colt hurls the timber away as he leaps to his feet. He breaks into a sprint, gasping through the pain of his hands, his chest, his every cell. It will all heal with time, something he doesn't have at the moment.

Reaching the trucks, Colt skids to a stop. Nothing moves apart from the wisps of ashen smoke coiling up from the crater. Bodies littered the road, all dead. Their demonic aura gone.

He's too late.

Asmodeus steps around the SUV with the smashed windscreen, dusting off his sleeve. "Well, you put up a good fight, Geryon." Asmodeus chuckles good naturedly. "It wasn't your finest hour, but at least Belphegor won't think you helped me."

"I didn't help you," he snaps. "We needed them alive and talking."

Asmodeus looks at Colt in question. "Oh, oops?"

Colt shakes his head. He stalks to the nearest body and squats down. "We needed answers, Asmodeus," he growls in frustration.

Something catches his attention and he leans in closer. A mark is etched into the side of the man's neck. Peering closer, Colt notes it's an insignia—two concentric circles with a line slashing across them. One he recognizes.

"These demons are Belphegor's," he notes.

"We knew that," Asmodeus states, sounding like he's rolling his eyes.

Colt's fingers hover near the mark. "But these demons didn't take possession of the humans willingly. They were summoned into these bodies."

Asmodeus appears beside him. "What are you saying?"

"These marks are summoning marks. Demons were forced into these humans."

"Why would Belphegor do that?"

"I'm not sure he did." Colt pushes to his feet, his eyebrows pulled low. "What if someone powerful summoned the demons loyal to Belphegor and forced them into these bodies?"

The archdemon doesn't respond, either unconvinced, or just as troubled at the prospect as Colt. Another suspicion climbs up Colt's spine.

He strides to the nearest truck and wrenches the rear door open. Nothing but cavernous, spotless emptiness greets him. "They're empty."

"What?" Asmodeus shouts, stalking over. "That's not possible. This was the consignment my spies informed me of."

He stops beside Colt, seeing what is undeniable. These trucks contain no demonic weapons. There's a gust as Asmodeus darts away, the clang of the rear doors on the other trucks piercing the air as he checks. A second later, he's back beside Colt, a vile curse drowning out any other sound.

"This was a distraction," Colt says. "They somehow knew that the consignments would be checked en route to wherever Belphegor intended to stash these weapons."

The archdemon curses. "We were betrayed."

Colt shrugged. "Or they expected this."

"What do we do now?" Asmodeus bellows. "We lost our only lead."

"Not our only lead," answers a female voice Colt immediately recognizes.

He turns, a smile already climbing up his face. Gabby stalks toward them, dragging a man behind her, looking undeniably strong. Formidable. Sexy.

"What's she doing here?" Asmodeus growls, clearly not echoing Colt's sentiment.

Gabby throws the chained man onto the ground. "Tell them what you told me."

The man flinches, seeming to prefer to look at Colt and Asmodeus rather than the wrathful angel standing over him. "Beelzebub," he squeaks. "It was Beelzebub!"

5
GABBY

Gabby pushes a curl out of her face impatiently. The last thing they need is another King of Hell surfacing on Earth. She drags her gaze from the coward who spilled the moment she showed her wings to Colt and almost gasps.

"Your hands!"

He glances down at the scorched skin, then at Asmodeus. "We had a disagreement."

Gabby glares at the archdemon, then stalks over to Colt. "Here," she says as she clasps his palms in hers. "Let me take care of that."

She closes her eyes and connects with her angelic essence, allowing the light and warmth to flow through her. Her hands heat and tingle, almost making her smile. Instead, she channels that healing heat into Colt, enjoying the way his hands relax in hers.

Gabby opens her eyes a moment later, beaming at the skin that now looks completely normal.

Colt turns his hands over to clasp hers. "Thank you."

She looks up, a "you're welcome," ready to go, only to stop

short. The swirling emotions in Colt's chocolate eyes take her breath away. Gratitude. Warm tenderness. A hot shot of attraction.

Asmodeus clears his throat. "When you're done," he says in disgust.

Gabby arches a brow at him, annoyed at the interruption. She wants to lose herself in those eyes for a few lifetimes. "Actually, I'm only just starting."

Colt chuckles softly, glancing at the man cowering between them. "So, he works for Beelzebub."

Asmodeus curses. "What in the name of Hell is he doing here?"

"Apparently stealing weapons from Belphegor," Gabby replies. "Everyone's after them."

Colt lets out a puff of air. "If Beelzebub is here, that's bad news."

"He's worse than Belphegor?" Gabby asks, noting the weight in Colt's words. Another archdemon in the possession of demonic weapons that could go nuclear is dangerous, but one who makes even Colt nervous is the last thing they need.

He regards her. "Belphegor knows mercy. Beelzebub doesn't really care much for it. He's ruthless and prone to anger and violence. He rules the upper levels of Hell, so he fancies himself superior."

"He's also reclusive," Asmodeus adds. "And is known to be a strong tactician and a strategist. He's only ever lost one battle."

Gabby notes the look that passes between Colt and the archdemon. "What battle?"

"The Battle of Dunabar," Colt mutters, his gaze falling away.

"The Battle of Dunabar?" Conscious there are some serious undercurrents here, Gabby waits. But Colt's eyes settle on their captive and don't move away.

"Dunabar is where the dark power first originated and corrupted Hell," Asmodeus says, filling the silence. "It's a place even demons try to avoid. But Beelzebub once tried to take its power and failed spectacularly. The credit goes to Geryon here."

"Geryon?" Gabby asks, wondering why the archdemon just indicated to Colt.

"My name in Hell," he offers, frowning at Asmodeus. Seems the memories of whatever they're talking about aren't pleasant. "We need to focus on the issue at hand," he continues. "The third King of Hell is on Earth and he has the weapons. And that means our world is in grave danger."

Conscious that Colt's changing the subject, Gabby decides not to push. She just has to hope she doesn't get impatient and demands to know what happened before Colt decides to tell her himself. "Beelzebub presents a danger to us all," she agrees, not pointing out that Asmodeus does, too. "He must be taken care of."

Asmodeus looks up, his eyes unfocusing as his dark brows pinch. "I cannot sense him."

"He could be cloaked?" Gabby suggests.

Asmodeus pulls his full sleeve half-way up his arm, revealing a tattoo of a strange creature with three heads, a snake-like body, and dinosaur-like claws.

"The mark of the Kings of Hell," Colt explains. "Three heads for the three Kings of Hell. Snakes depict immortality, and claws represent their ferocity."

"He's right," Asmodeus says. "With this mark, I can sense any of my peers, whether they are cloaked or not. Which means Beelzebub is nowhere on this earth."

"He might have returned to Hell then," Gabby offers.

"Highly likely. Beelzebub prides himself on appearing before Satan worshipers, encouraging them to pray to the goat-headed form of Lucifer, then disappearing."

"He's been visiting, even without the Tear?" she asks.

Asmodeus nods. "He can't stay for long, but he can get through the veil between our dimensions. I have no idea how."

Gabby's jaw tightens. She doesn't like the fact that an archdemon could flit in and out of this world so easily.

Asmodeus crosses his arms. "How did you learn of Beelzebub's involvement in the first place?"

Gabby looks at Colt and smiles. "Well, we suspected the organization might use a decoy."

"Why?" Asmodeus asks, his eyes narrowing.

Gabby's focus returns to Colt, remembering last night. "We went out to dinner," she says, her voice turning husky. Like a regular couple, although she barely remembers what she ate. In fact, all she wanted to do was leave the quaint little Italian place so she could have Colt to herself.

"Afterward, we were in an alleyway, cloaked, when..."

In fact, the first opportunity after they'd stepped out and started walking back to his car, she'd pushed him into a deserted alleyway and cloaked them. Her blood heats as she thinks of their kisses. The way their hands had roamed. The way desire had swallowed her whole.

And judging from the burn in Colt's eyes, he's thinking the same.

A strangled sound comes from Asmodeus. "The platonic version," he says in disgust. "I definitely do not want to know anything about your union, something I suspect hasn't gone well with either angels or demons."

The reminder has Gabby's core body temperature cooling. "We're well aware of that." She raises her chin. "But I don't hold the same biases angels and demons do."

"Then you're an exception to the rule," Asmodeus concedes. "No doubt because you were raised in this world, rather than in

Heaven." He waves his hand in dismissal. "Anyway, the story please, and give me the YA version."

Unfortunately, that's as steamy as the story got, Gabby thinks, disgruntled. Someone had approached from the other end of the alley, speaking into their cell. She would've ignored him if his words hadn't caught their attention.

"We overheard a man talking into his phone," she says. "He said there was going to be another robbery."

Asmodeus arches a brow in interest.

"He said his master wants the demonic weapons Belphegor has been stealing from Hell."

Gabby and Colt had stood so still, they'd stopped breathing.

"He spoke of a consignment coming out of the Tear and a mercenary organization transporting them after it reached Boston by ship."

Colt nods. "So Gabby came up with a plan."

"A plan?" Asmodeus asks.

"I suspected Belphegor would be expecting another attack seeing as his last two shipments were stolen," Gabby says. "The best way to address this was to use a decoy."

Asmodeus's eyes flicker to the trucks behind them, confirming her suspicion. This convoy was a decoy.

"So I came here," Colt continues. "Just in case the assumption was wrong."

Gabby smiles at him, wondering if he realizes what a kick-ass team they make. "While I went to Boston. By the time I'd tracked it down, Beelzebub had attacked and taken over." She glances at her captive. "There was one survivor."

The man cowers, trying to curl into himself. "I was just following orders."

"Beelzebub's orders," she snaps.

Asmodeus studies the captive. "Are you sure? He could be lying."

"He has Beelzebub's mark," she says, reaching down to yank his sleeve up and reveal the tattoo of an eagle with crimson eyes.

Asmodeus's gaze flies to Colt. "You told her of the Kings of Hell's marks?" he asks, aghast. His brows slam down. "Hell's secrets shouldn't be told to an angel."

"I don't serve Hell anymore, Asmodeus," Colt replies evenly. "I'm only helping you because I don't want to see Belphegor bring any more demons into this world. And I want to save these weapons from the people who would use them for all the wrong reasons."

The archdemon glares at Colt for long seconds but he doesn't back down, making Gabby's chest flush with pride. With another disgusted snort, Asmodeus returns his focus to her. "And where are the weapons now?"

"Somewhere safe," she responds curtly.

Asmodeus stills, his features tightening. "And that is?"

"Somewhere you won't find them."

He takes a threatening step forward. "Hand them over." He tries for a conciliatory smile, but it's more of a constipated sneer. "I'll see them safely back to Hell."

"No can do," Gabby says. "I don't trust you."

"Those weapons are dangerous," Asmodeus says, obviously trying for a different tact. "If they ever fall into the wrong hands..."

"They won't. The place it's going to has powerful wards and guards."

Asmodeus clenches his fists and Gabby senses Colt draw his energy tighter around him. He's ready to protect her, and yet is letting her stand up to Asmodeus on her own.

What.

A.

Guy.

Asmodeus looks like he's about to implode with impotent fury. With a curl of his lip, he morphs into black smoke. The inky cloud writhes on the spot as if trying to convey exactly how pissed he is, before shooting for the sky and disappearing over the trees.

Colt lets out a breath. "So the weapons are safe?"

"They're on their way to the safehouse we discussed." Gabby takes a step closer, wanting to touch him. "Kalisha's driving."

His eyes pop wide open. "Kalisha? Why would you involve her in this?"

"She insisted." Gabby lifts a hand as Colt goes to speak. "Everything you're about to say, I pointed out to her. This is dangerous, she's human, this is dangerous. But she wouldn't listen. Said she wanted to be part of the good fight, especially after what Samandriel did to her and Maya."

Colt frowns. "I'm not sure that was a good idea."

"Me neither, but short of tying her up, I didn't get a choice. She followed me and climbed into the car." She tries to smile. "Plus, Moroni sent over some angels."

"I suppose that's something," Colt concedes.

Gabby's about to assure him, and herself, that everything will be fine when her phone rings. She presses the screen to pick up the call. "That's Kalisha now."

"Gabby," Kalisha gasps, the pain and panic in her tone freezing Gabby's blood. "The consignment. We were attacked."

6

GABBY

Gabby rushes into her dorm room, Colt close behind her, gasping the moment she sees Kalisha curled up in bed. Her hair is a tangled mess, her face pale and pinched. Gabby's father is standing in the corner of the room, which is a surprise she doesn't have time to figure out right now.

She kneels beside the bed, too scared to take her friend's hand. "Kalisha, what happened?"

Her friend groans as she presses her face more fully into the pillow. "Someone hit me on the back of my head."

"But I sent angels to protect you," Gabby says, horrified that she allowed this to happen. "They were supposed to guard you and the consignment."

Kalisha frowns as she peeks up at her. "What are you talking about, girl? Angels? Consignment? You make it sound like I was on some supernatural drug run."

Gabby glances at Colt, seeing he's just as nonplussed as her. Maybe Kalisha's hit to the head was a significant one. "You insisted, remember?" she asks gently. "Wouldn't take no for an answer. You said you knew how to drive a truck thanks to your uncle, meaning you were the best person for the job."

"I'm the one with the bump on my head." Kalisha frowns even deeper, then winces as the motion causes her pain. "I would never volunteer to be part of something like that. I may be a bit kooky, but I sure as hell ain't crazy, girlfriend."

Gabby sits back on her haunches. "I don't understand..."

Kalisha glances at her father. "Mr. Davenport found me. I'd been knocked unconscious and buried alive!" She shudders, then winces again. "If he hadn't turned up, I'd be dead right now."

Colt crosses his arms, growling three words. "The shape-shifter."

Gabby looks up at him, knowing it's the only thing that makes sense. But that means the shape-shifter has the demonic weapons...

Her father steps forward, his focus on Kalisha. "You should rest, dear. You're safe now."

"I'm not sure I'll ever sleep again after—"

One wave of Gabriel's hand and Kalisha's out. Her body sinks into the mattress and Gabby gently pulls up the duvet before standing. "You'll heal her?" she asks her father.

He grunts. "It's already done." The peaceful expression on her friend's face confirms his words. "This is serious, Gabrielle. Kalisha was nearly killed, all to get you off campus."

Gabby holds up a hand, not wanting a lecture from the father who hasn't been present for most of her life. "I was tracking the demonic weapons."

He arches a brow. "Someone wanted you away from here so they could murder the cupids."

She almost does a double-take. "The what?"

"Pesky little angels tasked with spreading love and uniting

lovers," he says, on an impatient sigh. "Most humans know of their existence."

Colt moves closer to Gabby, a scowl making him look ferocious, but no less hot. "And they were killed?"

Gabby's father throws him a sour expression, looking as if the closer Colt is to his daughter, the harder he's sucking a lemon. "Yes, that's what I said." He returns his focus to Gabby. "A group of cupids arrived a few days ago wanting to speak with you, refusing to talk with anyone else. No matter how hard I tried."

"A few days ago?" Gabby asks, narrowing her eyes. "Why didn't you tell me?"

Her father throws another baleful glare at Colt, answering her question. He didn't want the little love angels to bring her and Colt closer together. She takes his hand, making sure her father notices. Cupid or no, Colt is hers and she's his.

"That's irrelevant right now," her father snaps. "While you were off with *him*, I discovered every single cupid had been brutally murdered. It took me quite a while to clean up."

Her father says it coldly, but his shoulders contract, giving a hint that the loss had an impact. Gabby suppresses a shudder, not wanting to think of what he saw.

"Someone wanted to ensure their message wasn't relayed," Colt says with a frown. "It must've been important."

"And now we'll never know," Gabby adds. Because her father didn't want her and Colt to get closer together.

Well, he can get in line with everyone who's failed.

"When I was returning to the academy, I felt a magical disturbance and found Kalisha buried." He glances at the sleeping girl. "She was very close to death."

"Thank you," Gabby says, meaning it. She doesn't want Kalisha's death on her conscience.

There's a subtle softening around her father's eyes. "I

brought her here. Not long ago, she became frantic, saying she needed to make a phone call."

Gabby glances at Colt. "To tell me the consignment had been stolen."

His lips thin. "The bastard wanted you to know. He conveyed the message through Kalisha."

He was bragging. Gloating.

The prick.

"A shape-shifter, you say?" Her father rubs his chin. "They are nasty creatures, fond of trickery."

"And now he has the demonic weapons." Gabby rubs her temples, deeply uneasy at the thought. "This isn't good."

It's pretty crap, actually.

Colt unwinds his arms. "Although his connection to Kalisha could be the advantage we need."

Gabby's father straightens. "Yes, we could."

"If a shape-shifter's victim survives, they develop a connection," Colt continues. "If the shape-shifter communicated through her after it had finished imitating her, then a link must exist."

Gabby glances between them, deciding against noting aloud they're almost working together.

"Good thing I found her and saved her life," Gabby's father points out.

Gabby looks away before she rolls her eyes. Of course her father had to ruin the fledgling moment. Instead, she focuses on the thread of hope that was just woven. "So, we can use Kalisha to track the bastard who stole the weapons?"

Her father nods. "I'll show you."

GABBY STANDS on the rooftop of the Mercy Academy, squinting at the low hanging sun. "Myrtle Beach, huh? That prick's really high-tailed outta here."

The delve into Kalisha's mind had been quicker and easier than Gabby expected. In fact, she'd found traces of the shape-shifter outside of Kalisha's consciousness, like a sticky film. There had been no need to dig deeper into all the private stuff like memories and thoughts, which was a relief. Doing that without Kalisha's knowledge would've been wrong, meaning they would've had to wait for her to wake to gain permission.

But the faint thread connecting her to the shape-shifter was easy to find. A locator spell meant Gabby could trace where they need to go—a small coastal town called Myrtle Beach.

Colt scans the horizon next to her. "All the more reason to fly. We'll catch up to him."

The way he says the words, all hard and determined, has a shiver slipping down Gabby's spine. Is intimidating meant to be sexy?

"Four hours by boring, old petrol power, but less than an hour when you have a set of these." Gabby snaps out her wings with a grin.

Colt does the same as his eyes trace hers. "I'm looking forward to this."

Holy heck, the huskiness in his tone is connected straight to somewhere deep in her belly. The last time they flew had been to leave the cemetery after Kalisha and Maya were kidnapped by Samandriel. It had been exhilarating, and far too short.

Now they have almost an hour of just the two of them and the sky trying to contain the emotions this delicious demon elicits in her.

The cloaking spell is almost unconscious as Gabby lifts into the air. Colt does the same, and they hover a few feet above the roof, even less distance between them. Their gazes lock as they gently lift higher. They unconsciously drift closer.

I love you.

The words don't whisper through Gabby's mind, they're a declaration. A promise. An undeniable truth.

She may be an angel, and he may be a demon, but it's never mattered. This feeling transcends Heaven and Hell. It's so much bigger than that.

But now's not the time to tell him. Not when there's a shape-shifter to track down and a consignment of Hell's weapons to find. But soon...

Flashing Colt a smile, Gabby pumps her wings and shoots higher into the sky, smiling even wider when Colt also turns into a blur of movement. She angles west, chasing the setting sun and flying toward Myrtle Beach.

Just like last time, flying with Colt is a thrill, but this time, there's the chance to enjoy it. Gabby swoops close to him, her heart somersaulting before she even thinks of executing one herself. He twists so his body is angled, his focus totally on her.

"You take my breath away, Gabby," he murmurs huskily.

She dips in closer, the silver tips of her wings brushing the crimson edges of his. "Ditto," she says, because that's all her lungs will allow her.

Colt in flight is magnificent. All power and strength and unconscious grace. Man, she'd like to kiss him senseless.

As if he reads her mind, Colt turns so he's on his back, his ebony wings expanded as he coasts through the dusk. His eyes twinkle, daring her.

She grins, awareness of every inch of his muscled body dancing through her veins.

Dipping low, she hovers above him, her own alabaster wings outstretched. The deep orange and faint peach of their surroundings seem to hold them, blessing this moment. One where they're mirrors, one white winged, the other black. Light and dark. Born of Heaven and born of Hell.

And it doesn't matter one bit.

Gabby lowers as Colt rises, their lips feathering a sweet caress over the other. It's a whisper of a touch. A brush of sensitized skin.

And yet, it's everything.

It's proof that gray exists in a world where black and white have been warring for centuries. It's proof that no divide is too great.

A giggle bubbles up Gabby's throat and she throws her arms out wide, executing a somersault for real this time. Air rushes over her face and through her hair, wisps of cloud making her skin tingle. Colt's husky laughter, so rare and so precious, follows her, filling the air and climbing into her heart.

They shoot forward, smiles reaching from horizon to horizon. They twirl and twist, dip and dive, starting a mid-air dance that's not only fun, but a total turn on. It quickly morphs into a game of tag where both want to be caught. A race to see who's the fastest, neither wanting to win.

Despite the distance, they reach Myrtle Beach long before Gabby's ready. But the moment the blue haze of the ocean appears ahead, they both sober. They fall in side by side, taking in the gentle hills, the street lights flickering on as twilight turns the sky a deep purple.

Gabby summons the location the spell scried and angles right. "This way," she says, all playfulness gone.

They need to find the shape-shifter.

Colt nods, the dusk creating somber shadows on his handsome face. He narrows his eyes, seeing a small chapel sitting on a rise. "There?"

Magic tugs at Gabby, drawing her to it. "Yes. There."

They land outside a rusty old gate, a dilapidated path

stretching on the other side to the chapel. Even in the twilight, the peeling paint and cracked stained glass windows are visible. Seems the chapel was abandoned some time ago.

Glancing at each other, Gabby and Colt step through the half-open gates. They're immediately surrounded by musty, choking air. Magic hangs heavily, corrupted and evil. Colt's nostrils flare and she wonders if he recognizes it. But before Gabby can ask, thirteen demons materialize from the shadows, surrounding them.

Each with the mark of Beelzebub stamped on the side of their necks.

Gabby and Colt glance at each other, an understanding passing between them. These demons are about to discover numbers don't matter. Not when they're up against an angel and a demon who face far greater trying to tear them apart.

The same dance they gloried in up in the sky is played out on the ground, but this time, with far more deadly consequences. They twist simultaneously, their backs only a few feet apart, their wings always touching. When one moves, the other mirrors.

Thirteen demons aren't enough to defeat the fortress they become. Neither Gabby nor Colt is willing to see the other hurt, meaning they make every strike count. With every punch and kick, they both have a defender as they become an attacker.

Within minutes, still bodies are littered around them. Gabby's barely panting as she turns to Colt, noticing he hasn't even broken a sweat.

They make one heck of a kick-ass team.

His chocolate eyes warm in the way that she loves. "Let's get the bastard."

She nods. "I like the way you think almost as much as I like the way you move."

Lips twitching, Colt shakes his head as he tucks his wings

away. He falls into step beside her as they approach the chapel. "I like everything about you," he says quietly, the words barely louder than the silence.

But they lift Gabby's heart far higher than her angelic powers ever have.

She brushes her hand over his as they reach the steps.

I love you, her mind whispers back.

But it's too soon to say it. Rejection by Colt is one hurt she won't recover from. Her response when she thought he betrayed her is proof enough. She needs to be sure...

Colt pushes the doors open and they step inside. Rows of wooden benches are coated in dust. A large cross hangs on the opposite wall, spider webs clinging to it, and the only movement in the place is the small black insects scrambling over the fine threads.

The chapel is empty.

Gabby focuses within as she tries to connect with the link she'd followed, but there's nothing. "I think he severed the connection. I can't feel anything."

"Skata," Colt growls. "He realized how we traced him."

Gabby's tempted to kick the nearest pew, but it looks like it could shatter if she even looks at it too long. "Great, he could be anywhere."

Colt's gaze roams over the chapel restlessly. "I suspect the shape-shifter works with both Beelzebub and the organization. Beelzebub was always trying to one-up Belphegor, and once he learned Belphegor was stealing weapons from Hell, he decided to steal them for himself. An alliance with the organization gave him the manpower to do it."

"And the shape-shifter?" Gabby asks. "Why work with him if they're so hated?"

"To cause chaos. Either as a distraction, or to help in securing the weapons." Colt angles his chin up, his focus turning inward. "I cannot sense Beelzebub on Earth. Asmodeus would've too. So he's definitely back in Hell."

"That kicks him down the priority list, then."

Colt nods. "We have more immediate threats."

She slips her hand into his and braids their fingers. "The shape-shifter. He could lead us to this mysterious organization."

His face turns hard. "We need to find another way to locate him."

Gabby steps in closer, a smile dancing on her lips at the prospect of spending more time with this demon. "We need to research."

7

COLT

Colt hasn't been to Veritas very often. As a library dedicated to the supernatural, he's avoided it, even if it meant learning everything he has the hard way. Fighting a shape-shifter, or discovering that angels hate demons with the power of a thousand suns may be painful, but he was still alone. There was no one to let him down.

There was no one to let down.

But as they pass through the run-down facade that hides Veritas, Colt's aware of how much things have changed.

He's no longer alone.

And he doesn't want to be.

He presses a hand into the small of Gabby's back as she enters first, and he instantly feels her awareness spike. It's in the way she stiffens slightly, yet subtly melts into his touch. In the way her breath hitches, then holds.

It's in the way she glances over her shoulder, her blue eyes glinting with warmth and promise.

And in the way the heart he thought was long frozen responds. It beats harder than it ever has. Heats in ways he didn't know were possible. The emotion within it swells beyond the containment of his chest.

As they're engulfed by the sheer size of Veritas, Colt realizes exactly how much Gabby has changed everything. And he's grateful for it. Humbled by it.

Determined to protect and nurture it.

But in these uncharted waters, he doesn't know how...

"Everything okay?" Gabby asks.

Colt realizes he's stopped just inside. "Sorry. I was just thinking."

She angles her head, her blonde curls shifting over her shoulder. "About what?"

You.

Us.

A future that has you in it till the end of time.

"Moving forward," he says, conscious he's hedging, but unsure what else to say. He squeezes her hand. "And taking care of the shape-shifter is the first thing on the list."

Gabby's brows twitch as if they want to frown. "Yes, it certainly is." She looks as if she wants to say more when a voice interrupts them.

"A shape-shifter?" Nim wheels out from between two nearby shelves, most definitely frowning. "That's bad news."

Gabby turns to her. "Yeah. And the prick stole the gem that can close the Tear."

Sierra appears, too. "That's a worry."

"Shape-shifters are rare," Nim says, stopping a few feet away. "But dangerous. They love to cause chaos just for the sake of it."

"We need any information you have on it," Colt says.

Nim winks. "You've come to the right place." She spins right and wheels herself toward more shelves.

Gabby's aunt follows, rolling her eyes. "She loves to say that."

They pass rows and rows of books of every size, some smelling of new leather and paper, others looking aged and worn, their spines barely legible. But each volume of work has something in common—it holds information on things most humans don't know exist. Magical things. Often fantastical things. Sometimes dangerous things.

Nim stops at the end of a tall set of shelves and removes a fat tome from a middle shelf. She passes it to Sierra. "Chapter two."

Sierra shakes her head. "Do you know the contents of every book in this place?"

"Either that or the spirits give me a heads up every now and again so I make sure I know where the relevant information is," Nim says with a wink.

Sierra opens the tome to the second chapter, her eyes quickly darting over the typed words. "They're a rare species," she says. "Ones who like to create problems for people."

Colt waits to hear something he doesn't know. Maybe avoiding Veritas wasn't a great loss.

Sierra flips to the next page. "They don't remember their original face if they continue to shift often." She skims her fingers over the lines of text. "They shed their skin when they turn into another person, but the spell wears over time and they revert to their previous form. So, they keep their victims who they want to transform into close by. By touching them, the shape-shifters replicate their DNA and become them."

Also information Colt is familiar with.

"How do we identify one?" Gabby asks with a frown, no doubt realizing exactly how hard it's going to be to find this slippery enemy.

"Most lores say they leave behind transparent skin when

they transform," Sierra answers, glancing at the page. "Some also say they leave fluorescent, colored skins, but there's even less evidence of that."

Gabby's shoulders tense, as if she's trying to keep them from drooping. Right now, nothing is news and all they're learning is that their task is more impossible than they'd like.

Sierra squints as she peers closer. "Their love for chaos is due to their primordial nature. They derive from a powerful entity of hate."

That piques Colt's interest. He hadn't known this. But before he can ask if there's more, a powerful aura tingles across his tenses.

"They certainly do."

Blaise appears at the end of the row, her hair a brilliant red, just as her dress is. She moves closer, brushing her hand over Nim's shoulder as she stops beside her. Colt inclines his head, conscious his skin is prickling. It's what happens whenever a powerful witch comes near. And Blaise is indeed powerful, descended from an ancient line of witches.

"We believe the shifter is after the demonic weapons," he tells her.

She nods sagely. "A shape-shifter could cause the ultimate chaos with something like that. Although shifters are averse to both demonic and angelic weapons, which will limit what it can do."

Gabby lets out a breath. "At least that's something."

Blaise frowns. "Unless the shifter in question is the original one."

"Original one?" Gabby asks, going from unwinding to tensing once more.

"Yes. Legend has it that all shifters derive from a powerful entity of hate. The story is so ancient that the being's name is no longer known."

"And can this original entity use demonic weapons?" Colt asks, his stomach tight.

Blaise looks at him, then Gabby. "I believe so, although it's so powerful that I don't know why it would feel the need for such weapons."

Gabby focuses back on her aunt. "What does the book say about the entity?"

But it's Blaise who answers. "There are no books that can tell you more about this original shifter. Even among supernaturals, it's barely spoken of. For all we know, that creature is a myth."

Assuming that is a risk they can't take.

Not when the original shifter is as powerful as Blaise is suggesting.

Gabby's eyebrows contract as she chews her lip. "And you say the entity is born of hate," she muses. She looks up, watching Blaise closely. "Would it want to murder cupids?"

Blaise blinks as Sierra moves in closer to her. Colt holds still, impressed that Gabby made the link between this new information and the killing of the cupids.

"It's possible," Blaise murmurs thoughtfully. "If the original shifter is molded from hate, then it stands to reason it wouldn't be too fond of the angels of love. Although it's said cupids can sense whenever this hateful entity is in their plane." She smiles weakly. "Once again, that's only a conjecture. Our lore on the original shape-shifter is literally nonexistent."

"Where would we find more?" Colt asks. He can feel it in his marrow that this is significant.

"I don't know. None of the Archivist chapters have that kind of information. Maybe some angel books or demon tomes, but those would be hard to find on Earth. Maybe even hard to find in Heaven or Hell."

He grits his teeth. They don't have time to scour every

dimension, especially with no guarantees the information has been recorded somewhere.

Gabby's thoughtful gaze falls on him. "I should see if my father knows anything."

Archangel Gabriel could know something—he's certainly old enough. And arrogant enough.

Colt suppresses a sigh as he thinks of someone else just as old and arrogant. "I'll talk to Belphegor."

Gabby nods, her lashes fluttering. It's best if they don't accompany each other for these respective talks. Their presence would end any information sharing the moment they stepped in the room. They're both being reminded they hail from two very different dimensions—Heaven and Hell.

"We'll meet back at the academy?"

It surprises Colt that Gabby's words are a question. "Of course." He's already resenting the time they'll be apart, no matter how foolish it is. He can't be by her side *all* the time.

A small smile touches her lips. "Good." She steps closer and presses a sweet kiss on his lips. "I'll see you later."

Gabby's slipped past him before he snaps out of the spell she cast on him. He turns, wanting for their goodbye to be a little more...more, even if they'll only be apart for a few hours, when someone speaks.

"Colt."

His name is said slowly, with meaning. Almost like a warning.

He looks back, finding there are three women looking at him with their hands on their hips.

He straightens, wondering what he's about to be accused of, no doubt because he's a demon. "Yes?"

Sierra narrows her eyes. "What are your intentions toward my niece?"

He blinks. "I beg your pardon?"

"I could've whispered that and you would've heard me." She steps closer. "I saw Gabby when she thought you'd betrayed her—"

"Which I didn't."

Sierra's eyes flash at being interrupted. "She jumped to the conclusion because the thought of you deceiving her terrifies her."

Blaise crosses her arms. "She held herself together, but only because she's tough. Not because she wasn't hurting."

Nim wheels forward an inch. "She won't be able to do that again if you betray her for real, Colt. It'll break her."

Any defensiveness melts under the fierce heat of the three women's protectiveness. "Do you really think a demon would do everything I have, if he hadn't fallen for a very stubborn, beautiful, determined angel?"

He directly disobeyed Belphegor.

He's risked his life.

And he will again, over and over, if that's what he needs to.

Sierra holds him in her steely gaze for long moments, but Colt doesn't shy away. The truth should never be hidden.

"Have you thought of telling her?" Sierra asks, arching a brow.

Both of Blaise's eyebrows rise. "No matter how scary it is."

It's Nim's brows who pinch. "She needs some reassurance, Colt."

Colt remains still as a statue, but for a whole new reason. Fear has never stopped him from making choices that needed to be made.

But is that exactly what's happened with Gabby? Has he not been open about his feelings because it would make him vulnerable?

To his surprise, Sierra smiles. She glances at the other two women and they nod approvingly.

"Anyway, you have a shape-shifter to track down," she says brightly, patting his arm as she walks past.

Nim grins, wheeling behind her. "Good luck."

Blaise flips a length of glossy, red hair over her shoulder as she joins her fellow Archivists. "Don't make Gabby regret choosing you."

Colt still doesn't move for long seconds after he's been left alone. He feels a little railroaded, but in a strange way, glad for it.

Gabby needs reassurance.

Spinning on his heel, Colt strides through Veritas and out the doors. He'll talk to Belphegor. He'll work on finding the shape-shifter.

And through it all, he's going to find a way to make Gabby glad she chose him.

8

COLT

Colt's surprised to find Belphegor has a secretary sitting behind a high desk in the room outside of his office. He's not surprised to realize she's a demon. No doubt her role is to take his appointments, make coffee, and kill anyone who's a threat.

"He's not currently in his office," she says. "You can wait inside, though. He won't be long."

The smile she gives Colt is one of pity, confirming that Belphegor isn't happy with him. He'll want to know where his weapons are. And where the shape-shifter is.

Neither of which Colt is able to tell him.

With a curt nod, he enters Belphegor's office and leaves the door ajar behind him. Unable to stand still, Colt paces. He doesn't care if Belphegor is furious. He wants to know if the archdemon holds any more information on the shape-shifter, and then he wants to get back to Gabby.

Restless energy buzzes through his veins as Colt prowls around the large chamber. It could be the size of a thousand rooms and it wouldn't be enough to contain the edginess nipping at his nerves. Even though Gabby is near, probably in the supernatural club her father established beneath the academy, it's too far away.

Colt finds himself beside the bookshelves lining the entirety of the left wall and he barely glances at the spines marching across in orderly lines. They're not the electric blue eyes and luscious blonde curls he wishes to see right now.

Except as his gaze passes a particularly thick spine, he pauses.

Bound in faded leather, it's clearly old. But it's the embossed symbols on the spine that catch his attention. He's seen them before.

A very long time ago.

Mazikeen cranes her neck as she assesses the sheer cliff they're standing before. "It's the only way."

Geryon grunts, uncomfortable with the fact he's even here, the closest to Dunabar he's ever been, but knowing he has no choice. He's indebted to Asmodeus.

Which means he's taking part in this suicide mission.

The eastern side of Dunabar is nothing more than a glistening, onyx bluff. If the jagged walls of black stone that reach several furlongs high wasn't enough of a deterrent for anyone foolish enough to consider entering the castle, then the warding around it certainly does. The spell is designed to diminish a demon's powers, and it's working. He feels weak in a way he really doesn't like.

"This is crazy, even for you, Mazikeen," he growls. "Why are you doing this?"

The demoness smiles, revealing white teeth that contrast sharply with her dark skin and ebony hair. "Because Asmodeus is right." She slips closer, her gaze roaming over him. "Whoever holds the power of Dunabar, holds sway over the Kings of Hell."

Which would mean Asmodeus would control Belphegor and Beelzebub.

Mazikeen sashays straight past, her shoulder and hip brushing his chest and groin. "How else are we going to be free of the evil that rules us if the Kings of Hell don't unite?"

She lifts a foot into a shallow shelf of rock and leaps, gripping an even smaller node a few feet above.

With little choice, Geryon follows, even as his curiosity is piqued. Uniting the Kings of Hell would mean a measure of peace in Hell.

He leaps higher than Mazikeen did, dangling from his fingertips as they gouge into a groove. "How will Dunabar help achieve this?"

Mazikeen's dark eyes glint. She knows she has him intrigued. "This is the very place that the darkness spread from and corrupted Hell." She taps the flat expanse of wall almost affectionately, then springs higher up with a sharp, graceful move. "The place that was once paradise."

Geryon digs his fingers in and uses that small point of contact to launch himself up. "That was a very long time ago," he grunts, clasping a jagged protrusion and hissing as it cuts his palm.

Mazikeen grins, scrabbling up a few more feet. "We must never forget our origins, Geryon. We are the children of Lucifer and Lilith, deemed abominations because of it. Lucifer created this dimension for us. It was the angels who corrupted it."

"When they threw the dark stone in," he mutters, his arms starting to strain under the force of holding his weight.

"Yes, an evil that has subjugated us to its will. Corrupted us." Mazikeen leaps, only to miss the handhold she was reaching for and skid down several feet, gouging lines in the rock with her sharp nails. She comes to a stop beside Geryon, grinning even harder. "You're strong, Geryon, I like that."

He squints, noting the flush to her cheeks as she pants. This demoness has spunk. "And you believe Dunabar is the key to ridding Hell of this evil."

"Asmodeus does. And I wouldn't be here if I didn't agree." She leans in closer, breathes in deeply, then leaps the highest he's seen so far. "Asmodeus wants to channel the well of dark energy here and use it to proclaim his rule over the other Kings. He might even defeat the evil that's controlling demons."

Weariness tugs at Geryon's muscles, trying to weaken them, but he grits his teeth and crawls determinedly up to Mazikeen. "That may not be possible," he grinds out. "The stone was thrown out when the rip opened between the worlds centuries ago, yet the corruption still exists."

He's just reached her when she flashes him a smile and leaps again. "You're right. Hell hasn't healed." She looks over her shoulder, dangling from nothing but a hand. "But I believe that's because of something else." Mazikeen turns back to the sheer wall and, spider-like, shimmies further up.

Unwilling to have a large gap between them, Geryon finds energy he doesn't have, determined to catch up.

Not to mention the demoness climbing with sultry confidence just gripped his curiosity in a way no one has in a long time. "An evil that isn't a result of the dark stone dropped here by the angels?"

Mazikeen doesn't look back as she continues to climb. "Yes, but with a similar power to the dark stone." She leaps, grunts, then leaps again. "I can sense its hateful aura. A formidable one."

Geryon frowns, focused on keeping up. "What aura?"

But Mazikeen doesn't answer. Either because she has no intention of telling him, or because she just hauled herself over the ledge of the cliff.

Geryon blinks in surprise. He'd been so absorbed in their conversation, he'd barely registered the dangerous climb. Mazikeen straightens then turns and bends over, extending a hand with a mischievous smile.

He ignores it, throwing her a baleful glare as he heaves his bulk onto the ledge. Drawing himself up, he finds Mazikeen standing close.

And that he's not inclined to move away.

Her eyes darken as she registers it, too. "We're going to work well together, Geryon," she purrs.

Spinning fast enough that her hair furls out and whips his chest, she stalks to the large door that dominates the wall they're now standing beside. Strange runes are etched into it, jagged and primal. One's Geryon doesn't recognize.

Mazikeen runs a black fingernail over one. "It's an ancient language," she explains without looking over her shoulder. "Now dead to all the world. Older even than Enochian or Adamic."

Geryon joins her, studying the deep lines.

"It's an ancient language rooted in primordial origins. Nobody knows its name." Mazikeen looks up at him, her eyes shining in a way he's never seen. "At least not anyone I've ever met."

He's about to point out that if they can't read it, they won't be able to enter when she presses both palms to the black door, muttering a strange language under her breath.

The runes glow with red fire.

And the door opens.

"That book won't save you from my wrath," growls a voice behind Colt.

He turns slowly, the threat meaning little as he regards Belphegor. "What does it contain?"

Belphegor curls his lip then turns away to sit in his leather chair. "All I'll tell you is the book is regarding Dunabar," he sneers. "And the shifter who stayed there, the same one you banished."

Shock ripples through Colt, although he doesn't show it.

Belphegor didn't directly answer his question, which means he can't read the strange symbols the book holds.

The same script that was on the door Mazikeen opened.

And even more surprising, is Belphegor's claim. Colt remembers his time with Asmodeus and Mazikeen in Hell, even if he'd rather not, but he has no memory of the shifter. The one the archdemon just claimed he banished.

"And here you are, siding with Asmodeus again," Belphegor snarls.

"I am on no one's side," Colt snaps back.

Belphegor snorts. "Because you are the most useless demon I've ever come across. The Tear is still open."

The insult no longer cuts like they once used to. Back when Colt served the archdemon, he was loyal. Even keen to please. But Belphegor tortured him for making a mistake.

And now Colt has Gabby.

"I couldn't sabotage the spell because a shape-shifter is involved. One who may be a primordial entity, the first shape-shifter."

Belphegor's gaze sharpens. "I doubt it's little more than a run of the mill, nasty shifter." He waves a hand dismissively. "Either way, I want that spell sabotaged, Colt. No matter what. I cannot afford for it to be closed."

Colt nods, holding the archdemon's gaze steadily even though he has no intention of betraying Gabby. He'll help her close the Tear for good. "I need to know about the shape-shifter to do that," he says. "In particular, I need to know if it's the primordial entity."

"Those legends are long lost," Belphegor scoffs. "No angel or demon tomes contain that information. The only people who can help would be those pesky little angels who pose themselves as the paragons of love."

"Cupids?" Colt asks, stilling.

Belphegor steeples his fingers, looking as if he's trying to summon patience. "Cupids have always known who this primordial entity is." He smiles coldly. "If you need to know more, I suggest you contact them."

Except Gabby's told Colt that several were murdered, at the

academy no less. It also seems Belphegor hasn't heard the news, meaning the angels have hidden the massacre well.

Colt crosses his arms. "Well, I'll need to find out soon. The shifter is the one who has your latest consignment."

Belphegor slams his fist down on his desk, making the phone sitting on it rattle as curses in every ancient language pepper the air. "I want my weapons back!" he roars. "Do you hear? Find them, and soon! I will not tolerate any more failure!"

Colt remains calm through the storm of fury. It no longer scares him.

The only thing that does is losing Gabby.

He inclines his head in a show of obedience. "As you wish," he murmurs.

Spinning on his heel, he takes the book with him, knowing it's a link to understanding the shifter, but a tenuous one at best.

Already looking forward to seeing Gabby, Colt strides past the secretary without glancing at her.

Hopefully, she's found out something more useful.

Because one thing is for sure. If this primordial entity is on Earth, it will be spreading hate to every corner.

9

GABBY

Gabby's father isn't anywhere on the grounds of the academy posing as Mr. Davenport, so she heads below ground to the supernatural club. But even there, he's not in the usual common or training rooms she'd normally find him in. Tracing his angelic essence takes her down labyrinthine corridors she hasn't been down before, deep into what must be the outskirts of this underground world.

She finds her father outside a room with Moroni. Magic tickles her senses, and she realizes the door is warded. Whatever's in there isn't something they want others to see.

"Gabrielle," her father says by way of greeting. "You found us."

She decides not to roll her eyes. "I'm not a total novice when it comes to spells."

He arches a blonde brow. "Indeed."

"What's in there?" she asks, indicating the closed door, wondering if her father will even tell her the truth.

"This is where the cupids were hiding as they waited to speak to you." He frowns. "It's where they were murdered."

Gabby takes an instinctive step back. "Oh. Well, once you're done checking out their dead bodies, I'd like to have a chat."

Moroni shakes his head. "Cupids turn to ash after death. The room will be empty."

She relaxes as she recovers the distance her horror had created. "Oh, okay. My Aunt Sierra was never great at cleaning. I'm pretty used to dust everywhere."

"That's good," says Moroni, clearly unsure how to respond to that. He turns to the door and waves his hand, muttering a few words. The magic that was prickling over Gabby's skin instantly disappears.

Moroni opens the door then steps back, allowing Gabriel then Gabby through.

They both stop the moment they enter.

Gabby's hand flies to her mouth as the need to be sick washes through her.

Bodies are scattered all over the room, heads at odd angles, limbs flung out in abandon. Some of the cupids have thrown themselves on others, one is right in front of them, it's throat shredded. Dried blood is peeling off their faces, their necks, their chests. It's sprayed on the walls, and pooled in cracked puddles.

Moroni slips past them, then also stops. "How?" he rasps.

"I thought..." Gabby gulps down the bile scorching her throat. "You said they would've turned to ashes by now."

Her father snaps out of his stupor, kneeling beside the nearest cupid. "I don't understand. Their bodies should've turned to ash by now."

Gabby wants to turn away, but she doesn't let herself. That would mean turning away from the sacrifice these beings made. It was her they were here to talk to. The least she can do is acknowledge them, even in death.

She walks to another cupid not far away. This one has his

hand wrapped around the companion beside him, the fingers tightly interlocked. She's surprised to find that despite the carnage, their faces are serene and composed. As if even death couldn't corrupt such purity.

Seems love can conquer even that.

Just thinking of Colt has her believing that's possible. What she feels for him will live on, no matter what. All she can hope is he feels the same for her...

She shakes her head. "I thought there was only one," she murmurs, shifting her focus from the greatest unknown in her life right now.

Her father straightens, his somber gaze scanning the bodies. "There are actually many cupids. Each works in a different territory, and not all of them are on Earth. Some of them even work their wonders in Heaven and Hell."

"So, cupids aren't angels?" she asks, surprised.

"Not exactly," her father says. "Cupids come from something primordial, but they were granted permission to make Heaven their abode, and for that, they usually follow the orders of the archangels. No one knows what really happened seeing as it goes back to the beginnings of Heaven. But we do know that the cupids came from a single cupid, whose true name has been long forgotten. He turned to ash at the hands of a powerful god, long before angels and demons and even Lucifer's Fall. Cupid's wife then pleaded with God, hoping to counteract the loss of love in the world, hoping to stall the entrance of something even more primordial than cupid himself."

She frowns. "Which is?"

"The antithesis of love—hate." Her father strokes his chin. "I believe the common name is Pothos, although it's never been confirmed that Pothos is indeed this entity that cupid was trying to prevent coming into the world."

"When he was killed," Gabby prompts, knowing without a doubt this is all connected to the shape-shifter somehow.

Her father nods. "Yes. But cupid left behind many sons, each possessing his power. So now there were more than a hundred cupids to spread the power of love. As it grew, Pothos became weaker. The gods were able to trap him in Hell."

"Hell?" Gabby stills, not sure why that's significant, but knowing it is.

"Yes. There was one place in Hell that was full of Light, which the gods hoped would neutralize Pothos, make him realize that love is the most powerful magic there is. Unfortunately, Pothos came into contact with a dark and evil power, this same dark evil power that corrupted Hell."

Moroni comes to stand beside Gabby's father. "And there's ample evidence to suggest it was the obsidian. Nothing else on this earth has the power to corrupt such pure Light."

Gabby curses inwardly. The obsidian again.

"Cupid's descendants turn to ash when they are killed, just like the original cupid." Her father indicates the bodies littering the room. The ones that shouldn't be here. "I don't understand why they haven't."

Gabby kneels down again to look at the poor soul who was murdered so brutally, and yet looks so peaceful. She frowns as she notices a strange mark on the man's shoulder. "Do they all have one of these?"

Her father and Moroni squat, studying the mark that resembles a spinning wheel. Neither have an expression that suggests it's supposed to be there.

"A summoning mark," her father said, scowling.

"Summoning marks?" Moroni asks, clearly confused.

"Yeah, summoning," Gabby says, proud she at least knows that. "As in angels summoned into human bodies."

He reels back in horror. "Possession? Angels possessing humans? Blasphemy! It's outlawed!"

Gabby looks to her father, seeing that Moroni's telling the truth. His scowl is growing deeper by the second. "Yes, it is outlawed. But these cupids obviously used the human bodies to visit you, Gabby. They must've known there is danger."

Gabby can feel her own scowl forming. "What danger?"

Neither her father nor Moroni are able to answer the question. Instead, her father sighs. "We can't track them, either. Their essence has evaporated and they would've fallen into a deep slumber so they can heal. All we can do is wait for them to reach out to you again, daughter."

She turns and exits the room, letting the scowl take shape. Waiting isn't an option.

"Where are you going?" her father calls after her.

"To talk to Colt," she shoots back, unsurprised by the silence that follows. Her father will never condone her relationship with a demon.

But it's only when she's with Colt that they ever make any progress, so too bad. There's too much coming at them at once.

The shape-shifter has vanished and there's no way to track him after he severed the link to Kalisha. And it seems he's allied himself with Beelzebub, a King of Hell. And possibly this mysterious organization determined to create chaos in an already chaotic world.

The death of the cupids can't be a coincidence. Especially when they knew they needed to protect themselves.

They need to learn who this shape-shifter is. And if it's the original shifter, one with primordial power, then they have one heck of an opponent on their hands.

They need answers.

And now.

10

GABBY

Colt opens the door to his cottage at the rear of the academy even before Gabby's knocked. She slips inside and the moment the door's closed, she throws herself into his arms.

Their mouths devour the other, almost as if Colt is as hungry for her as she is him. Gabby winds herself around him, her arms around his shoulders, her legs around his waist. Even as she tries to get impossibly closer, as every part of her molds to every plane of him, Colt tightens his hold. One powerful arm clamps across her back, the other spears into her hair and angles her head so he can have unfettered access. Their tongues duel and delight. Soft moans and groans become the symphony of their passion.

To her absolute dismay, it's Gabby who pulls back first.

Panting, she clings to his shoulders as she drops her jelly legs to the floor, needing a few moments for her muscles to want anything else but to claim the hot demon in front of her.

But her extreme response to the prospect that Colt betrayed her is proof she needs to slow down. That she needs to be sure.

Before she commits any more of herself, she has to know that Colt is in this as deep as she is.

Her emotions are forever.

No matter what.

She smiles. "We should..." She clears her throat when she discovers how husky her voice is. "We have a shape-shifter to track down."

Colt nods, his arms loosening. "Of course." His mouth twists into his own rueful smile. "If I'm not careful, I forget everything when I'm with you, Gabby."

Her heart soars at those words. She sways toward him, her good intentions fast evaporating. She doesn't want Colt to be careful.

But Colt steps back. "You're right," he says on a sigh. "We need to catch the shape-shifter. If he's who we hope he's not..."

Gabby suppresses her own sigh. "Then things could be bad," she finishes for him. She walks over to the couch and flops down. "My father doesn't know anything. The first shifter is older than even angels and demons."

Colt's mouth purses as he sits beside her. "Yes. Belphegor knows even less. Very little was recorded."

"Surely there's something, somewhere," Gabby huffs in frustration. "We need to know what we're dealing with."

Colt's gaze falls on a large leather tome sitting on the coffee table. "I found this in Belphegor's office. He believes it references the first shape-shifter."

"That's great!" she says, pulling it onto her lap. She runs her fingers over the runes embossed on the front. "I've never seen these before."

"Most haven't," Colt says heavily. "It's an ancient language. Older than most can read."

Gabby frowns as her cautious excitement dims. "Surely someone can."

To her surprise, Colt rises to his feet, looking edgy. She's never seen him edgy.

He clears his throat. "Back in Hell..." He clears his throat again. "I saw runes such as this at Dunabar."

Gabby watches him curiously. Something about the place definitely has Colt off kilter. And if it's a painful memory, he's probably not going to want to talk about it.

To her surprise, he continues without hesitation. "Dunabar is the source of all corruption in Hell. I was sent there by Asmodeus as I owed him after he rescued me from Belphegor's dungeons."

Gabby frowns. "You were trapped in Belphegor's dungeons?" She keeps her voice modulated, even as the need to pummel the King of Hell is overwhelming.

Colt's jaw tightens. "I gave him incorrect information after I was lied to. He believed I betrayed him and..." He shrugs as if it's of little consequence. "Demons aren't known for their mercy."

Gabby goes very still. That's exactly what she did.

Her stomach drops like it just turned to lead. How can she expect him to open up to her when she treated him the same way the archdemon did? She assumed guilt. And punished him for it.

Colt waves a hand. "The point is, I was at Dunabar because Asmodeus believed there was a way to free demons from its evil hold. Controlling its dark power was the way to do it."

Her heart still aching, Gabby rubs her temple, trying to focus. "Dunabar doesn't sound like a walk in the park."

"We didn't know it at the time, but it was the obsidian that corrupted Hell."

"The obsidian?" Her gaze snaps to Colt. "That evil really likes to get around."

He throws her a rueful smile. One that's short-lived as he

glances at the book again. "Those runes were on the eastern entrance when we arrived."

Gabby was about to open the book when she stops. "We?"

Colt does something she's never really seen before—his gaze slides away. "There was another demon with me. Her name is Mazikeen."

Gabby bites her lip so no words can shoot out before she can think this through. Colt's discomfort didn't just come from sharing whatever awfulness he experienced in Hell.

It's because of this demon.

A *female* demon.

Mazikeen.

Jealousy rips through her. Furiously accompanied with the drive to shred this Mazikeen, limb from limb. Colt. Is. Hers.

But Gabby breathes through it, some shred of rationality weaving its way through. Colt has a past. One that's centuries old. Of course he's had other relationships.

It's just that she's never had to think about him holding someone else. Kissing them. Some female knowing what it's like to touch—

Gabby clears her throat. "So you saw these runes with Mazikeen?" she asks, conscious of how polite her voice sounds.

Colt hasn't moved. "Yes. I couldn't read them, but she could. She explained it's a language founded during the primordial era of this universe. Nobody in the three realms can read it." His face brightens. "Belphegor thinks the cupids may be able to, seeing as they're also primordial entities. Is there some way to trace the others?"

But Gabby shakes her head. "The cupids who were murdered were using human bodies. They've fled and are in a deep sleep, so there's no way to track them. We have to wait until they reach out to me again."

"We have no idea how long before they do that again, considering the dangers," Colt growls.

"Exactly." Gabby grips the sides of the tome, not quite believing she's about to suggest this. "Decrypting this book is our only option, Colt. We need to summon Mazikeen."

He blanches, and if Gabby wasn't feeling so unwell herself at the prospect, she'd almost think the expression was funny.

Colt's scared.

Of Mazikeen? Or something else?

Gabby leans forward. "What happened between you two?" she asks softly. She needs to know, even if she doesn't really want to.

Colt drives his fingers through his hair. His gaze slides away once more, and she wonders if he's even going to tell her. And as much as any lies or deflecting will hurt, Gabby understands it. It's not easy for Colt to trust, and he has good reason for that.

Especially when she's one of the people who didn't trust him.

"She and I..." He trails off, then sighs. "We had a brief relationship. It was complicated, and it didn't end well." His chocolate gaze returns to her, steady and sure. "And it was over a long time ago."

Gabby finds herself smiling. Colt didn't avoid the question. And he wants to reassure her. It makes what she has to say that little bit easier.

"We need to summon her. We need to know what's in this book."

"She's crazy and manipulative, Gabby. And seeing as I broke it off with her, she most certainly won't do this as a favor. She'll want something in return."

Learning that Colt dumped Mazikeen shouldn't give Gabby a small flash of satisfaction, but it does. She even nurses it for a second or two.

But then she stands, trying to not make this personal. "Then we pay the price, Colt. We don't have a choice."

Colt's shoulders slump as he realizes she's right. "She's dangerous," he warns.

Gabby snaps her wings out, pulling up a determined smile. "Don't forget, so am I."

Colt. Is. Hers.

He moves toward her, his dark eyes shining in a way that warms her chest. "You are certainly a force to be reckoned with, Gabrielle Heartley."

"I feel invincible when I'm with you, Colt Grayson," she murmurs, slipping her arms around his shoulders.

"Good thing you have me, then," he murmurs back.

Gabby grins. Take that, Mazikeen. "Then let's summon this crazy bitch. We've faced worse."

Colt presses his warm lips to her forehead. "And won."

She holds him tightly for long seconds.

It's time to show Colt she trusts him.

DESPITE BELIEVING what she said to Colt, Gabby still finds herself nibbling her nail as Colt sets up the summoning spell. It took a little longer than anticipated seeing as he decided to use a witch-based spell that Blaise sourced for them rather than a demonic one. Seems no one particularly likes Mazikeen, and Colt didn't want to alert other demons, including Belphegor and Asmodeus, that the demoness was in this realm.

She appreciated him being careful.

And she liked that his ex-girlfriend isn't Ms. Popular, too.

Colt sits in the center of the triangle outlined in salt on the wood floor. The curtains are drawn, making his living room gloomy even though it's only afternoon. He's been solemn and silent since he began the process of the summoning spell. He laid a possession of his at each point of the triangle—dark t-shirts that have seen better days but seem to be his most prized possession—then three drops of his own blood. He hadn't even flinched as he sliced his palm, then squeezed the crimson blood at each point.

Now, Colt closes his eyes, going as still as a statue. Gabby also freezes, finding she's holding her breath. Unmoving Colt is just as enthralling as Colt in motion.

The soft shadows seem to wrap around him, almost caressing his skin. His chest barely moves. He looks like he's been carved from marble. Yet the power he wields is unmistakable. It's there in the corded muscles. The sense that his energy is barely contained.

It has Gabby entranced. Awed. And extremely possessive.

Mazikeen can ask for whatever she wants in exchange for reading the tome, but she's not going anywhere near this incredible, wonderful demon. Who. Is. Hers.

Colt begins chanting the spell, his sculpted lips only moving enough to murmur the words that sound like a mix between Latin and demoniac. Gabby has to remind herself to breathe as she waits to see what's going to happen. Blaise said it takes more power to summon a demon from the deeper levels of Hell. This will be straight forward if Mazikeen is somewhere in the upper echelons. Or it could be a draining battle to drag her up from the bowels.

And as much as a little part of Gabby—that part that's as far removed from being an angel as possible—is hoping this doesn't work, she doesn't want this to drain Colt. It would just be another reason to be pissed with Mazikeen.

A shudder ripples through Colt, making Gabby tense. His eyebrows contract a little, his lips thin.

He can't find the demoness.

Minutes pass. Then an hour. Restless energy thrums through Gabby, wishing she could at least pace, but she doesn't move from where she's sitting across from Colt. It's as if this is her way of helping. Or at least supporting him.

It feels like several more hours before he opens his eyes and lets out a breath. "I don't understand. Although I could sense her essence, I couldn't find her anywhere. It's as if she's not there."

A flash of guilt pierces Gabby. A part of her was hoping for this outcome.

Colt pushes to his feet and with one flick of his hand, the summoning triangle disappears. He sighs. "What do we do now?"

Gabby scrunches up her face. "We could ask my father if he can read the book?"

"Perhaps we should've tried that first." He slips his hand into hers. "It's more palatable than summoning Mazikeen."

"Wow," she jokes as they head for the door. "She's worse than my dad?"

Colt squeezes her hand. "It's possible she hates me more than he does."

Gabby smiles even as her gut clenches. Somehow, she doubts that. Her father has never liked Colt, no matter how unreasonable that is. Mazikeen most certainly liked Colt... which is totally understandable.

Pushing away the thoughts, especially now that facing the demoness isn't on the cards, Gabby updates Colt on what she learned about the cupids. His eyebrows contract as she tells him the cupids didn't turn to ashes like they're supposed to because they were actually possessed humans. He frowns even harder when she reiterates they have to wait for the cupids to find them.

Down in the supernatural club, they find Gabby's father stalking the corridors like a restless panther. His scowl only deepens when he sees Colt is with his daughter. Funnily enough, Colt doesn't smile back.

Knowing there won't be any social niceties, Gabby gets straight to the point. "Can you read this?" she asks, holding out the tome.

Her father takes it, his big body becoming still as his blue eyes survey the thick, aged cover. Without saying a word, he opens it, his gaze flitting over the lines of harsh-looking symbols.

"It's a language once spoken in the halls of Olympus. Prometheus taught me it, claiming it's a language from the primordial era, long before the faeries."

Gabby holds her breath. The faeries were the first entities known to inhabit this universe. And her father can read it! The excitement that sparks within her is quickly snuffed out by her father's next words.

"It's a dark book," he says soberly as he turns the page. "It talks of nothing but hatred."

Colt moves closer to Gabby. "What else does it say?"

Her father's so absorbed in the text that he doesn't even flash in annoyance that a demon dared ask something of him. "It is written by the original cupid, Kama." He looks up, the muscles around his blue eyes tense. "He writes of an entity named Pothos and his ability to shape-shift."

The same name he mentioned when telling her about the origin of cupids!

"What else does it say?" Gabby asks, knowing this is significant.

Her father flips another page, then another. His face sets in lines of concentration and as the seconds tick by, Gabby has to stop herself from going around and scanning the words he's reading. It's not like she can't understand it. It's more about her impatience, and her father isn't a fan of impatience.

He looks up after what feels like days later. "The book states that Pothos breeds hatred among humans. As the original shape-shifter, he's a primordial entity who can shift into anyone he touches. He basically clones DNA."

"It's him," Gabby breathes, any elation that they're getting close to the truth quickly dampened by the realization they're possibly dealing with an ancient, powerful entity.

One who may be in possession of the demonic weapons.

Her father's lips tip down at the edges. "It says here he's the antithesis of cupids, determined to annihilate them, which confirms what I'd already been told."

Colt narrows his eyes in thought. "And how do we know if Pothos is in our world? How do we differentiate between Pothos and any other shape-shifter?"

"Cupids," Gabby's father responds, closing the book. "Cupids are the only ones who can identify him."

Gabby clenches her jaw. Stalemate again. They're back to waiting for the cupids to turn up again. 'Then how do we beat Pothos?" she asks, changing tact to something they may have control over.

"He cannot be killed," her father answers. "He's primordial darkness. But he could be banished back to where he came from."

"Which is?"

"The primordial ether. A void that exists beyond the Light that gives life. There are a lot of names given to this void, this ether. I think today's scientists call it antimatter."

Gabby blinks, wishing she had more time to explore this fascinating convergence of science and the supernatural. Unfortunately, saving the world is kind of a priority. "And we'd need a spell for that?"

To Gabby's surprise, her father's gaze falls on Colt. "I've heard that a demon once banished a shifter during their time in Hell."

Gabby turns to look at Colt, unsure how she feels about this news. Surely Colt being familiar with this is a good thing...

"That was a long time ago," Colt growls. "And I have no memory of that time. Besides, each spell is specific to a shifter. We'd need someone who knows how to do that."

Gabby's heart thuds out a few furious beats before she asks the next question. "And who could do that?"

Colt's chocolate gaze flicks to her before darting back to her father. "Mazikeen," he says, his jaw tightening. "And we haven't been able to find her."

For the second time, they've come full circle. Not only do they need to wait for the cupids, but Colt's demoness ex-girl-friend is still needed.

"We need that spell," Gabby says aloud, as if she has to hear it just as much as Colt.

No matter how much the words leave a bitter film in her mouth.

Colt straightens, his dark eyes lighting up. "There's one other person who might know about the spell."

Gabby's spine also unwinds as she realizes who. They now have something to do while they wait for the cupids.

They may not need Mazikeen after all.

She almost smiles. "Let's go talk to Asmodeus."

II

GABBY

Turns out Asmodeus has high-tailed it to who-knows-where.

To all intents and purposes, he's disappeared.

Colt jams his fingers through his wine-colored hair, growling with frustration. "There's nothing to trace."

Gabby sighs as they stand on the lawns of the academy, the afternoon sun stretching their shadows over the manicured green. She'd started to think Asmodeus might be a reasonable King of Hell. He wants to return the weapons, and he tried to bring peace to Hell. Then again, he sent Colt to Dunabar to do his bidding.

If that's not bad enough, he's the prick who introduced Colt to Mazikeen.

And if he's MIA, then they need to find that demoness. Gabby's not sure she's ready for that.

She's not sure she'll ever be.

Colt's head jerks toward the parking lot. "I have an idea. Come on."

He takes her hand and Gabby willingly goes with him. She'd follow Colt anywhere. Especially if it means Mazikeen stays wherever she is. They reach his sleek black car and he unlocks it, his handsome face set in determined lines as they climb in.

Colt drives fast but competently. He barely slows for bends, yet the tires never lose their grip on the road. It's like he's part of the throaty engine that roars each time they accelerate. Both are barely controlled power wrapped up in a package that has heads turning. Gabby could sit here and revel in watching Colt's understated confidence for hours.

They've been driving through the streets of Mercy City for a few minutes before she realizes she should at least know where they're heading. "Where are we going?"

Colt slows and pulls over next to the curb. "Here," he says, indicating the house they're beside.

Gabby surveys the unobtrusive-looking place. With its green lawn, neat fence, and paved path that leads to the front door, there's nothing about it that's exceptional. And yet, there's a faint buzz of energy tingling over her skin… "Whose house is this?" she asks, curious.

"As you know, demons possess human bodies," Colt says, also scanning the house. "Well, Asmodeus took possession of the guy who used to live here. If I can find something that belongs to him, I can track the body instead of the demon."

Gabby grins. "Not just a pretty face, huh?"

He rolls his eyes, as unassuming as always. "There are strong wards around it," he observes. "It might take a while to break through them."

Gabby unclips her seatbelt. "Not when the two of us work our magic."

Colt's eyes gleam. "Very true."

They climb out of the car, yet have to stop before they've even reached the fence line. Although the barrier surrounding the house is invisible, it's thick and thrumming with energy. Asmodeus definitely doesn't want anyone in here.

Which makes Gabby want to get inside even more.

She stands side by side with Colt and they raise their hands. Gabby goes to cloak them only to find Colt already has. A soft cocoon of magic surrounds them, hiding what they're about to do. She flashes him a smile of thanks. She wonders if he even realizes how he almost unconsciously looks after her.

Focusing back on the task, Gabby spreads her fingers, the tips tingling as they make contact with the ward. She closes her eyes, connecting with the well of power known as her Grace. It flares instantly, flowing through her veins like electricity. White light heats her palms and appears at her fingertips. It branches out like lightning, crawling over the barrier, looking for weaknesses.

And doesn't find any.

Gabby opens her eyes, her brow pinching in concentration. Beside her, crimson energy pours from Colt's fingers, arcing out in the same way her angelic energy is. It crackles over the ward, also unsuccessful in finding a crack it can infiltrate through.

They glance at each other. Smile slightly. And return their focus to the ward.

This time, the gold and crimson energy shoot out simultaneously. They weave together, lines of light crisscrossing and merging to form a fabric of light and dark. Of love.

Gabby doesn't hear the crack. She feels it. The place where her own and Colt's powers mesh the most splinters. Crumbles. And the ward collapses.

Colt's face lights with triumph and something else. The same emotion crowding Gabby's chest. Pride.

Impulsively, she pressed a quick, hard kiss against his mouth. "Told you. Invincible."

He grins. "I see what you mean."

Turning back to the house, they walk up the path and Gabby's tempted to wrap herself around his arm. Except they're not off to a friend's house or a garden party. They're trying to track down a King of Hell. She resists biting her lip. She wants to tell Colt how she feels. That she trusts him. She should've from the beginning.

But the battle of good and evil keeps getting in the way.

One wave of Colt's hand and the door opens before they've reached it. The space inside is dark, so he conjures a golden light to lead their way. "The more personal the item is, the easier it will be to channel," he explains as his sharp gaze roams the interior of the house. "Rings, favorite clothes, coffee mugs all work well. It could be something he uses daily and attaches meaning to. A photograph could do."

Gabby nods, finding herself in a large, open plan lounge room. A chunky sofa and matching armchairs face a blank TV. Everything looks normal, but empty. "He hasn't been here for a while," she guesses.

"Yes." Colt walks around, squatting to peer under furniture, then running his hands between the cushions. "He's kept it looking like this so suspicion isn't aroused if anyone gets nosy."

Gabby walks to the tall bookshelves on the other side of the room, finding they're lined with mystery and thriller books. "Could they work?" she asks, pulling out a John Grisham novel.

Colt grimaces. "The less connection the human has to the item, the harder it will be to track them."

She sighs as she puts it back. "Let's hope we find something else, then."

They make their way into the kitchen, but it's emptier than the living room that functions as a false front for the neighbors. The cupboards are bare. The drawers are empty. There's not even a tea towel to be found. The dining room is nothing more than a heavy wooden table with matching chairs.

Upstairs, the three bedrooms are just as fruitful. Although they open every wardrobe and look under and around every piece of furniture, they come up empty-handed. Not even a lone sock caught behind a bedside table, mourning the loss of its mate.

Gabby's about to comment that they'll have to hope Grisham can come through with the goods when she notices a manhole above them as they stand in the corridor. "An attic," she says, trying not to get excited.

Colt narrows his eyes. "It's locked."

She flicks a blonde curl over her shoulder. "My turn," she teases. Focusing her gaze on the manhole, she purses her lips. Hopefully she can do it quickly and look like she knows what she's doing. The spell is pretty straightforward—

Click. The small door pops open and a wooden ladder slides to the ground.

"You're getting faster," Colt says, impressed.

She beams in a way she never does when her father gives her a compliment during their training. "I barely had to think about it."

"You're a natural, Gabrielle Heartley." He steps back and waves a hand. "M'lady."

She pretends to curtsy then clambers up the ladder, feeling very little like a lady as she makes sure to sashay her backside, just in case Colt's looking.

The inside of the attic is as musty and dusty as the house is clean and deserted. But it's also full of boxes.

"Bingo," Gabby breathes.

She stops beside the first stack and lifts the lid as Colt does the same with another beside it. He lifts up a tea towel. "This may take a while," he mutters.

But Gabby's box isn't the contents of the kitchen drawers. She lifts up a photo. "Double bingo."

The image shows the man Asmodeus has possessed with an old couple she guesses are his parents. The man's younger, and holding a trophy comprised of two golden tennis racquets.

"Will this do?"

Colt takes the photo and studies it carefully. "Yes, I believe it will." He closes his eyes, his lips silently forming a spell. They open almost instantly. "I've found him."

Gabby throws the lid back on the box. "Then what are we waiting for?"

But Colt doesn't move. "He's not on this continent, Gabby." His face tightens. "And I'm best going alone."

Her first instinct is to object, but she knows he's right. She can't disappear halfway around the globe right now. And Asmodeus is going to be as happy to see her as her father was to see Colt.

Once again, their heritage is keeping them apart.

"Fine," she huffs. They need that spell. "But tell Asmodeus if he ever tries to send you somewhere like Dunabar again, I'll personally shred him."

Colt's sculpted lips tip up in a smile. "I'll mention it if it comes up."

"Good," she says grudgingly.

With a sweet kiss that has her heart fluttering, Colt disappears. Gabby lets out a long sigh as she prepares to leave. She'll fly back to the academy, maybe see if Kalisha wants to get a hot chocolate and donut from the cafeteria or something. She's hoping to talk about Maya's upcoming birthday. Things haven't been the same since Maya lost her adoptive parents and blamed Colt for it. She even went as far as telling Gabby he was the one who betrayed her. And then Maya refused to believe the footage was fake. Hopefully a party will be a good opportunity to heal the fracture in their friendship. Maya's grief has to lessen its grip on her at some stage...

Gabby's just closed the attic when her cell phone rings. She picks up with a smile when she sees who it is. "Hey, Kalisha. I was just thinking about you. We totally need to start planning Maya's birthday party."

"Wow, we really were on the same wavelength. I'm ringing about Maya."

Except Kalisha's voice isn't light and chirpy. She isn't calling to talk about balloons and streamers. "What's up?" Gabby asks, her own tone dropping to match her friend's.

"She's just been acting a bit...weird. I thought it was just me after she came back from that trip out of the blue down to Miami and Key West."

Gabby frowns. "She went to the coast?"

"Yeah. Said it wasn't a big deal, that she just wanted to clear her head. I was hoping things would be better, so I just went with it. But then..."

Every cell in Gabby's body stills. "Yeah? But then?"

"I dunno. I decided to wash my sheets, and thought it would be nice if I did hers, too. But I found something in her bed."

Gabby waits, but Kalisha doesn't continue. "What?" she prods.

"It was gross, Gabby," she explodes. "Like a transparent shell or something. Like a clear, kinda sticky skin!"

The words ricochet through Gabby. But she goes from reeling and stunned to striding down the corridor, down the stairs and out of the house in a blink.

"Stay away from her, Kalisha," Gabby warns. "I'm coming back now."

"Stay away from her?" she asks, alarmed. "Why?"

"I'll explain when I get back. But she's not who you think she is."

Gabby hangs up, already weaving the cloaking spell around her so she can fly back. Maya went to Miami, which isn't far from Myrtle beach, the same place they tracked the stolen weapons to. The unreasonable hatred of Colt. The grief and denial that she was determined to cling to.

Then the fake video aimed at tearing Gabby and Colt apart.

All things that are out of character for her sweet, smart friend.

Gabby should've known something was amiss. Although, it turned out to be far more than that. The explanation is far more sinister and disturbing.

Maya is the shape-shifter.

12

COLT

The King of Hell chose the ruins of a village in India to hide in, surrounded by jungle and mosquitoes. Whether he's hiding from Belphegor, Beelzebub, or Colt himself, there's no way of knowing.

But it doesn't really matter.

Colt found him.

He strides through the thick undergrowth, any path to the village long ago reclaimed by palms and ferns and creepers, weaving a spell as he goes. The vegetation ends abruptly, revealing a clearing of moss-covered rubble. A hut sits at the rear, the pale stone and thatched roof looking incongruous amongst the decay of anything man-made.

A puff of black smoke pours out the door and straight for the sky, only to hit an invisible ward a few feet up. The one Colt just erected as he suspected the archdemon would try to flee. He didn't want to have to deal with tracking the demon king again. Not when he'd realize Colt tracked the vessel he possesses, making it even harder the next time around. Seething, the mass of black smoke drops back down and takes form.

A furious Asmodeus appears a few feet away. "What do you want, Geryon? Here to pretend we're working together again, when all you do is scheme with that angel of yours?"

Colt refuses to feel guilt. It's true he and Gabby had made a plan without Asmodeus's knowledge when it came to the shipment of demonic weapons, but it's no different to Asmodeus using Colt for his own gains. Nor can he blame losing the weapons on them—the secret organization used a decoy.

He pins Asmodeus with a watchful glare. "I'm here to learn about the shape-shifter."

The one they thought was little more than a troublemaker when it stole the gem used to power the Tear, only for it to steal the demonic weapons.

"What about it?" Asmodeus spits.

"I believe it may be quite powerful. The first shape-shifter, in fact."

Asmodeus frowns. "I have heard of it. Primordial in origin. Definitely powerful." He narrows his eyes in thought. "I originally thought the Shifter of Dunabar was one and the same, but I was never sure."

Colt doesn't want to dwell on the past. "Either way, you know the banishing spell we can use to be rid of it."

For some reason, that amuses the archdemon. "The one Mazikeen gave you?"

"Yes," Colt grinds out through gritted teeth. "That one. I can't seem to remember my time in Dunabar clearly."

"I'm not surprised after what happened there," Asmodeus scoffs.

That time in his life has always been hazy, but Colt's never delved too deeply as to why. A part of him knew he didn't want to relive visiting one of the darkest places in all the three realms.

"Well, it seems it's time you did remember," Asmodeus

says, a slow smile spreading across his face. "If you want to know the spell, that is."

Colt tenses, not liking the sound of that. But before he can demand Asmodeus simply tell him, especially if he wants those demonic weapons back in Hell, the archdemon moves. He shoots toward Colt, easily slips past the strike and block Colt throws out, and brushes a cold finger over his forehead.

Colt's legs give out and the world goes black.

The black corridor that stretches before Geryon looks like endless night. Yet Mazikeen strides into Dunabar, her long hair brushing her sashaying hips. "This way," she says, barely glancing over her shoulder.

Geryon follows, drawing his shoulders in tightly as he avoids the dark power pulsing in the walls. The air is thick with a foul stench that has him breathing as little as possible. Within seconds, it feels like his veins are turning black and corrupt. His muscles are also weakening, his strength slowly being corroded by the evil that lives here. Even his eyesight is affected.

Ahead, Mazikeen nimbly steps to the side, and Geryon realizes there's a hole in the ground. One glance reveals a bottomless drop, smooth onyx walls leaving nothing to gain purchase on. A drop would be certain death. Or worse. Endless torture once it was discovered what's at the bottom.

"This place is..." Geryon shakes his head. "Sick."

Mazikeen flashes him a smile. "This place is where the darkness that corrupted Hell originated, of course it's sick. Nothing grows here. No light can shine in this place. Not even that created by our magic."

"Then how are you navigating?" he asks, realizing she's right. It takes effort to be standing, let alone work magic here. He squints, watching for more deadly holes or any other nasty surprises. "I cannot even see clearly."

"I've been here before," Mazikeen says, sounding almost wistful.

"Long before, when it was not so dark. Demons used to live here before they went crazy and abandoned this place." She sidles closer, her hip brushing his hand. *"I've been lonely for a long time, Geryon."*

He doesn't answer. In part because his gut just clenched at the contact. In part because he knows what lonely feels like. Over time, he's become accustomed to it. But Mazikeen's dark eyes seem to remind him of the hollow that he's always carried. Either because she understands it.

Or because she's offering to fill it.

"Of course, something else lives here now," she says bitterly, stepping around another hole and tugging him closer so he avoids it, too.

"Something else?" he asks. *"Is that why Asmodeus wants us to check this place out?"*

Mazikeen nods. *"Asmodeus wants to use this power to drive out the corruption from Hell. The seven Sins are intent on ravaging the earth, and something needs to be done about them."*

"And both of you think that this dark power will help you do that?"

"The Sins have been influencing this place for a long time, but they're becoming ambitious. It's why the Kings of Hell are fortifying —in order to make their cities safe from the influence of the Sins. It's dividing them even further."

Geryon pulls Mazikeen close when she almost brushes against a wall. She grins up at him as if she was testing him. He shakes his head, refocusing on their conversation. *"And you said someone lives here now?"*

"Those primordial runes you saw weren't there before," Mazikeen says as they reach an intersection. She turns left without hesitating, now holding Geryon's hand as she leads him. *"Someone with knowledge of a banned language carved them there. It means the entity is ancient. Maybe even powerful as nobody can actually stay here for any length of time, and yet they've done so."*

"What for, is the question," Geryon thinks aloud. No one would choose to remain in this evil den unless they needed to.

Mazikeen takes a right Geryon barely noticed through his hazy eyesight, then another sharp left. "Asmodeus thinks the entity is preparing for some kind of ritual that involves the channeling of demonic weapons."

An evil entity channeling demonic weapons has uneasiness crawling over Geryon's skin alongside the dark evil of this place.

Mazikeen halts, then presses her length against him. "That's why we're here," she purrs in his ear. "To stop it. It's the only way Hell can be saved."

He shivers. The words themselves are ambitious. But so is the demoness gently gyrating against him.

With a low chuckle, Mazikeen turns and walks ahead. Geryon discovers they're no longer in a corridor, but in a large cave-like room. One lined completely in books. He executes a slow turn, marveling that so much evil and knowledge can co-exist in one place. Huge, leather-bound tomes hug the rounded walls, giving the sense of a strange sort of womb. Geryon knows without a doubt that some of the most ancient and legendary books of Hell are here.

Mazikeen walks to her right, then gracefully leaps and grasps a spine. She's already opened it as she lands, flicking her onyx hair back over her shoulder. Instantly immersed, she flips the pages, one by one.

Geryon prowls the room as he waits, wondering how she's even able to read the text. Even with his demonic vision, everything here is clouded, as if a thick shroud has been pulled over his eyes. He glances at the door they entered through. "Won't the entity know we're here?"

"Most likely," Mazikeen says mildly, not looking up. "But I've cloaked us enough that it won't be able to pinpoint our location. We're that annoying fly you can't seem to find."

"We need to hurry, then." Geryon paces back to the door. Mazi-

keen may be careless with her own life, but he hasn't reached that stage yet. "What are you looking for?"

This time, Mazikeen looks up. She smiles with relish. "A banishment spell." She holds up the book. "The one I just found."

He finds himself drawn to it, curious despite himself. Even though this isn't his fight.

Mazikeen points to the lines of demoniac. "One you'll need to memorize. You'll be casting the spell."

He reels back. "What?"

"The fact you can see at all in here is proof of your power, Geryon. You were mentored by Belphegor, his star pupil. You have an archdemon's blessing."

It's true. Even though Belphegor has now turned his back on him, he's taught him things no other demon knows.

"Asmodeus hasn't granted you the same?"

She shakes her head. "I'm not the great Geryon," she murmurs, her eyes raking over him. "Although I can certainly see why you were chosen."

Mazikeen passes him the book and to his surprise, he takes it. "Memorize it," she says huskily. "Then you will be the one to cast it."

His gaze scans the lines, memorizing them easily even as he knows he's likely being used and manipulated. Despite that, freeing Hell of its corruption would change his world.

"What will happen?" he asks, needing to know. "Once I've cast the spell."

"The shifter won't die, obviously, but will be sent back into the void from where he came." Mazikeen slips in close and runs her finger along his jaw. "Trust me, Hell will be freed."

He closes the book and passes it to her, his decision made. "Where to now?"

Mazikeen's eyes gleam, her teeth flashing a moment later as she smiles. "This way."

One somersault and she returns the book. Two flips and she's *back at the door. Geryon follows, cold determination settling in his gut as he repeats the spell in his mind.*

They've taken two turns through the labyrinthine corridors when he realizes something. "You're following the stench." It's growing stronger with each step.

Mazikeen throws him an appreciative glance. "Yes. I remember it from when Kama, the first cupid, penned a book about this entity. He called it by a name I can no longer recall, Po...something." She waves a dismissive hand. "Kama's offspring and the gods combined forces to trap the entity in Hell, long before it was corrupted by the darkness. They built Dunabar as a prison to contain it back when this was known as the Underworld."

But as Mazikeen continues to talk, her voice fades, even though the distance between them doesn't grow. Geryon frowns, sensing something now in the corridor with them. Something evil.

The power that corrupted this dark place.

And powerful it is. Geryon can feel it. A voice whispers through his mind.

"You are meant for great things, Geryon."

Suddenly, images crowd his vision. He's sitting on a throne of legend, one that only exists in the deepest bowels of Hell. One no demon would think of coming close to. A throne meant for the ultimate ruler of Hell. And it's the most tempting image Geryon's ever seen. Power swells through him, seductive and dark.

"You would be unstoppable," the voice promises.

Shame scorches Geryon. He's never thirsted to sit on Lucifer's chair. He shakes his head, pushing away the traitorous thoughts. They weren't his own. They can't be.

Instead, he recites the spell over and over, branding the words in his mind.

Colt sits up, drawing in a sharp breath. He blinks as the sounds and the smells of the jungle register once more.

Asmodeus was right. The memory had been within him all along.

A quick glance around the rubble reveals the archdemon is long gone. Colt growls in frustration, the sound quickly tempered by the knowledge he got what he came for.

He knows the spell to banish the shape-shifter.

13

GABBY

Gabby enters the head of security's office with determined strides. Her father, posing as Mr. Davenport is there, someone with him. Although she registers the veneer of a young man in a matching security uniform, she recognizes Moroni beneath it, in the same way she now sees her father's true form beneath the illusion of a graying, old man. They're leaning over a set of architectural plans spread out on the desk but the moment she enters, Moroni rolls them up.

Her father smiles at her as he steps slightly in front of his lieutenant. "Hello, daughter."

They're hiding something from her, but Gabby knows asking is a waste of time. Her father may be in her life, but he has his secrets. She suspects he always will. His duty as an archangel has always been his priority.

It's something that will always define their relationship, she thinks, surprised by the bitterness that jabs at her chest. She thought she'd accepted that.

Shaking her head, she pushes the revelation away. There are more important things to focus on apart from her daddy issues. "I need a spell," she says, getting straight to the point.

Pothos needs to go. By taking over Maya's life, his drive for chaos just became personal. And a little more complicated. Before they can use the banishment spell that Colt's sourcing, they have to find Maya and make sure she's safe. What's more, they'll need to sever whatever link exists between them.

Which means she needs to talk to a cupid.

Her father straightens. "What kind of spell?"

"To talk to the cupids—"

"I told you," he says a little impatiently. "You need to wait for them to contact you. They are sleeping so they can heal."

Gabby holds her ground. "Well, I can't wait." Maya's life may depend on it. "Surely there's a spell that would allow me to contact them whilst they're asleep."

"What you're suggesting is extremely risky," her father says, frowning. "You're suggesting entering an angel's mind, which is dangerous. You could be trapped."

She takes a step forward. "So there is a spell!"

He nods grudgingly. "Yes, there's a spell that allows you to dive deep into a being's consciousness, whether they are human or more. But once you enter, you're in their territory and have little control."

Gabby shrugs. "Sounds kinda like real life right now."

Moroni shakes his head. "It's one thing to delve into a human mind, Gabby. Angelic dreamscapes are different. More protected, and therefore harder to leave." He glances at Gabriel. "Although there are ways to mitigate the risk."

Gabby almost rubs her hands together. Now they're talking. "Which are?"

"Every individual has their individual dreamscapes, the place of their dreams and nightmares," he explains. "While human dreamscapes are easy to enter, angelic ones are surrounded by a shell fueled by their Grace. It takes significant power to get past that."

Gabby waits, wondering when the 'this is possible' part kicks in.

"If you breach the wall to the dreamscape, their Grace will register you as a threat. It will trap you, refusing to let you leave with whatever secrets are held within the dreamscape."

She crosses her arms. "Mitigating the risks, remember?"

Moroni glances at her, not liking being prodded. "There is someone who can help you enter dreamscapes," he offers. "They may even be able to help mask you once you're in there."

And there it is. Her risk mitigator. "Who is this being?"

Moroni glances at her father, who's stony, yet hasn't stopped his lieutenant from sharing the information. "They're called the Sandman."

TURNS out the Sandman is a she.

A she who lives in a cute little apartment in Philadelphia, Gabby notes as she rides the elevator to the fifteenth floor. Although the inhabitants may be questionable, she thinks as she ignores the stare of the goth-looking guy sharing the small space. He exits on the twelfth floor, muttering what sounds like his phone number under his breath. She almost rolls her eyes.

No guy will ever compare to Colt.

Finding apartment number twenty-three, Gabby knocks on the door. There's the sound of footsteps on the other side and the door half-opens to reveal a young woman of similar age, a mass of brown curls framing pretty features. "Yes?" she asks, wary.

"Hi," Gabby says brightly. "My name's Gabrielle Heartley. I was hoping to chat."

"About?"

Gabby's more than happy to get straight to the point. "I need help getting into a dreamscape."

The young woman tries to slam the door but Gabby jams her foot in.

She keeps her smile up as she continues. "I know you're the Sandman and that you can help me." She drops her voice. "It's urgent."

The young woman hesitates, then lets out a long-suffering sigh. She opens the door fully. "Fine, then." She turns, speaking over her shoulder. "My name's Mira, by the way."

Gabby follows her inside, relieved. "So, you can help me?"

"Of course I can," Mira says, stopping in an entrance accented with shades of purple. "But that doesn't mean I'm going to. I don't just take anyone into dreamscapes. There's this little thing called privacy."

"Fair enough," says Gabby. "I respect that." She angles her head, then gives the lowdown on everything. Pothos, the first shape-shifter. Maya. Cupids being the key. "I need to speak to one of them," she finishes, hoping she conveyed exactly how many lives may depend on it.

Mira's face settles in grave lines. "A deep dive into their dreamscape is a risky endeavor, even with my help. They're angels. If you're trapped, I can't help you. You'd be left in a vegetative state, and I'd feel responsible."

Gabby waits, wondering what her next move is if she gets a no. Can she force Sandman to do this?

"Luckily for you, Fate visited me," Mira says.

"Fate?"

"Yes, the goddess of the loom of life. She told me you'd

come. The fact you're here is proof that I'm supposed to help, even if I think this is dangerous and risky."

Gabby grins. "You sound like you've been talking to my father."

"He obviously cares what happens to you." Mira turns before Gabby can respond, although she's not sure what she'd say, anyway. Caring isn't how she'd describe her father.

Mira leads her into a living room dominated by two large couches. Both long enough for a person to stretch out and lie on. Like a psychotherapist might have. Mira sits on the one on the right and indicates to Gabby to take the other. "Make yourself comfortable. I'll take us to the Crossroads, where I'll track the cupid's dreamscape. Luckily, it shouldn't be too hard. There aren't many on this mortal plane."

Gabby does as she's told, stretching out on the couch, not surprised to find it's soft and inviting. The couch is more like a bed. One designed to draw you into slumber.

Into dreams.

"Now, close your eyes," Mira says, her voice low and soothing. Almost hypnotic. "Relax and open yourself to your subconscious."

Gabby's not sure whether she's just realized she's tired, or whether she's primed to fall asleep fast because she's knows there's a ticking clock counting down the seconds before the shape-shifter unleashes itself on the world, because consciousness falls away and she finds herself suffused by golden light.

"Your dreamscape," Mira says, appearing beside her. "Come, it's the Crossroads we want."

Gabby follows, but her gaze is drawn to the flickering images around her. They're all strangely familiar, even if she doesn't remember them. She realizes they're her dreams. The fantasies her subconscious weaves, largely beyond her memory.

Colt's there, just as she knew he'd be. Her heart clenches as she realizes they're standing close together as she cradles a baby. He leans down, pressing a kiss to the child's forehead.

Then there's another image, of the two of them flying high over snow-capped peaks. Their wings beat in unison, their gazes spending far more time on each other rather than the breath-taking views below. They come together, wings outstretched, gliding soundlessly as they kiss.

Then there's images of Arielle and her at the mall, sharing a banana split. And another with Kalisha and Maya and Klae, all laughing as they dance at a party.

Gabby notices Mira is smiling almost wistfully. The moment she notices Gabby looking, the softness in her face dissolves. "No, I don't know," she tells her.

"Don't know what?"

"What your mind was wondering. I can't tell which dreams come true, and which don't."

Gabby realizes that's exactly what she was hoping Mira could tell her.

Because she wants every one of those images to become reality.

Another door appears and Mira steps through without hesitation, Gabby right behind her. She finds they're at the Crossroads. Hard-packed dirt, countless feet compacting the soil over centuries of use, divides into two roads ahead, their destinations obscured by mist.

Mira does a slow turn, looking thoughtful. She looks one way, then the other, although Gabby's not sure what at. All that surrounds them is dirt road and mist.

"This one," Mira says, taking several steps down the road, away from the intersection.

"Which one?" Gabby asks.

But even before she's finished, the outline of a door appears at the side of the road. Bright light seeps through, a faint, scarlet tinge to it.

"This is the entrance to one of the cupid's dreamscapes," Mira says, watching Gabby closely.

Gabby nods, not letting herself think too deeply about what she's going to do.

"Remember," Mira says, suggesting she's not going to let Gabby off that easily. "You need to get out before their conscious mind gets a hold of you."

"Dodge consciousness. Noted."

Mira shakes her head, almost looking amused. "Here," she says, passing her a golden coin. "This will help cloak you. It'll buy you some time as you seek the answers you need."

Gabby takes it. "Thanks," she says, meaning it. Her deliberate denial of the dangers of this venture isn't entrenched enough to realize she needs every advantage offered to her.

Mira indicates to the door with her chin. "Good luck and be quick."

Gabby steps through before she allows herself to think this through any further. Denial is actually preferable. It has her believing this is totally doable.

Inside, the door closes immediately, enclosing her in a sterile, white room. A single bed sits in the center, the starched sheets just as glaringly absent of color. The only thing that breaks the endless alabaster is the tall man lying on the bed, unblinking eyes staring at the non-existent ceiling.

Gabby approaches him. "Hello? Can you hear me?"

He doesn't move. Doesn't even blink.

Yet, the moment she speaks, something shifts in the room. The air thickens. The white deepens. It goes from ethereal to gaining substance. A cranky substance.

Gabby steps closer, urgency filling her. There's even less time than she thought.

Desperate, she grips his shoulders and shakes. "Please! Wake up!"

The man sits up with a gasp, his eyes flying open. He blinks as he looks at her. Then blinks again. "Gabrielle, finally."

The moment he speaks, the walls settle. The air becomes easier to breathe.

She smiles with relief. "Yes, that's me. Gabby."

Cupid swings his legs down, his gaze intent as he studies her. "You found me here?"

"Yes. I need to speak to you."

He nods. "As we did you. We arrived at the academy in our human vessels, searching for you."

Gabby leans forward. "Yes. You wanted to tell me something."

"We did. Something important." He glances around warily. "It has to do with the dark entity now in the mortal plane."

"I know. Pothos."

Cupid grunts. "Yes. Manipulative, evil thing that he is. He likes to prey on the vulnerable."

"We've discovered that. He's taken over my friend's life. We'll have the banishing spell soon," she says, having no doubt Colt will be successful. "But we need to know how to keep my friend safe."

Cupid grimaces, his hands clenching the white sheets. "He keeps his victims close. The key will be to identify who the real Maya is. When you close in, Pothos will know this. He'll try to trick you." He glances at the bed. "My kind can tell the difference, but it will be some time before we recuperate and our slumber ends."

Gabby tenses as she registers a change around her. Although the walls seem to have no substance, they suddenly feel closer. Harder. Like they're frowning.

She clasps her hands, trying to be patient. "Which means I need a Plan B."

Cupid nods, seeming unaware of the change around them as he looks thoughtful. "There's a spell that could sever the link between Pothos and your friend. Between the real and the false. When that happens, Pothos will keep shifting through the myriad forms he's taken in the past and you'll identify him."

"Yes," she says, leaning forward. "That's exactly what I need."

Except the moment she moves, their surroundings twitch. The frown turns to a scowl. And this time, Cupid notices.

He shuffles forward, looking earnest. "You must be careful with the spell. Pothos will expect it. He'll try to stop you."

The sound of cracking has Gabby tensing. Small fissures appear in the walls that are now most certainly hard. Yet thin as eggshells. Whatever's on the other side is about to smash through.

"The spell," she says urgently. "What is it?"

A crevice appears above the cupid, and a sinuous, snake-like vine of midnight winds through. Cupid spins and lifts his hands, trying to stop it. But the tendril doesn't even pause, determined to end the foreign entity posing a threat. Cupid isn't strong enough to stop it.

He spins back to Gabby. "You must go! Leave here!"

Because if she doesn't she'll be trapped in this white room, her body in the real world little more than vegetable.

But still, Gabby hesitates. "I need the spell!"

"I'll transfer the memory to you! Go!"

Not knowing if that's even possible, she turns and sprints for the door. The sounds of destruction amplify. The air shudders. Something brushes her hair, and another cold tendril touches her shoulder, making her skin crawl. She yanks the door open and launches through, slamming it behind her.

The silence is stark after the roar of destruction she just left, leaving Gabby panting.

Mira blinks. "That was close."

Gabby's out of control pulse is proof of that. "I was hoping for more time." The door behind her shakes, making her leap away.

Mira frowns. "Well, it seems like time's up."

"But—" Gabby dives into her pocket for the gold coin that was supposed to cloak her presence, yet the moment she pulls it out, it turns to dust.

She blinks, suddenly finding herself back in the apartment, the soft couch beneath her.

And Mira's already standing above. "Did you get what you needed?"

Gabby stills as she scans her mind. Cupid said he'd gift her the memory of the spell.

She straightens as the words clearly rise in her mind. "I have it," she breathes.

The final weapon to defeat Pothos is now part of their arsenal.

14

COLT

Once the decision had been made to find Pothos, nothing could've stopped Gabby and Colt. Gabby broke through the shifter's cloaking spell with determination. Then he used a locator spell to find the bastard.

Turns out Pothos is in a chamber right beneath Maya's dorm. Which is also Gabby's dorm room.

The malaka was far closer than Colt would like.

Gaby stares at the floor of her room. "We have the spell to distinguish between the shape-shifter and Maya. We have the banishment spell." She looks to Colt. "And you've faced him before."

"All I remember is what I've told you," he says. "I don't recollect coming up against the shape-shifter. And I don't even know if I was successful."

"You've remembered the spell, and that's what counts," she assures him.

Except Colt's not convinced. The reason he's only remembered the events once they've been triggered or forced is a concern. Especially when he doesn't know what that reason is.

Not that it matters. They don't have time for the last of the fragmented memories to return. Maya's life is at stake.

Gabby squats down and presses her hand to the carpeted floor, coming to the same conclusion. Colt's about to kneel and help when a pulse of light explodes from Gabby's palm, burning through the layers of the barrier protecting Pothos's lair. Colt's once again reminded of Gabby's power. A power predicted by a prophecy because she's the seventh daughter of an archangel. For a brief moment, Colt wonders about the other six children. All Gabby's siblings.

The light flares like a sun, blazing through the room, and Colt instinctively shades his eyes. He lowers his arm a moment later, discovering they're in a room that mirrors the one they just left.

Except it's a prison.

The bunk beds are cells, the walls are cement. And there are two people trapped here.

A young man sits up in one of the cells, blinking groggily. "Colt? Gabby? Is that you?"

Colt recognizes him. It's Donald, the tour guide who he'd noticed loitering around Gabby a few times. What is he doing down here?

Gabby gasps as she registers Maya in the second cell. She rushes to her, but Maya doesn't move where she lays on her bed. "No," Gabby whispers.

"She can't hear you," Donald croaks. "She's been like that since she arrived."

Colt squats beside him. "Who did this to you?" he asks, even though he knows. "What happened here?"

"Pothos happened," Donald spits. "He trapped me here the day he arrived at the academy, then picked Maya up a couple of days later. Maya's been in a trance ever since. She believes she's living life as normal."

Gabby joins Colt. "You know about Pothos?" she asks, shocked.

Donald sits up and adjusts his dirty shirt. "I'm a cupid. Of course I know that vile creature."

Gabby's eyes widen. "Learning to trust your heart is key," she murmurs.

"You remembered our conversation," Donald notes. He looks at Colt then back at her. "Did you take my advice?"

Confused, Colt glances between them. But Gabby just shakes her head, her cheeks slightly pink. "I have now." She clears her throat. "So, Maya is under the illusion she's still living life at the academy?"

Donald nods, glancing at Maya's immobile form in the other cell. "Pothos has woven an illusion so he could keep her alive."

Colt pushes to his feet. "He's fond of illusions," he growls.

"Yes, I am, Geryon," says a voice behind him.

Colt spins around as Gabby leaps to stand beside him. Pothos stands on the other side of the room, everything about him familiar in a way Colt wishes it wasn't. The tall, darkling figure. The bow in one hand. The quiver holding green-tipped arrows.

The need to end Pothos before he comes anywhere near Gabby is one of the most powerful urges Colt's ever experienced, but it's those arrows that keep him where he is, despite the roar of anger shooting through his veins.

Every form of hatred is embodied in those arrows. But seven of them are his prized weapons, each one embodying the Sins.

And with recognition come flashes of memories.

The dark walls of Dunabar. Shadows far deeper and more ominous than he'd ever seen. The stench becoming stronger the closer they got. Coming to a large chamber that had Mazikeen shifting closer to him.

The evil had been so strong Colt could feel its pull. Dark whispers had woven through his mind, spinning images of him sitting upon a throne of legend. One that existed in the deepest bowels, so deep he'd never seen it. One meant for the ultimate ruler of Hell.

Fighting it had taken strength. Sitting on Lucifer's chair wasn't an ambition he thirsted for, but the temptation had risen, nonetheless.

Another of Pothos's illusions. Just like Maya's experiencing.

Pothos lowers his bow, his black lip curling in his black face. "I hope you're not planning on banishing me again, Geryon." He waves a dismissive hand. "You think I won't be prepared this time?"

Colt doesn't respond, even as his gut clenches uncomfortably. Pothos knowing what happened all those years ago gives him an advantage.

The darkling turns to Gabby. "Ah, the underdog angel who took care of not only Samandriel, but also the Grigori." He tilts his head in fascination. "The daughter of an archangel and the child of the prophecy. I'd be impressed with that resume if you hadn't allowed me, the harbinger of hate, to come into this mortal plane."

"Liar," Gabby snarls. "I'd never do that."

Pothos smiles indulgently. "Not on purpose, you wouldn't." He moves closer to the cell holding Maya, the evil smile growing. "But you did. When you used celestial fire for the first time, dear Gabby, you opened the door for me to return."

Gabby doesn't answer, her hands curling into fists. Colt also remains silent, intently watching Pothos as he desperately tries to summon the memories he knows are vital.

"What? No theories from the unlikely twosome?" Pothos goads. His black eyes glint with anticipation. "Well, let me educate you, then. Ever since Geryon disrupted my plans back in Dunabar, I've been looking for a way to return. Especially when I learned you were here on Earth."

The hatred in the room swells and Colt and Gabby move closer together, seeking to shield the other.

Pothos notices, and his whole body twists in disgust. "And then the chance came," he seethes. "When Gabby used celestial fire to expel the Grigori, I saw my chance. I channeled the energy your spell released and used it to cloak myself from the cupids as I returned. What's more, you gave me the ultimate way to exact my revenge."

Gabby slips her hand into Colt's, showing without words that Pothos won't be dividing them.

"You were so amazing, he had no choice but to fall in love with you," Pothos sneers.

Gabby stiffens and Colt wishes she was learning the truth in a different way. He lifts his chin. "It's true."

Gabby's intake of breath is almost imperceptible, but he hears it. How he wishes he could face her and say the words.

Except his words only have Pothos grinning more widely. "It meant I could wreak my havoc on your disgusting abomination of a relationship."

Gabby's gaze darts to the cell Pothos is standing beside. "Maya," she breathes.

Colt suppresses the growl clawing up his throat. Maya has done everything she can to break them up, including showing the fake video of Colt betraying Gabby. "It didn't work," he spits out, that knowledge helping him keep calm.

"It doesn't matter," Pothos snaps, his black eyes once more glinting. "The stronger your love, the stronger your hate will be."

"Never!" Gabby shouts.

As the word rings out in this dungeon room, Pothos moves.

He yanks a yellow-tipped arrow from his quiver, notches his bow, and shoots it at Gabby.

"No!" Colt cries.

But even though he's right beside her, the arrow is faster. Moving with more speed than a bullet, it impales Gabby in the chest. Colt shouts her name. She drops to the ground, her face twisted with pain. As he catches her and brings her to the ground, he suddenly remembers.

He remembers everything.

"Leave, shape-shifter," Geryon snarls at the entrance of the chamber they've reached. "You do not belong here."

The shifter stalks forward, a tight grip on his bow. "That's not what the pagan gods who put me here said." He angles his darkling head. "Although I could say the same for you, Geryon. You do not belong here. Then again, you haven't come here willingly, have you?"

Tension coils through every one of Geryon's muscles. He's going to need to be fast. "Who do you work for, shifter?"

"I serve the void," he hisses. "I am a soldier of the dark powers, the horrors of which you have never experienced before. The same power that speaks to you, Geryon."

Mazikeen raises her fists, ready to fight. "You lie," she shouts.

The shifter turns his hard gaze to the demoness. "Worried, Mazikeen? You know he's beyond you. That you can never have him. That he's destined for far more than someone like you." He turns back to Geryon. "Join me. You'll never be beholden to another King of Hell. You'll be lord and ruler." He takes a step forward. "Help me and you will become all that. And just to sweeten the deal, the dark powers that infest this place would be gone."

"Don't listen to him," Mazikeen shouts. "He manipulates. He lies."

"I do not lie, demoness. I tell nothing but the truth." The shifter's eyes glint with malice. "But that's what has you worried, doesn't it?

You don't want Geryon to know you were told to do whatever it takes to bring him here. To cajole him. To seduce him."

"Ignore him," Mazikeen pleads. "Use the spell. Banish him."

Geryon stills as he realizes Mazikeen didn't deny the accusation. That it makes sense. That it had all been an act.

"Geryon," she says, sounding desperate. "Yes, I was told to seduce you. But I had no intention of doing that. Despite what Asmodeus thinks, I'm no whore. Everything I did and said was because I wanted to."

The shifter snorts. "You're going to claim you have feelings for him? That anything but hatred and manipulation could exist here?" He curls his lip. "That the first buds of love have flourished in this den of evil?"

Mazikeen growls low in her throat. "I will never explain myself to the likes of you."

The shifter returns his focus to Geryon, already looking triumphant. "So, Geryon, what answer do you have? Will you join me?" The dark power that Geryon had felt earlier swells again. "I can help you. Open yourself to me."

His answer is a single word. A short, sharp syllable. "No."

The shifter moves instantly, as if that was the answer he was expecting. He spins, simultaneously notching a yellow-tipped arrow in his bow. He releases it with a cry and it pierces Mazikeen's chest a split-second later.

She falls to the ground with a cry, writhing in pain.

"Hate will fill her now," the shifter says with glee. "It will power everything she does."

Furious, Geryon lifts his hands, shouting the banishing spell with such ferocity that it echoes throughout the chamber. Power courses through him, searing him from the inside out, suddenly multiplying exponentially. He throws back his head, teeth gritted and lips peeled back. Something else has entered him.

The dark power.

But Geryon's been trained by an archdemon. He controls whatever's happening to him through sheer force of will. White light explodes from his palms then twists into a single beam. It streaks straight at the shifter.

"No—"

The shifter tries to run, but he can escape it as well as Mazikeen could escape his arrow. The beam hits him just as a portal opens behind him. He struggles for a moment, his midnight body stretching and distending as he's drawn in. But there's a giant pull, like a massive indrawn breath from the portal, and he disappears within.

The portal closes, leaving the chamber empty and dark.

Geryon falls to his knees beside the still-writing Mazikeen. Furious red veins streak from where the arrow is impaled in her chest, climbing up her neck, over her shoulder, and down her arm. He yanks it out, eliciting a cry of pain from Mazikeen, but the red doesn't lessen. In fact, it continues to spread.

Scooping her up, Geryon turns and leaves.

Hoping the curse of hatred can be reversed.

Colt watches in horror as the same red veins spread over Gabby's pale skin, each one a river of poison.

"Her love for you is strong," Pothos sneers. "Which will make her hatred just as powerful."

Colt yanks the arrow out even as he knows it won't make a difference. Even as he knows what Pothos is saying is true. He can't siphon the magic out. He can't lessen the pain. None of it worked with Mazikeen, no matter how desperately he tried.

Rising to his feet, he roars his rage. History is about to repeat itself in one way only. Pothos is about to be sent from this realm. Colt raises his hands, rage fueling the words forming on his lips.

Except Pothos is no longer standing across from him. Maya is. And the other Maya is stepping out of the prison cell to join her. "Which one will you banish?" they taunt simultaneously.

Colt halts the spell. If he focuses on the wrong Maya, the real Maya will die. Except the two girls are carbon copies of each other. Identical twins. There's no way to differentiate which one is Pothos, and which is a human being controlled by him. Especially now that Gabby is hurt. She was the one who knew the differentiation spell. Except...

Donald is a cupid. He can tell the difference!

"Donald," he cries. "Which one is Pothos?"

"That one!" Donald shouts, pointing to the Maya on the right. Except the Maya beside her leaps in front, spins them so fast they're a blur, then separates again.

Before Colt can ask again, a cry is wrung out of Gabby, one drenched and twisted in pain. Her body contorts on the floor, bending back at an impossible angle before jackknifing as she curls into herself. Colt's heart feels like a vice has gripped it. He needs to go to her.

And yet, he needs to stop Pothos.

Donald crawls to her, reaching out through the bars. "I can't siphon the hate," he says, looking at Colt. "But I can turn hate to love."

Colt nods, barely able to breathe. His chest is too crowded with fear. Donald grabs the arrow in his hand, and as he stares at it, it progressively turns red. Slowly, decisively, turning hate into love.

Turning back, Colt focuses on the two Mayas, realizing Donald needs time. Plus, one of the twins on the other side of the room is Pothos, the one who did this to Gabby. And for that, he will pay.

Colt stalks toward the two girls, his hands flexing at his sides.

"A demon in love," one Maya scoffs. "Who would've thought."

"It has made you weak," says the other.

The first Maya glances at Gabby with distaste. "And it has made her weak."

"What you have cannot defeat the power of hate," they say in unison.

Colt breaks into a run, the determination to prove them wrong a roaring through his bloodstream. The Mayas leap, eyes flickering a twin black as they attack. He blocks and parries, taming the need to end this until he knows which is the human Maya. The dual attackers fight with symmetry, in one moment striking simultaneously, one punching high, the other kicking low the next.

But Colt wears any hits that get past his defenses. He's in a holding pattern until Gabby can be healed. Then Donald can identify the real Pothos so Colt can banish him.

One of the Mayas glances past Colt. "No!" she screams.

They split, one throwing herself at Colt, the other leaping over him. He's knocked to the ground where he fights her, doing everything he can to get her away so he can get to Gabby. Maya throws a fist at his head and he ducks to the side. The fist powers into the floor, a shudder rippling through the cement. Colt grabs the arm, pulling and twisting simultaneously, throwing Maya across the room.

He leaps to his feet, discovering that the other Maya is about to throw herself on Gabby. Colt launches forward, even as he knows he won't get there in time. His heart howls a denial. His soul rejects a reality where Gabby's not in it.

Donald sees Maya flying at Gabby, teeth bared, and he lifts the arrow high then slams it down into Gabby's chest. Maya screeches in fury, an arm reaching through the bars to grab his throat. She lifts Donald until he's kneeling, then snaps his neck with a sharp flick of her wrist. His eyes roll back as his body crumples back to the floor.

Colt reaches Gabby, his pulse pounding ferociously. "Gabby!" he pleads, although he's not sure what for. If the cupid's arrow didn't work, he knows without a doubt she'd rather be dead than a creature fueled by hate. She'd be everything she's fought since learning she's an angel.

Gabby's eyes flutter open. They focus on Colt, the haze of pain and confusion quickly dissipating. Impossibly, she smiles. "By the way, I love you, too."

His breath whooshes out as relief tidal waves through him. Even more impossibly, he finds he's smiling back.

Gabby focuses beyond him, then starts mouthing a spell.

The spell to differentiate the real Pothos!

Colt leaps to his feet, bringing Gabby with him. She continues to murmur her spell. He prepares to say his own. The moment the link is severed between Maya and Pothos—

It happens almost immediately.

One of the Mayas slump to the ground. The other becomes a flickering image of countless bodies. Male. Female. Old. Young. Wearing rags then lavish velvet then tight leather then flowing robes.

"No!" Pothos screams as he cycles through the thousands of bodies he's replicated through the ages.

But Colt's already reciting the spell, the same one he spoke hundreds of years ago back in Dunabar.

Pothos snarls and leaps, only to be yanked back as the portal opens. Just like last time, his body is sucked back into it and it blinks out, as if it was never there.

The shape-shifter is once again gone. Banished.

Colt and Gabby move simultaneously. They clasp each other and hold tight, silently breathing in the realization they've won.

That their love was far from weak.

In fact, it was Pothos underestimating it that was his undoing.

They pull back, smiling softly.

"Colt—" she starts.

"Gabby—" he says at the same time.

"Colt? Gabby?" Maya's voice interrupts their growing grins. "Ah, what are you doing here?"

15

COLT

Colt tugs on the sleeve of his black collared shirt, adjusting the cuff around his wrist. He has to admit, formal attire from this era is far more comfortable than it was in times gone by. Stiff, high collars and heavy wool suits were something he avoided whenever possible.

Realizing he's fidgeting—and he's never fidgeted—he leans against the base of the staircase in City Hall. He still can't believe the lengths Kalisha went to organize Maya's birthday party, but if he were a dramatic young woman with a flair for the extravagant, he probably would've done so too.

Especially after everything Maya's been through.

It had taken a few days for Pothos's illusion to completely wear off, and when it did, she learned everything she did while under his influence. She was devastated, and Gabby and Kalisha had spent many hours convincing her she wasn't at fault. Neither of them is sure they'd been successful.

Hence the lavish party that's about to start. This is Kalisha and Gabby's way of showing they care for Maya. And judging by the silver and blue balloons scattered on the floor, the sparkling glitter everywhere, they care a whole lot.

Colt's gaze roams restlessly over the crowd that's already assembled. Mostly young men and women from the academy, there are also adults mingling around. Kalisha invited anyone and everyone, wanting the room to be full of life and fun. The more the crowd grows, the more agitated he becomes, though.

He's never liked congregations of people. There are too many eyes. Too many scents. And too many opportunities to be caught unawares. If it weren't for Gabby...

Colt shakes his head. He's barely seen her over the past few days. After Pothos was banished to the ether, there was still much to do. While Gabby focused on healing Maya, he'd turned his attention to the threats still hanging over them.

The demonic weapons. The gem that would close the Tear.

And a mysterious organization they still know little about. Apart from the fact it wants something as dark and evil as the obsidian.

But he'd come up empty-handed. He even tried to trace Asmodeus again, but the crafty archdemon had cut all links, including those to his human body. Everyone had covered their tracks, determined to disappear.

And now the birthday party is about to start. As much as Colt's not been particularly looking forward to it, he'd enjoyed watching Gabby take pleasure in coordinating it with Maya and Kalisha. After Pothos, it's nice for her to have some snippets of normality.

His gaze wanders to the doors, impatience and the need to fidget again tightening his muscles. He's barely seen her today as setting up the ballroom in City Hall has taken most of the day. After everything they've been through, being apart for too long makes him edgy.

Although he suspects the circumstances don't matter. He doesn't like being apart from Gabby, period.

Those words have been hanging between them since Pothos was banished. Waiting to be honored in the way they should be, not being flung around by a being fueled by hatred. Colt's been waiting for the right moment.

And tonight might be it.

That is, if Gabby turns up. He tugs on his cuff before he's realized he's done it, then scowls. Maybe he should just go looking for her.

Something has him looking up. A change in pressure. A thickening of the air. A hike in temperature.

Gabby stands in the doorway, her gaze already on him, as if she found him the moment she entered. Colt stills. He doesn't blink. Doesn't breathe. Is barely conscious of a pulse.

Gabby's wearing a pale blue, glittering dress. It hugs her torso, then flares out into a full skirt that brushes the floor as she approaches him. The closer she gets, the more his chest tightens.

The more he wants to touch her.

Colt finds he's moving, wanting to extinguish the distance between them. Their gazes hold each other, acting as a beacon, drawing them in. They stop close enough that Gabby's skirt brushes his loafers.

"There are not enough languages to capture how you look right now," he murmurs.

Gabby smiles softly, warming every corner of his heart. "First thing that came to mind when I saw you was hawt dang."

Colt's hand lifts, brushing a loose curl from her bare shoulder and he watches in fascination as her blue gaze darkens. "Not even close," he says, his own smile starting somewhere in his soul.

"You, looking at me like this, says it all." She traces his face with her eyes. "This is all I'll ever want, Colt."

The need to kiss her thrums through his veins. He leans down, his heart already thudding in anticipation.

The round of applause that rises from the crowd jars them apart. Colt almost instinctively steps in front of Gabby, protectiveness coiling his muscles at the loud intrusion, but he relaxes when he sees Maya has entered the room. Shouts of "Happy birthday" bounce around and she blushes even as she grins.

"I knew she'd love it," Gabby murmurs, tucking into his side.

Proudly sashaying in a white dress with a cherry red sash around her middle, Maya falls into welcoming smiles and outstretched arms, her smile impossibly growing. A couple of guys joke that they're more than willing to be one of her seven dwarves.

"You've done well," Colt says, squeezing her so she's pressed in close.

"It was all Kalisha. I just did as I'm told." Gabby looks around, noting the silver streamers winding up the railing of the staircase they're not far from, more balloons dangling down every few feet. "She knew this fairytale theme would be amazeballs."

"It's certainly captured my interest," Colt murmurs, his gaze nowhere but the beautiful, magical creature that is Gabby.

She looks up, her face softening even as her eyes twinkle. "What has?"

He chuckles, knowing exactly what she means. Their surroundings are fast becoming white noise. He leans down, her parted lips his new center of gravity, and she leans closer.

"You know, two of Kalisha's older cousins are event managers," comes a voice to their left.

They pull apart, and Colt has to work not to scowl at the

second interruption. He takes in the woman regarding them, one dressed as Puss In Boots right down to the tight britches and flowing top.

Gabby angles her head. "You know Kalisha?"

It's then that Colt notices the ring on the woman's finger. He raises an eyebrow. "The Knights Templar?"

The woman inclines her head, the movement contained as her eyes remain shrewd. "Yes, although we now go by the Order of the Knightly Rose."

Gabby throws a surprised glance at Colt, but it's clear she knows who the woman's referring to—a secret sect of vampire hunters. She smiles in welcome. "Hi, I'm Gabrielle. Nice to meet you."

"Kenna de Voe," the woman responds, her eyes narrowing as if she's assessing them. "Head of the Order."

"My name's Colt Grayson," he volunteers, wondering why this woman's here even as he appreciates her direct manner. Angels could take a few pointers from this woman.

"So, you know Kalisha?" Gabby asks, seeming to be wondering the same question.

Kenna turns so she's standing beside them, her back no longer to the crowd. "Yes, a couple of years ago my nephew, Caleb, was being a little over-enthusiastic during training and flung a set of nun-chucks through her bedroom window. We fixed the window, and next thing I know, I get a text invite to some fairy tale party."

Colt glances at her costume. "I wouldn't have picked it as your kind of thing." Especially when she barely knows Kalisha.

"It isn't. But then I realized the party's connected to Mercy Academy." Kenna angles them a glance. "And things have been happening at that place. I wondered if it may have something to do with the scumbuckets I'm hunting."

Gabby stiffens. "Vampires are at the academy?"

Kenna waves a hand. "Probably, but not the trouble-making ones as far as I can tell." She sighs. "I can't believe I'm saying this, but I'm hunting something, or someone, just as dangerous."

Colt's back to being tense. They don't need another foe on their hands. "Who?"

"The Tenth Legion," Kenna spits. "Humans who worship dark powers."

Gabby's eyes widen. "The Tenth Legion?"

Kenna's lip curls in disdain. "Yeah. The bastards who stole the demon weapons coming out of Hell. Lead by that piece of shit, Malcolm Hunsecker."

Gabby grips Colt's hand. "We've been trying to locate them too," she says, her voice both hard yet excited.

"I suspected as much. Which is why I'm here, wearing this," Kenna says in disgust, glancing down at her black shiny boots. She looks up, that shrewd glint back. "It's time we join forces, Gabrielle Heartley."

Gabby nods, but before she can answer a hoot lifts from the crowd. They turn to find three Prince Charmings trying to help a Tinkerbell fly, even though she's laughing too hard for them to be able to lift her up very high.

"It's going to be an interesting party," Colt observes.

Gabby giggles, but it's cut short when she turns back to discover Kenna is gone. "Urgh! I didn't get her number."

Colt scans the crowd, but he's unsurprised that he can't see the small, intense woman. Kenna is someone who would only be found if she wanted to. He shrugs. "I suspect she'll find you when the time's right."

"Which is fine by me," Gabby says, her voice dropping in a way that tugs at his gut. "We should dance."

He smiles broadly. "We should."

Her eyes twinkle as she moves in close. "I want an excuse to put my hands on your body."

His nostrils flare as he instinctively draws in her rose and lily scent. "All my centuries on this earth couldn't have prepared me for you, Gabrielle," he murmurs. "I never stood a chance."

She leans in close, pushing up so their lips are close and their breaths mingle. "You really didn't."

He chuckles, his palms already warming at the thought of holding her. For a brief second, he considers disappearing every last person in this room to some alternative dimension but he refrains. Gabby put too much work into this for him to ruin it.

Unless he distracts her with a kiss first...

"Gabby darling!" Kalisha's voice ruptures the spell that was weaving around them. "There you are!"

Kalisha shimmies toward them, a sultry, garish version of Alice in Wonderland's Queen of Hearts. She waves her glitter, heart-shaped wand. "The cake's arrived! And you thought five tiers were too many!"

Gabby lets out a slow sigh as she steps back. "No, I said having every Disney princess on it was too much."

"Do not start, young lady," Kalisha says haughtily, flicking the large white collar framing her dramatically high hair. "There had to be all forty of them. Especially after Tinkerbelle was given an honorary princess title because she committed an act of bravery. "

Gabby rolls her eyes even as it's clear she's suppressing a smile. "It's just that when I googled it, there were twelve Disney princesses, fourteen max."

Kalisha flicks her heart wand in dismissal. "I'll update the Wikipedia page if that makes you feel better." She takes Gabby's hand and tugs. "Now come on, I need your advice. Personally, I don't believe Queen Nala should be on the fourth tier."

Colt suppresses the need to hold onto Gabby tighter so Kalisha can't pull her away, even forcing a smile onto his face. Kalisha grins at him, either unaware of his disgruntledness, or enjoying it. "Nala is the queen in Lion King. She can't just be put in any old place."

Gabby giggles as she lets herself be led away. She glances over her shoulder at Colt. "You owe me a dance."

Kalisha also looks back, raking her heavily made-up eyes over Colt. "I can't blame you. Black is most definitely his color."

Gabby giggles again, leaning in close to whisper, although his sensitive demon ears still hear. "You should see his wings."

Kalisha makes a show of fanning herself with her heart wand and this time it's Colt who rolls his eyes. They blend into the crowd and he steps back, closer to the side of the wide, rounded staircase that goes to the second level, muttering under his breath, "A queen is not a princess, anyway, irrespective of species."

He returns to scanning the crowd, his gaze pausing when he finds a young woman turning away from where Gabby and Kalisha just disappeared to look at him. The moment she realizes he's looking at her, she inclines her head in acknowledgement, then walks away.

For a moment, Colt considers following her, but he quickly changes his mind.

He's not going to go look for trouble.

Not when he's waiting for Gabby to come back for that dance.

16

GABBY

I t takes far longer to decide where Queen Nala should sit on the freaking cake, but eventually Kalisha decides on putting the lioness beside Mulan after Gabby suggested she just go in alphabetical order so there's no favoritism.

When she finally heads back to Colt, she pauses as she catches sight of him. He's talking to someone. A *female* someone.

Thoughts of Mazikeen have her picking up her pace, clacking agitatedly across the parquetry floor in the glass slippers she magically created just for tonight. There was no way the Cinderella outfit was going to be complete without them. She doesn't stop until she slips in beside Colt, wrapping an arm around his waist and placing a soft kiss on the side of his jaw for good measure.

She turns to the young woman with black hair dressed as Ursula from the Little Mermaid, the bell shape of her octopus skirt only emphasizing her tight bodice and itty-bitty waist. "Hi, I'm Gabby. It seems you've met Colt." She dials up her smile. "Who's mine."

Colt looks down at her, amusement glinting in his chocolate eyes. "It's true," he murmurs. "I'm hers."

Gabby's smile goes from strained and artificial to warm and genuine the instant the words are spoken. "And I'm his," she vows.

Colt presses a tender kiss on her head before turning back to the woman. "Gabby, this is Lydia," he says, amusement lacing his voice. "She's been working with Kenna in hunting the Legion. She's also a witch."

Gabby knows she should be abashed for her blatant possessiveness, but she's feeling too gooey about Colt's response. So instead she smiles as if moving on is the most natural thing in the world. "Wow, you work with Kenna?"

Lydia nods. "Kenna had to leave before she could introduce us—the Order keeps her busy. But she wanted me to connect seeing as we're both hunting the same target."

"The Tenth Legion," Colt growls.

"They've been a thorn in our side for a long time," Lydia says bitterly, adjusting her strapless bodice as if she's uncomfortable with it. "We're still not sure what their end game is, but they're the cause of many a war in this world and they worship evil. If they have their hands on the demonic weapons, then they have something big planned."

Gabby frowns, wishing she was surprised. Hasn't every evil entity they've fought thirsted for apocalyptic level chaos? "Do you have a lead on them?"

"All of my spells have hit a wall," Lydia says in frustration. "The Legion has cloaked itself with a powerful warding spell. I don't think any supernatural creature could breach it."

Colt's fingers drum just above Gabby's hip as he thinks. "But this warding must be originating somewhere."

Lydia nods. "True, but the exact location is hidden. I can pinpoint the general area, but that's it. Even if we did find it, breaking through the warding spell would be almost impossible."

"How can you be so sure?" Gabby asks, thinking that she and Colt have managed to overcome insurmountable obstacles.

Lydia smiles, but the motion is sad. Almost bitter. "Because I know the witch who cast the spell and she's quite powerful and skilled in dark magic." Her lips twist. "Something she learned from our mother."

Gabby can't hide her surprise. "The witch who's defending the Legion is your sister?"

"Yes. She's lost her way thanks to our mother's horrible influence. I want to stop the Legion, but also stop her before she does something she won't be able to recover from. She's been corrupted, drawn to the dark power the Legion worships."

Like destroying the world.

Colt's fingers tense at Gabby's waist. "They worship a dark power?"

Lydia nods again. "Nobody knows where it is, but lore has it the dark power came into this world during the Resurrection when a rip opened between Hell and Earth. It took the form of a dark stone. And then an angel broke it into seven pieces, hiding it among seven families. It's known as the—"

"Obsidian," Gabby finishes for her. It always comes back to the evil piece of rock. "Well, the Legion won't get their hands on it, just like the Grigori didn't. As long as they don't have the parchments retrieved from the families, they won't be able to trace the obsidian's location."

Lydia lets out a breath. "That's something." But then she's frowning again. "But there's another way. The demonic weapons are tainted by the same dark power. If they have enough weapons, my sister could use the power to trace the obsidian. We need to stop the Legion."

"Which brings us back to the warding," Gabby says, trying not to get frustrated that they're back to the start—being stuck.

Lydia glances around, tugs at her bodice, and moves closer. "I've heard of someone who can defy supernatural laws, and is supernatural themselves."

"And that is?" Colt asks, sounding guarded.

"Legends call him the Skeleton Man. He's the key to bypassing the warding."

Gabby glances at Colt, also trying not to get too optimistic. There's always a catch. "And how do we find him?"

Lydia's shoulders drop an inch. "That's the issue. No one knows."

Gabby's once more looking up at Colt. She presses a hand to his chest. "Huh, what seems like an impossible task."

His lips twitch. "Our favorite."

She's tempted to kiss him again—that little spot on his jaw was particularly delicious—but she returns her focus to Lydia. "So we find the Skeleton Man," she says brightly, as if they've just decided to meet up for high tea.

Lydia smiles. "Great." Before they can speak she steps back. "Now, I'm off to get this awful costume off. This is all they had left."

With a wave of her hand, she disappears among the other Cinderellas and Belles and Pocahontas's, one of her stuffed tentacles brushing over an Ariel mermaid tail.

Gabby steps around so she's facing Colt, her arms around his waist. "And we start tomorrow," she says firmly. "Tonight is about forgetting all that for a few hours."

He quirks a brow. "Forgetting what?"

She grins. "Right answer." Then she leans in so all of her is pressed up against all of him. "And I think we should have that dance somewhere else. Away from interruptions."

Although Colt's eyes heat to a delicious shade of melted

chocolate, Gabby braces herself for her level-headed demon to point out this is a party she helped organize, or that the Skeleton Man needs to be found before the Legion get hold of the obsidian. Or some other 'we can't forget our responsibilities' gibberish that's valid, but really not what she wants to hear.

He leans forward, his palms slipping around her waist and leaving a scorching trail of heat straight through her bodice. "Your wish," he murmurs, "My command."

In the space of a blink, City Hall disappears and they're standing in Colt's cottage. Before her startled, but pleased, gasp is finished, the lights have dimmed and soft music is playing.

Gabby winds her arms around his neck, pulling his face down to hers. Her every nerve is instantly thrumming. "I changed my mind," she says huskily.

Colt's hands tense. "Very well."

But before he can jump to conclusions and transport them back, Gabby takes his lips in a searing kiss. "I don't want to dance," she says against his mouth, then seals the words with their unique brand of passion.

He groans, sinking into the kiss as if he's drowning. As if he wants to.

As if she's his new oxygen.

Gabby melts against him, swept up in the same passion, every trembling gasp pulling Colt deeper into her lungs. He's not just her oxygen. He's her reason to breathe.

Colt's arms band around her back, hauling her up against him. Loving the heat and pressure, she spears her fingers into his hair, the material of her skirt crinkling as she wraps a leg around his. Colt grabs it and lifts, fitting her softness to his hard planes.

Gabby almost internally combusts. Heat licks across her skin, sears through her veins, and burns away anything but sweet surrender to what's been unleashed. She can barely think, all she can do is feel. Taste. Touch.

And revel as Colt does the same to her.

She yanks off the pretty shirt he was wearing, discovering the ridged muscles beneath are far more fascinating. Driven by desire, Gabby runs her mouth along his jaw line as her hands explore every ridge and valley. Colt's skin quivers. His breath shudders.

"Gabrielle," he groans.

And then he's lifting her completely. She kisses him, wanting to hear him say her name like that again. As if he's almost in pain. As if, just like her, he couldn't stop even if he tried.

It's only when something touches her back that she realizes Colt's brought her to his bedroom. She looks up at him, all edgy darkness and shadowy sexiness. "I love you," she says, her voice soft but undeniably ringing with truth.

Colt does something that takes the moment from beautiful to exquisite. He smiles, his lips stretching tenderly across his face even as his eyes flare with sultry fire. "And I love you, Gabrielle. With every beat of this mortal heart, and every breath of this immortal soul."

She pulls him down, sealing their vows with a scorching kiss. The passion flares again, now so much more potent that they've laid their hearts bare. There's nothing between them anymore. It brings tears to Gabby's eyes, although they evaporate before ever having a chance to be born. Every inch of her skin is on fire.

Their clothes disappear. Hands roam as mouths taste. Pleasure fills the air with their gasps and moans and groans.

As they become one, Gabby makes Colt hers in every way she can. With her mouth. Her body. Her heart.

Only to find that she gives as much as she takes. She

becomes Colt's with such totality, that she's not sure where she starts and he ends. There are no boundaries between them, no dark or light.

Just love.

As they find the peak of their pleasure, Gabby cries out Colt's name. A cosmos of stars explode behind her eyes as she clings to him, reveling in the shudders wracking his strong frame.

They collapse, panting, and Colt scoops her into his arms. Gabby wraps herself around him as a smile curls up her lips. She snuggles down into his chest, tired and replete.

Colt presses a soft kiss to the crown of her head. "I'll always love you, Gabby."

She lazily nuzzles his chest, suddenly too exhausted to even open her eyes. "I'll love you longer," she murmurs through the smile.

As sleep steals her consciousness, contentedness wraps around her. That was amazing, and she wonders if it's just because of the depth of her feelings for Colt. Or because she wanted to do this within weeks of meeting the hot demon she's holding.

Or if it's because what just happened was the product of the impossible love between an angel and a demon.

17

GABBY

GABBY

Gabby stands outside of her childhood home, not surprised to find herself here. After she spent a beautiful, but short morning in Colt's arms thanks to him having a martial arts tutoring session with a client, she'd found out she has the morning free of classes.

But the thought of going to the cafeteria and joking with Kalisha and Maya as if everything was the same just wasn't something she wanted to do right now. Not after last night. The memories are so colored by love that she wanted to be with the people who defined the word for her as a child.

Yet as she reaches for the doorknob, Gabby hesitates. It's only now she's remembering that the last time she saw her mom, things had been tense. She wasn't willing to accept Gabby's angelic side. What would she do if she learned Gabby has fallen deeply and irrevocably in love with a demon?

That they're now just as physically connected as they are emotionally?

Heat climbs up Gabby's cheeks as memories of the glances,

the sensations, the sweet sounds from last night rise through her. They're quickly followed by images of drowsy Colt as he'd woken up, of smiling Colt when he'd registered her in his arms, then sultry Colt as he'd kissed her, the echo of last night's passion still clinging to him.

Gabby's hand tightens on the doorknob and she enters her home, flicking her hair over her shoulder. Maybe now that things are so great with Colt, she wants to have peace at home, too. Or maybe she wants to tell her mom she finally understands why she'd pine for her father for all these years. Gabby would wait for Colt until the end of time.

But the only person in the living room is her cousin, Arielle. She's sitting on the couch and the fact her feet are up on the coffee table instantly tells Gabby that neither her mom nor aunt Sierra are home. So is the fact that Arielle's wearing headphones and staring at the laptop screen on her lap with a goofy grin on her face.

It's clear she's supposed to be studying, but isn't.

Gabby snaps the door shut loud enough to startle Arielle. "How's the study going?"

Arielle leaps, her hand shooting to her chest, then relaxes when she sees Gabby. Pulling off the headphones, she rolls her eyes. "Even if bacteria are older than dirt and more numerous in our bodies than our own cells, I can't get interested, okay?" She waves at the screen. "Bacteria can never compete with *Friends*."

Gabby plants her hands on her hips. "You need to study, Ari. It's important."

Ari rolls her eyes again. "You're starting to sound like your mum."

"Where is she, by the way?" Gabby asks, glancing around.

"Gone to the store. She decided she wanted to make cappuccino cupcakes. Said they'd make me study better." Arielle pushes to her feet as she places the laptop on the coffee table. "But do you know what will make me study better? A break. Specifically, a shopping break."

Gabby's already shaking her head. "No way, Ari. I'm sure you've got assignments galore."

Arielle's shoulders sag as she pouts. "Wow, and here you were saying you wanted to spend more time with me..."

"Are you emotionally blackmailing me?" Gabby demands, hiking her hands further up her hips.

"Of course not," says Ari, full of mock indignation. "I was just pointing out that we have an hour or two that you could use to show me how much you miss me."

Gabby's giggling before Arielle's finished. She hesitates, tempted. Some time with Ari would be nice...

Her cell dings and she pulls it out, trying to buy some time. Responsible Gabby would put an end to this. A text from Colt appears on the screen and Gabby opens it, a warm sensation blooming in her chest.

Seems it's true. Love knows no barriers.

Gabby practically swoons on the spot. She's about to tap out a gushy reply when her phone is swept out of her hands.

Arielle ducks around the couch. "I've never seen that look on your face. You've got a boyfriend!"

Gabby's hands are back on her hips. "Give it back, Ari. Now."

"Only once you agree to take me to the mall." She glances down. "And buy me churros."

"Outright blackmail, huh? Not happening, sis."

Ari's eyes dance playfully. "Well, you might reconsider when you realize I'm replying." She holds up the cell, her thumb dancing over the screen.

"You little terror!" Gabby cries, leaping over the couch in one jump.

She yanks the cell out of her surprised cousin's hand, the motion making Ari's thumb slip over the send button.

Gabby gasps. "What have you done?"

Arielle's a mass of giggles. "I was trying to type 'help, I can't live without you' and you grabbed it!"

Meaning one word was just sent to Colt.

Help.

A moment later, loud thumping has the front door rattling. Arielle's eyes widen. "What the..."

"That's Colt," Gabby says, striding to the door. "Thanks to you, he's here to check up on me."

Arielle frowns. "That was quick."

"He was...ah...waiting for me outside," Gabby says, thinking fast. She yanks open the door, her heart stuttering at the sight of a glowering Colt, ready to slay dragons. "False alarm," she assures him, hooking her thumb over her shoulder. "Arielle got hold of my phone."

Every muscle in Colt's body visibly unwinds. He's about to say something when Arielle shoves past Gabby and extends her hand. "Hi, I'm Arielle, Gabby's cousin. Nice to meet you."

Colt takes the offered hand and shakes it with a smooth smile. "Likewise. I'm Colt."

Unable to help herself, Gabby tucks into his side and presses her palm to his chest. "My boyfriend."

Arielle beams, then leans in. "Is he the one you were really into?" she asks in a conspiratorial whisper.

Gabby grins back. "Yep."

"I knew it!" Arielle turns back to Colt. "I'm glad it was all sorted out."

Colt, looking a little bemused by Arielle's energy, simply nods. "So am I."

Arielle angles her head. "Sorry you came rushing over.

Gabby and I were just heading to the mall to do some clothes shopping."

"Actually, you were going to study," Gabby says pointedly.

Arielle turns back to Colt. "Don't you think Gabby could use some time to unwind? Just for an hour or two?"

Colt looks down at Gabby, his lips twitching in amusement. "You've certainly been working hard..."

She narrows her eyes at him. "You're taking her side?"

"I'm looking out for you," he says, now almost smiling.

"Please?" Ari asks, stretching the word out over several, whiny seconds.

"Fine," Gabby huffs, actually looking forward to spending some time hanging with Arielle. "But only for an hour."

Arielle's already spun around to race up to her room, squealing with delight.

Gabby's once again narrowing her eyes up at Colt. "You did that to get on her good side, didn't you?"

He grins. "I figure I have to gain the favor of at least someone in your family. I mean, apart from Sierra. Your mother is still uneasy with the supernatural, and your father, well, he hates me on principle."

Gabby sighs, acknowledging that's true. She shifts closer, her skin tingling everywhere they touch. "And you came because you thought I needed help?"

Colt brushes his knuckles along her cheekbone, his eyes now serious. "Of course."

"Thank you," she murmurs, pushing up on her toes to press a kiss to his lips.

Colt melts for a beautiful second, but then pulls back. "Arielle's returning," he murmurs, the hint of longing in his voice calling to the same yearning tugging at her insides. "I'll return to Veritas where I was researching the Skeleton Man. You go shopping and have fun."

Before Gabby can answer, he takes a step back so he's out of view of the living room, and disappears.

Gabby sighs. One lifetime really isn't going to be enough with that demon.

Arielle appears, practically hopping from foot to foot. "There's a pair of shoes I want to check out."

Smiling, Gabby leads the way to her car. "And how many churros would you like with those shoes?"

THE MALL IS RELATIVELY QUIET, meaning Gabby and Arielle wander through the levels without any real goal. They window shop, munching on the churros dipped in chocolate sauce. They reminisce about the times they played house, never occurring to them that a male should be part of the cast after being raised by single moms who are sisters. Ari teases Gabby about Colt, predicting their seven children will all have red curls and blue eyes.

And Gabby loves every minute of it.

It's proof she can know things like the Legion exist, that demonic weapons are out there, that something like the Skeleton Man has a name, but also have things in her life like girl time, giggles, and chocolate-dipped churros.

They reach a trendy little clothes store and Gabby grabs a t-shirt off a rack, holding it in front of her. "I like this one for you."

Scrawled across the front of the bright pink shirt, it says *One day, I'll save the world.*

Arielle rolls her eyes and steps away. "I don't even know what I want to do after high school."

Gabby reaches out to press a hand to her cousin's shoulder

before she can create too much distance. There was something in Arielle's voice. "Fate has a plan for you, Ari. Just like she does for all of us."

Gabby could never have guessed hers was to be an angel. A prophesied daughter of an archangel, no less. But it's now a life she welcomes. She has purpose.

She has Colt.

Arielle smiles weakly. "The way I'm going, my fate will be to try and come up with cheesy lines like that one for shirts."

Gabby puts the top back, remembering what it was like to be standing at the end of your school life, wondering what's in the big abyss called *your future*. She squeezes Arielle's shoulder. "Trust your heart," she advises, conscious she's quoting Donald. It seems like a beautiful way to honor the cupid's sacrifice. "It'll know."

Arielle chews her lip as she nods. She looks up, and her face breaks into a smile. "Right now, my heart is telling me to get my favorite bagel."

Gabby snorts. "I'm pretty sure that's your stomach."

"I'll be back in a sec," Arielle says, wrinkling her nose. "Study food."

Gabby shoos her away good naturedly, smiling as she watches Arielle walk to the stall in the center of the walkway.

Clasping her arms, Gabby lets her gaze roam over the brightly lit stores, the moms pushing prams, the elderly couple who were sharing a vanilla slice. After the serial murders, the hell fires, the hostage situation at City Hall, then Pothos, she needed this. In some ways to remind her what she's fighting for. In some ways, just to take a breath.

Arielle stands at the back of the line at the bagel shop, and Gabby registers the large clock dangling from the ceiling above. Although it's telling her they need to get back, she realizes she doesn't mind. She's okay with this cute interlude being over.

She's keen to see Colt, touch him, and find out if he's learned anything about the Skeleton Man.

Especially after Pothos's last words. "They have returned."

Who has returned? The Grigori? She doubts it. If they had, she would've known. They're most definitely in their prison cells in Hell, waiting to be judged for their crimes. Which means Pothos's declaration is even more of a mystery.

Turning as if she can physically push the thoughts away, seeing as the last thing she needs right now is more questions without answers, Gabby catches sight of herself in the glass of the clothing store she's standing beside. She frowns. The reflection staring back at her has the same mass of blonde curls, the same black tank top and tartan miniskirt—her favorite outfit.

But that's where the similarities end.

The luminous, slightly see-through Gabby in the glass is standing straight, her chin held high. And she's holding a spear.

Taller than her, its tear-shaped tip gleams. Ornate and golden, it seems to hum with power.

Although she's never seen it before, Gabby instantly knows what it is. The Spear of Destiny.

Moroni mentioned it months ago, saying it was broken into three shards, each location only recorded inside the golden plate Samandriel has hidden. Yet, the spear her reflection is holding is complete. Whole.

But how?

Gabby shifts uncomfortably, unsure what this all means, but her reflection doesn't move. She stares back at her, blue gaze intense as if she's trying to tell her something.

"So rude!" Arielle gasps behind her.

Gabby spins around, registering that her cousin has coffee spilled all over her top. "What happened?"

Arielle spins furiously, pointing to a guy and a girl on the other side of the bagel store, walking away. "They happened," she huffs. "The girl was laughing as she ate mac and cheese, of all things, when she bumped the guy. He then stumbled and spilled his coffee all over me! They burst into laughter and kept going. Talk about rude!"

Gabby looks a little more closely. The girl is mocha-skinned with unruly hair, while the guy is tall and strong, black hair looking like it could also use a cut. There's something about them... She wishes Colt was here. He'd be able to read the young man's aura. It's as if Fate is clinging to him, waiting to unleash his destiny on him. They disappear around the corner, snapping her out of her reverie.

A quick glance over her shoulder reveals the Gabby she's always known looking back at her. No spear. No 'bring it on' attitude.

Arielle wipes at her shirt in agitation. "If this stains..."

Gabby suppresses a smile. This reminds her of the first time she met Colt. She'd been annoyed and frustrated then, too. She shakes her head. Now she's imagining the beginnings of another great love story.

She loops her arm through Ari's, tugging her in the direction of the parking lot. "It'll come out. But we'd better get back and get you changed before my mom gets home."

And maybe Gabby needs to get some sleep.

18

COLT

Colt shifts position on the faded couch tucked in a corner of Veritas Library, placing his foot on his knee. He turns a page, even though he's not expecting to see anything he doesn't already know.

Or anything on the Skeleton Man.

Yet, if Skeleton Man is their only way to take down the Legion, they need to find him as soon as possible. And then somehow convince him to take down the warding protecting the Legion. Flipping the page he just skimmed over, Colt decides they'll address that issue when they come to it. They need to find the elusive being first.

Lydia appears, carrying another stack of books. "I found these in a section Nim hasn't looked in yet," she says as she places them on the low table between the couch and two matching armchairs. "I'll get started on them."

Colt huffs, suppressing the need to snap the tome he's holding shut. "Judging by the countless books we've already gone through, I doubt it. There's nothing on the Skeleton Man." He rakes his fingers through his hair. "Have we even confirmed he's real?"

Lydia peers at the large text she just opened, her finger running down the yellowed page. "It seems he is."

Colt launches to his feet, alert. "What book is that?"

Lydia glances at the cover. "*Shames of the Supernatural World*," she reads aloud. "I doubt it's full of good news stories."

"What does it say about this Skeleton Man," Colt asks, his gut tense.

"Not much," Lydia says, back to scanning the page she was on. "There's little more than a paragraph on him. Almost more of a footnote really." She frowns, peering closer as she reads. "Back in the twelfth century, a witch siphoned massive amounts of power from anything she could get her hands on then channeled it into the people of the Great Lakes region. Everyone died except for one."

"And?" Colt asks, his eyes roaming over the same words.

"That one person became immortal." Lydia angles her head, looking baffled. "But the witch managed to kill it with dark magic." She flips the page, then another, then looks up. "That's it."

"How can you be sure that minimal information refers to the Skeleton Man? It does not call him as such."

Lydia taps her finger on the page. "This does."

Colt moves around to stand at the back of the armchair Lydia's sitting on and peers down. A crudely drawn picture of a skeleton has been scrawled beside the text. He leans closer as he stares at it, thinking it could've been drawn by a child. Or decades after the book was printed.

"Colt?"

He straightens, his heart taking on the new rhythm it always does when Gabby's near. As if it's coming to life.

Except she's looking at him with one eyebrow arched, her pointed gaze drifting to Lydia as she sits not far away. Unable to help himself, he smiles as he walks toward the angel who's touched his soul. He's never had anyone feel possessive about him, and as illogical as it is, he likes it. "How was the shopping?" he asks, pressing a kiss to her cheek.

"Mine," Gabby growls softly, her hands gripping the front of his shirt.

He nods, willing to pacify her jealous side. Too much has tried to tear them apart. "Always."

She relaxes. Even smiles a little. "That'll do for a start."

His lips twitch. "So Lydia can live?"

Gabby giggles, glancing over his shoulder. She wrinkles her nose. "For now."

Taking her hand, he chuckles as he draws her over to the small study area. "We've found something, but it isn't much."

Lydia passes Gabby the book, her own eyes glinting with humor. "A book I found, by the way, which suggests keeping me alive would be useful."

"Thanks." Gabby smiles as she shrugs a shoulder. "I probably only would've broken some bones as a warning, anyway."

Lydia inclines her head, humor and respect glinting in her dark eyes. "It may help to know that demons aren't my taste. And neither are males."

A light flush creeps up her cheeks as she takes the book. "Your bones should be safe then."

Colt moves over to stand beside her, pointing at the passage of text with the drawing of the skeleton beside it. "This is it," he says, bringing the focus back to why they're here.

It only takes Gabby a minute to read it. She looks up. "It's interesting, but it's not much."

"Nor do we have any way to verify its reliability," Colt says. "We've looked through almost every book that may have something, and this is all we've found."

Gabby chews her lip in thought. "Maybe we ask our respective elders?"

Her father, Archangel Gabriel, and whatever King of Hell Colt can find. He nods slowly. "It's worth a try."

She beams and reaches up on tippy toes to press a kiss to his jaw. "I'll go find my father now." She passes the book back to Lydia, then sashays away, her tartan skirt brushing the top of her thighs.

Colt watches until she's out of sight, images of the night before crowding his mind. He's been alive for a long time, and experienced many things, but making love to Gabby was world-altering. Just when he thought the fierce tenderness or powerful protectiveness couldn't grow any stronger, they'd connected even more deeply.

There's nothing he wouldn't do for Gabby.

Lydia snorts as she settles back in the armchair, flipping the page in the book. "Man, I pity any woman who's actually a threat to that angel."

Colt's about to say that Gabby may be emotional, but she wouldn't hurt an innocent person, but new images are crowding his mind.

Images from a past that keeps revealing itself, whether he likes it or not.

Geryon covers as much distance as he can between himself and Dunabar before finally placing Mazikeen on the dusty earth. Behind him, the castle still rises, standing strong and unapologetic. Although he's banished the shifter, evil still clings to the onyx walls. It still holds Hell in its corrupt clutches.

It hadn't worked.

Geryon kneels beside the unconscious Mazikeen, registering that the red spidery veins fanning out from the wound have thickened and darkened.

"Fool," hisses the voice in his mind. "You could've been great."

Geryon ignores it. "Mazikeen," he says hoarsely. "Wake up."

"*Stop wasting your time. You can still do it. You, Geryon, could imprison all three Kings of Hell and make yourself lord and master.*"

A sharp, throbbing pain pierces Geryon's temple. He doesn't want that power. Nor does he want this evil voice inside of him. Against his will, a vision rises before him of him leading an army against the Kings of Hell. And succeeding. In the next scene, he's unlocking the doors of the Cage and releasing the Devil. Then two archangels are battling, one quickly gaining the upper hand. The second angel dies, triggering a swirling portal to rent open the sky above them. An army of horrors pour out, teeming with terrible monsters the likes Geryon has never seen.

Then he's being rewarded for his allegiance. For being the one to make all this possible.

"No," Geryon moans. "Never."

"*Very well,*" sneers the voice.

The next images reveal the Kings of Hell continuing to quarrel amongst themselves, just as they are now. This time, a Tear appears between the demonic and mortal plane, unleashing the Sins on the world. Humanity is reduced to nothing but their most base emotions. Wars destroy. Hatred kills. The apocalypse comes, destroying everything with it. Including Geryon.

"*That will be your punishment,*" the voice hisses. It breaks into throaty laughter, triggering more piercing pain.

Geryon grits his teeth, ignoring the evilness that's now inside him. "Mazikeen," he tries again, this time a little louder. "You must wake up."

When there's no response, he shakes her gently even as he remembers the shifters promise that she'd now be filled with hate. If that's the case, then he'll have to help her. He cannot let her be the collateral damage of all this ugliness.

Mazikeen's back arches as she draws in a startled breath. Her eyes fly open and she looks around, confused. "What...what happened?"

"The shifter's gone," he answers as he watches her closely. "He's been banished from Hell, but you were struck by his yellow arrow."

Mazikeen frowns, glancing down at the wound that's almost healed. A twisted scar sits at the center of the vein-like red lines. "That's...I don't feel so good..." She massages the area near her wound with her fingers. "It all feels so hot inside, as if every cell inside me is raging. Burning."

Although he wants to frown, Geryon stops himself. Mazikeen is certainly looking flushed. "It's the poison from the arrow."

She curls her lip as her gaze falls on Dunabar. "I want to burn it down. Drown it in flames."

"No, Mazikeen," Geryon says. "Let me help you."

But she shuffles back, her body vibrating with rage. "Geryon," she gasps. "I...I can't..."

With a flash of movement, she streaks away, her face twisted with wrath and regret. Geryon stands, intent on following her, but Asmodeus appears in front of him, his hand extended.

"Let her go. The primordial powers possessing her are too difficult to cure."

"But not impossible," Geryon points out.

Asmodeus shakes his head. "Demons are easily affected by such influences. It's what we Kings have been battling since they came to Hell."

Geryon's hands compulsively clench into fists. Asmodeus may be willing to turn his back on Mazikeen now that she's served his purpose, but he won't do that. "I—"

"No, you won't," Asmodeus snaps, his gaze flaring with the power of an archdemon. "Those powers are seeking to rule Hell, Geryon. If the Sins succeed, we are all doomed."

The ominous words hang in the stale air. Geryon's jaw is so tight it could snap. The shifter may be banished, but they still face a formidable challenge. "Then we end the Sins."

Asmodeus grunts. "The Sins cannot be killed by any weapon we possess. They require special daggers, which aren't in our dimension. Yet, if we don't stop them, they'll spread their evil to other dimensions."

The mortal world.

"Then how? How do we end them?"

"We bring a truce between us Kings and we rally our forces against the dark powers."

Geryon nods, even though that seems like an unlikely solution. Beelzebub appears determined to go to war.

"Come," Asmodeus says. "We shall return to my castle and plan."

He turns and walks away, assuming Geryon will follow. He hesitates, glancing in the direction Mazikeen ran. He knows he can't go after her, not when the entirety of Hell is under threat, but that doesn't mean he doesn't want to.

With a sigh, Geryon falls in behind Asmodeus. He just has to hope the hatred she now holds doesn't wreak its own damage.

A frustrated sigh jolts Colt out of his reverie. He looks around, blinking at what now feels like the harsh lights of Veritas. After the darkness that surrounds Dunabar, the white walls and well-lit shelves are a sensory shock.

"Nothing," Lydia mutters, shoving the book away. "Apart from that little passage, there was nothing."

Mentally shaking away the disturbing memory, and glad the witch hadn't noticed him lost to the happenings of the past, Colt strides to the couch, picking up another book on the way. He sits down and opens it, scowling. "There must be something."

Except the book holds nothing on the Skeleton Man. And neither does the next. And the next. Colt tries to remain hopeful as they scour texts that are more and more distantly linked to what little they've learned.

But their research is fruitless. Information on the Skeleton Man is elusive as the being himself.

Colt stands, his muscles objecting to all the inactivity. He paces to a nearby window, frowning when he sees that night is falling. He wonders if Gabby will be returning soon. All this feels far more possible when she's within touching distance.

Something about the view catches his attention. Something's off...

Lydia joins him, peering out into the darkness. "What? What do you see?"

"Nothing," he murmurs. "Which is the issue. It's dark. Far darker than usual." In fact, there's a hint of red to the black, as if it's a shade of crimson off midnight. "I've seen this before."

"Where?" Lydia frowns, scanning the nothingness.

"It was just after I banished Pothos the first time," Colt says, his gut tightening. "Something evil was happening..."

Geryon stalks through the darkling woods surrounding Asmodeus's castle. Back when he'd been sent here to spy, he'd spent many hours roaming through these blackened trees, at times with Asmodeus himself. The King of Hell spoke of how he'd planted a forest such as this in every level he ruled in. His vision was to return Hell to the paradise it once was. Of course, right now it was little more than decaying wood, gnarled branches, and desiccated leaves.

Still, when they first returned, Geryon couldn't bring himself to step over the threshold and follow Asmodeus inside. Not when the voice was painting images of him stabbing the King of Hell between the shoulder blades then standing over him, relishing the shock on Asmodeus's face as he spun. Then collapsed. Then died.

It had felt so good.

Geryon's lip curls, disgusted at himself. He hardens his determination against the parasite that's infested him. The focus is the Sins and the danger they pose. They must be stopped.

A faint sound, little more than a whisper, has him freezing. His fists are already raised when a slight frame steps from behind the peeling bark of a tree. "Hello, Geryon."

He straightens, dropping his fists to his side. "Ran, what are you doing here?"

"Looking for you," says the demoness.

"So you can lie to me again?" he growls.

The little demoness inclines her head. "I'm sorry about that," she says mildly, not sounding the least apologetic. "You were sent here by Belphegor to spy. I couldn't have you ruining Asmodeus's plans. He has a good heart and wants what's best for Hell. This darkness and corruption need to be handled and cleansed. Hell must return to the Paradise Lucifer envisioned it to be."

"I betrayed Belphegor because of the false information you gave me," Geryon snaps, memories of the dungeons still haunting his mind.

Ran clicks her tongue, looking as if she's had enough of discussing the topic now that she's made a show of a shallow apology. "But Asmodeus knew his vision of Lucifer and paradise wouldn't come to pass until the darkness was driven from Hell."

"So, he rescued me," Geryon says, realizing how he was forced to play a part in this again.

"Yes, and sent you to Dunabar."

Geryon pins her with a glare. "It didn't work. I banished the shifter, and the darkness is still here."

Ran steps closer, her dark eyes shining with knowledge. "And it came at a cost."

The evil inside Geryon pulses with agitation. "Kill her and this conversation is over."

He takes a step back. Surely Ran can't know that the darkness took hold of him when he banished the shifter.

"You have the darkness within you," she says, taking another step closer and looking him over. "I can feel it." She walks around

him, not seeming to notice she barely reaches his shoulder as she surveys him. "But you'll still do."

"Still do for what?" he spits.

Ran points up at the sky. "See that Geryon?" He looks up, registering the blackness through the scraggly branches and dried leaves. Although light barely survives in Hell, the totality of the darkness is unusual. As is the red tint, as if congealed blood had been brushed through it.

"The same darkness within you is growing," she continues. "Even if the Kings of Hell unite to defeat it, where will they drive it to?"

"The mortal world."

Ran nods. "Which is exactly what the Sins want. They'll corrupt Earth."

"And what does that have to do with me?" Geryon asks.

Ran stops in front of him, looking up with intensity burning in her eyes. "They've found a way out, Geryon. They've discovered a spell that can create a rip between the two words, much like the one that occurred during the Resurrection. The Sins intend on escaping through this Tear to wreak their havoc."

He frowns, the consequences of that settling in his gut like lead. "The demons tainted by the Sins will escape. Hundreds of them, probably thousands."

Yet Ran's expression says that won't be the end of it.

That there are more dire consequences coming.

"And the Tear will implode," she states flatly. "The mortal world will be plunged into an apocalypse."

"Colt?" Lydia's voice pierces his consciousness. A hand lands on his arm. "Is everything okay?"

He shakes his head, taking a step back. "I just remembered what the sky means," he says, his heart thundering against his ribs.

"Another memory?" comes Gabby's voice from behind him. She walks over, looking up at him in concern.

His pulse slows a little now that she's back. "Yes." He glances at the red-black night. "It's happening again."

Gabby frowns. "What is?"

"The darkness has been trying to escape from Hell for centuries, but this time, the Tear has already been created for it."

She nods, watching him closely as she waits for more. Lydia stands behind her, looking just as intense.

"Demons have been pouring out of the Tear, wanting to escape Hell. If they continue to do so..."

Gabby goes still. "If they continue?"

"If the Tear isn't closed, it will implode, Gabby," Colt says heavily. "And it's going to happen soon."

19

GABBY

"Implode?" Gabby gasps. "Soon?"

Colt nods somberly. "The dimensions of Hell and Earth will collapse onto each other. They'll become one."

She's pretty sure her heart stutters at that. "We can't let that happen," she breathes.

"No, we can't," he agrees, that steady determination that is Colt soothing her spiking stress.

Gabby clenches her fist. "It's more important than ever that we find the Skeleton Man."

Lydia steps forward, waving an arm in the direction of a stack of books. "We haven't found anything."

"Me neither," Gabby huffs.

She spoke to any supernatural she could on campus to see if anyone had heard of their mythical target. But no one had. The closest she got was her father and Moroni scratching their heads as they mused they'd heard something about a Skeleton Man, but they have no idea who or what he is.

Colt slips his hand into hers and interlaces their fingers.

"We'll find him," he promises, the strength in his voice and stance feeling reassuring.

Even if they have no way of making that promise comes true.

"Not with those books, you won't," comes a voice from behind them.

Gabby and Colt spin around, registering Blaise walking toward them. She's wearing a flowing, yellow dress with bell sleeves, and her matching sunshine-colored hair is braided. She glances at Lydia. "You must be Lydia. Blaise, lovely to meet you."

Lydia straightens as if she's just been spoken to by her headmistress. "Yes, I am. Lovely to meet you, too."

Blaise angles her head. "I've heard a lot about you. Various covens speak highly of your power and have competed to have you join their ranks." Her gaze sharpens. "But you've refused them all."

"Covens are overrated," Lydia says, shrugging. "They love their rules too much."

Blaise chuckles. "True. They have them for a reason, but I also prefer not to be stifled by a coven." She continues to watch the younger witch closely. "And yet you've still gone after the Legion."

Lydia's jaw tightens. "They're the ones who corrupted my sister. They're a dark and dangerous group. We both want the same outcome—to end them. I'll free my sister from their grasp, and you get the demonic weapons back. "

"Exactly," Blaise says. She turns to Gabby and Colt. "And Nim tells me the warding surrounding them is powerful."

"Yeah," Gabby says. "That's why we've been trying to find the Skeleton Man. He has the power to break through it."

Blaise's brows hike up her forehead. "He's a legend, even in witch circles." She glances at Lydia. "I can see why you suggested him."

"Yet we have found little information," Colt adds.

"Yes, a dark history surrounds the Skeleton Man," Blaise says. "Not much is written about him."

Gabby watches Blaise closely, realizing she's talking about the Skeleton Man with far more familiarity than anyone else they've spoken to. "What do you know about him?"

"I read about him in a book some time ago."

Colt's hand tightens around Gabby's. "What book? We've managed to find very little."

"That's because this book is at one of the Archivist's libraries," Blaise answers. "One that's about a day's drive from here."

"We don't have time for that," Colt growls.

Lydia straightens as if she just thought of something. "Blaise, you could transport us. You come from a long line of some of the most powerful witches who ever existed."

Blaise's brow furrows. "It would take a lot of energy to transport four people over that distance."

"Four supernatural people," Gabby points out. "Each with their own power to add to the mix."

Blaise smooths the yellow skirt of her dress. "There's a reason I work the color of focus and willpower. We're going to need it." She indicates for the others to move closer. "We'll have to hold hands."

Gabby can't help it. She slips past Colt so she'll be the one holding Lydia's hand, rather than him. She flicks her hair when she notices Colt's lips twitch. At least he finds her possessiveness amusing.

Blaise clasps Colt and Lydia's hand, while Gabby clasps them on the other side, creating a circle. "Close your eyes," Blaise murmurs. "And connect with your energy."

Gabby does as she's told, instantly feeling her power well within her. It rises like a tide, warm and electric, filling her veins and heating her skin. Then she feels Colt's power in their clasped hands, harder and hotter than hers, yet the same in some indefinable way. Although her eyes remain closed, she senses when they decide to send it to Blaise. Their energies flow into each other, twisting and blending like they have before, then rush away. Gabby thinks she hears Lydia gasp as it passes through her, then Blaise as she receives the double bolt.

Then Blaise is murmuring in what sounds like Latin. Colt's hand tightens around Gabby's as the ground disappears from beneath their feet. But it's only gone for a second, and she wonders if she imagined the second of weightlessness.

"We're here," Blaise says quietly.

Gabby opens her eyes, discovering they're on the outskirts of some town, a large, abandoned field stretching out before them. Sitting in the center is a multi-story building, looking even more abandoned.

"I would've thought it was a little better hidden," Gabby muses. Although there wouldn't be much traffic, many a curious history buff or ghost-hunter would want to check out the old building. The cracked windows and peeling cement don't look strong enough to keep out a fly.

Blaise smiles. "The building is hidden. All a human can see is a barren patch of land, and if anyone inquired about purchasing it, they'd find it's not for sale." She looks at the crumbling place almost fondly. "There are several spells warding it. You can see it because you're supernatural, but also because I've allowed it."

Gabby wrinkles her nose. "Thanks." She should've worn different shoes.

They cross the field and the building looks even worse the closer they get. The cement walls are cracked and flaking, the windows are more gaps than glass, and even the scraggly weeds sprouting wherever they can look like they could use a good water.

Blaise doesn't seem to notice as she picks her way to the front door. It opens with a creak and she enters, assuming they'll follow. Inside, it's dark and dank, but she strides with purpose to the stairs on the other side of the foyer.

"There was a time that Archivists used this place on a regular basis." Blaise stops on the second floor, indicating toward the corridor with a door on each side. "There are two apartments on each floor. We'd use the place as a stop-over during various missions. There are other buildings like this all around the world."

One of the doors is missing, and Gabby gets a glimpse of sagging, faded furniture and more flaky walls. It's as if the building has a severe case of eczema.

Blaise continues to the third floor. "But as our numbers have dwindled, the buildings have fallen into disrepair. Money ran out along with recruits."

Gabby notes the edge of sadness in Blaise's voice. As far as she knows, Blaise, Nim and Sierra are the only ones now part of the centuries-old group of scholars committed to chronicling the supernatural. Gabby steps around a chunk of cement that's fallen from the ceiling and smashed all over the floor, now knowing why the last three Archivists have based themselves at Veritas. They can no longer maintain all their outposts.

"One more floor," Blaise tells them over her shoulder, even putting her hand on the railing as she ascends.

Gabby keeps her hands to herself, thinking this place is as dark and morose as the skies are turning. Remembering why they're here has her stepping more determinedly, no matter what crunches underfoot.

The Tear's growing.

But that growth isn't infinite. As it expands, it's stretching, weakening.

And when it collapses, it'll be the end of the world as they know it.

They reach the fourth and top floor, discovering that it's even more unkempt than the lower stories. Broken furniture is scattered around the corridor and the ceiling sags dangerously. What's more, it smells...off.

Gabby wrinkles her nose. "Ah, what's that smell?"

Blaise grins over her shoulder. "Sometimes spells don't always work out the first time."

She walks to a door half-way down the corridor, her sunflower dress and hair a sharp contrast to the dark, decaying surroundings.

Pushing open the door, she steps back. "I did figure it out on the second attempt, though." She waves her arms toward the room she just revealed. "And here we are."

All thoughts of the spell gone wrong and unfortunate smell are wiped from Gabby's mind as she follows Colt into the room on the top floor. "It's...massive," she breathes.

The area opens out, expanding for yards and yards as if they're on the ground floor of Veritas.

"The building is designed to look much smaller than it really is," Blaise explains as she walks past them. "The apartments have the same enchantment. The whole place is really quite big."

Gabby takes a few more steps in. "I can see that." In fact, she can feel the power hanging in the air, almost electrifying it. She stops when she almost collides with a stack of books. The top floor may be the same size as Veritas, but it's certainly not as well organized. Books are lined on shelves, but there doesn't seem to be any order to them. More sit on the floor in haphazard piles that look like they could topple any minute. Others lie open on desks or chairs or on the shelves themselves.

Blaise weaves her way through the semi-ordered chaos. "Sorry. I always mean to organize the place, but then get sidetracked." She glances over her shoulder, her eyes shining. "Just the other day I found an interesting spell on trapping a person's consciousness in a book."

Lydia steps forward. "Interesting! I'd love to learn it."

Blaise turns to face the fellow witch. "Trapping someone in a book would be quite the punishment."

"Yes, it would," Lydia says, her voice hard.

Colt rubs his chin. "You're thinking of doing this to Malcolm Hunsecker?"

She nods sharply. "He wants to unleash chaos on the world, and he's using my sister to do it. Damned straight, I do."

Colt is still looking thoughtful. "Men like Malcolm are slippery. He'd find a way to escape. Better to kill him than imprison him."

He says the words matter of factly, almost dispassionately. And yet Gabby can't help but agree. She's learned some evils need to be stopped, period.

Lydia shrugs. "I'd still love to learn. Just in case the whole killing him plan doesn't work out. Like you said, he's a slimy prick."

Blaise waves her hand in the direction of the countless books they're surrounded by. "I'll teach you, but first, we focus on why we came here."

To learn what they can about the Skeleton Man.

Gabby does a slow turn, glad they've found another lead, but a little overwhelmed.

All they need to do is ferret out the needle in the bookstack.

20

COLT

Blaise and Lydia walk in opposite directions, eyes scanning spines and covers as they move.

But Gabby hesitates. "This, ah, could take a while."

Colt rests a hand on her shoulder. "Follow your magic, Gabby. Your instincts will guide you."

"I freaking hope so," she says on a sigh, striking out straight ahead.

Colt can't help but appreciate her unconscious grace as she disappears between some shelves, the edge of her skirt brushing her thighs. The night they spent together, the bond they've forged, only cements his determination to defeat the Legion.

Opting to cover the east side of the floor, Colt slips in between two lengthy shelves. He's about to run his finger over the leather spines as he reads the embossed text when something catches his eye. A glimmer much further down.

Frowning, he walks toward it, conscious that he's delving deeper and deeper into the bowels of this expansive library. And that this section of the library is darker, more encased in shadows. Colt reaches the book, discovering it's the insignia on its spine that is glinting with light. An insignia from Hell.

An insignia that belongs to the demon lord named Dagon.

Colt's hand reaches out, even as he can feel reality slipping away, the memory of seeing this book before becoming his world.

Ran pushes open the door to the castle's library, the monstrous size of the room only making her look smaller. She still enters with confident strides, though, suggesting she's been here before, or isn't a demon to show hesitation.

Geryon follows, his gaze roaming over the ceiling-high shelves brimming with books. Some are the familiar texts chronicling the history of Hell, others are clearly grimoires holding demonic spells. Ran ignores them all, moving deeper into the room.

He watches her, wondering if he can trust her. The small demoness carries a power about her that belies her size. But she's deeply loyal to Asmodeus. She will always choose him first, would die for him.

She stops beside a bookshelf and points to a thick tome several feet up. "That one."

Geryon uses his magic to summon the book to him, and as it lands in his palms, he notices a strange insignia emblazoned on the hardcover.

"It once belonged to the demon lord, Dago," Ran says. "He was Beelzebub's minion. Did all his dirty work for him."

Yet it's in Asmodeus's library. "What is it doing here?" he asks.

"Dagon was doing anything he could to incite the demons into warring against both Asmodeus and Belphegor. To prevent such a war, Asmodeus took Dagon out of the equation." Ran shrugs. "Of course Beelzebub was furious. But he has yet to retaliate."

"It will only be a matter of time," Geryon points out.

"Which is why we need to unite them before the Sins win, then unleash Hell on Earth."

Geryon almost scoffs. Does Ran not see how impossible the task is? "And how will we do that?"

She shrugs again, as if it's simple and straightforward. "We find a neutral place. We bring the three Kings together and we tell them what's at stake. Then, once they reach a truce, we fight together to free demons from the thrall of the Sins."

Geryon shakes his head. "I always knew there was something about you, Ran, but I couldn't quite place it. Now I know. Your mind is touched by madness."

She rolls her eyes. "Just open the book."

He does, and is instantly forced to slam his eyes shut by the blinding light that assaults him. He closes it, then opens it far more cautiously. Squinting, he makes out a diagrammatic representation of a demonic spell. "What is it?"

"The spell the Sins are going to use to open a rip between the worlds." Ran glances over at the shining page. "They'll be a force to be reckoned with once on Earth as they won't be weakened."

"A Tear, you say," he muses.

"Yes. I suspect it's their only way to reach the mortal plane. Especially now that you've banished the shifter."

"Then we need to stop them."

"We don't have that sort of power. Not unless the Kings unite."

Geryon grunts. "We're going to need a back up plan."

To his surprise, Ran grins. "This is why Asmodeus likes you, Geryon. You're as clever as our enemy."

He arches a brow at the little demon, not entirely sure that's a compliment.

Grinning even wider, Ran leans over to turn a few of the pages in the book. "In fact, you're almost as clever as me."

"This book contains a spell to stop the Tear?"

Shaking her head, she taps her finger on another spell once more diagrammatically represented on another page. "I have something better." Her pixie-like grin is back as she looks up at him. "A spell that will put the Sins to sleep."

The sound of footsteps snaps Colt out of the memory. Blaise stops beside him, angling her head as she looks at the book curiously. "Interesting," she muses, her gaze roaming over the insignia on the cover. "This book has a strange history as to how we found it. On the day we created the Tear and tried to stop Cain from acquiring what we thought was the Holy Grail, it appeared on Gabby's doorstep. Her mother found it and gave it to Sierra, thinking the book was hers. Sierra had never seen it before, but she took it anyway." She glances at Colt. "Do you recognize it?"

"Yes, I do," Colt says, the memory still fresh in his mind. "I saw it in Hell a long time ago. It's a demonic spell book."

Blaise's eyes light up. "Well, it seems it's found its home. You should take it."

"Thank you," he says, tucking it under his arm. "It may come in handy."

He's not sure why or how it's managed to land in his hands again after all this time, but he does know it's significant.

Blaise pats his arm. "Let's focus on the book we actually need." She plants her hands on her hips. "Which I think may be in this section, too?"

Colt doesn't reply, wondering to himself whether her mind is as well organized as this place. The book could be here, or in any other section of this mammoth library...

Gabby's excited voice carries from several yards away. "I think I found it!"

Colt almost shakes his head in amusement. Of course she did. Fate seems to throw everything her way.

He and Blaise join Gabby just as Lydia does. Gabby holds up a thick tome, eyes alive with excitement. "There's a whole chapter on the Skeleton Man!"

Blaise takes the book, smiling herself. "Yes, this is the one." She opens it, instantly immersed as she turns the pages.

Lydia peeks underneath, reading the title on the cover. "*Monstera Legendarium.*"

"Yes," Blaise says, not looking up. "It lists and describes every monster ever seen on Earth. Including witches."

Lydia straightens indignantly. "Rude!"

Blaise shrugs nonchalantly, still not looking up. "Some of our kind have done great things, but some have done terrible things."

Lydia's mouth clamps shut, probably thinking of her own sister who's aligned with the Legion.

Colt clears his throat, trying not to get impatient. "And the Skeleton Man?"

Blaise's eyes finally rise from the book. "I think we should sit down."

"It sounds like we should've brought popcorn," Gabby says, her eyebrows twitching a little higher.

Blaise smiles, but the motion is thin and stretched. "This way."

She leads them to an alcove with a couch and a couple of armchairs, but doesn't sit down. Colt takes the couch and pulls Gabby onto his lap. "It's dusty," he says by way of explanation.

Her lips arc up as they soften. "Much appreciated, gallant knight."

Blaise clears her throat, although her attention is already back on the open pages of the book she's holding. "Apparently, there are several little-known mythologies that reference the Skeleton Man. North American folklore calls him Baykok. Korean folklore calls him Pah-guk." She flips the page. "But most of the references are from Algonquian mythology. Seems he's well known to the tribes that are settled in the Great Lakes region."

She turns the page again and Colt and Gabby glance at each other. There's a lot of page flipping, and not a lot of information.

"And?" Lydia asks where she's perched on one of the armchairs. "Where can we find him?"

Blaise looks up, her gaze heavy. "This chapter isn't information on the Skeleton Man. It's a history of the Great Lakes tribes."

Gabby sags against Colt. "Seems we didn't need the popcorn after all."

"We're going to need more than that," Blaise says ominously. "This chapter is also a map that will take us to the tribe who know of the Skeleton Man."

Gabby shoots to her feet. "That's great! We can go talk to them!"

Blaise is already shaking her head, prompting Colt to also stand, but far more slowly. He braces himself. "What's wrong?"

"Yuma is the leader of this tribe, and he's indeed a knowledgeable man," Blaise says. "But this tribe is well versed in the supernatural. And they refuse to have anything to do with it."

Gabby frowns. "I'm sure we'll be able to convince him once he realizes how important this is."

Colt tenses, knowing the next hurdle is about to be revealed.

Blaise slowly closes the book. "That's assuming we can get past his guards."

21

GABBY

Awall of unfriendly faces greet them at the reservation. Men and women of all ages exit their houses, arms crossed and brows low. A few hold rifles.

Colt is tense beside Gabby, protective energy coming off him in waves.

Blaise is just as alert. "They sense your demonic energy, Colt. We need to be ready for anything."

Gabby keeps her hands open at her sides, trying not to look like a threat, even as she prepares to use her magic at any moment. The challenge is to be faster than a bullet.

"Yuma's house will be at the center of the village," Blaise continues, her voice low. "It may be a fight to get in."

They continue on, keeping as a tight group with Blaise and Colt at the front, Gabby and Lydia right behind them. The people who were already sitting outside their homes stand, others exit, the sound of screen doors slamming piercing the tense silence.

Yet none of them move. No one twitches, let alone attacks.

"They're trying to trap us," Colt growls.

Gabby swallows. By allowing them to enter the village more fully, it'll be harder to escape.

Except they need this information on the Skeleton Man. Badly.

So they continue on, walking cautiously but steadily down the road riddled with potholes. A white house appears ahead, not much larger than the others, but the large carved owl perched on the letter box suggests they have the right place.

As do the two tall men standing on either side of it, each holding a double-barrel shotgun across their chests.

"Fools," Colt mutters. "The only people who are going to get hurt are them."

Gabby's chest tightens. Hurting innocent people in the name of fighting evil isn't something she wants to do.

To everyone's surprise, the two men step back, revealing the brick path leading to the house.

"It could be a trap," Colt warns.

One they're going to need to walk straight into if they have any chance of learning about the Skeleton Man.

Blaise and Colt pass first, bodies vibrating with tension, holding the gazes of the guards until they're past. Gabby and Lydia are next, and she notes their stony expressions. It's clear they don't intend on attacking, but they don't like having these intruders here, either.

The door opens as they approach and a man appears, leaning on one of those crutches that clamp around a person's forearm. Gabby quickly realizes it's because he's missing half of his right leg.

Blaise dips her head in deference. "Yuma."

He nods, stepping back silently in the same way the guards did to indicate they should enter. Gabby wonders if Colt is going to snap from the tension tangling his muscles. They're about to be well and truly trapped.

Yuma follows them, his crutch tapping hollowly on the timber floor. They enter a homey but sparsely furnished living room. Thick red rugs cover the floor, while more carved animals sit on shelves and side tables. The tribal leader takes a seat in an armchair that looks like it's molded just for him, leaning his crutch beside him. Beside it is a prosthetic leg, which he obviously decided not to wear.

Gabby also discovers he's staring at her. To the exclusivity of anyone else.

"We're here to—" Blaise starts.

But Yuma lifts a calloused, wrinkled hand, stopping her. "An angel, huh?" he says to Gabby.

Colt's barely twitching a muscle, he's so wired. If Yuma recognizes Gabby as an angel, then he knows Colt's a demon.

Gabby nods. "Yes, I'm an angel." She smiles, trying to lighten the mood. "Although I've never actually been to Heaven."

Yuma nods, stroking his chin. "Interesting, an angel born on the mortal plane." His aged eyes scan her from head to toe. "You bear a powerful aura, girl. Even more powerful than those descended from the Pearl City. You're destined for great deeds," he says matter of factly. "Yet I still see evil ahead for you."

Gabby waits, hoping he's talking about the Skeleton Man.

He inclines his head. "You may yet escape with the seven black stones."

That has her stilling. Yuma's talking about the obsidian?

Before she can ask, he turns to Blaise. "And yes, I know why you're here. The spirits foretold your arrival. You wish to know about the Skeleton Man."

Blaise nods. "Yes, we haven't been able to find much."

Yuma grunts, then arranges his stump of a leg before indicating for the others to sit. Colt is the last to do so, and Gabby knows he'd probably prefer to stand. Although they've here without a hitch, in fact, Yuma was expecting them, sitting means a split-second to standing and defending.

"The knowledge of the Skeleton Man was buried a long time ago," Yuma says once they're all seated. "He was the product of a dangerous experiment. One we didn't want repeated."

Gabby leans forward. "But you know about him."

The old man nods sagely. "He was once one of us."

Everybody waits, breaths held. Yuma holds the information they need, and not only did they not need to shed blood to hear it, he seems willing to share.

"He—his name is long forgotten—was approached by an ancient organization a very long time ago," he says, absent-mindedly scratching his stump. "The leader promised he could help us defend ourselves from the demons of the forest."

Colt stiffens, but Yuma remains relaxed in his armchair. "They turned out to be werewolves. They wanted our territory and no matter how sacred this land was to us, we were losing."

Blaise nods. "The reservation lies over a powerful hotspot. The confluence of ley lines is a strong one."

"The leader of the organization brought brujas, witches," Yuma continues. "They spoke of a ritual, an experiment that would grant us magical powers which we could use to protect ourselves and our lands. And they showed us a mask. At first we resisted, my ancestors could sense the evil in it, but eventually many agreed."

Gabby frowns. This is all sounding a little too familiar, which means she knows what's coming next...

"Most died," Yuma says, glancing down at his stump. "Some were mutilated and disfigured, and those genes remain in our population."

Gabby's heart constricts. Yuma's people are still living with the effects of something that happened hundreds of years ago.

"The nameless one stole the mask from the organization, I'm not sure whether to protect his people, or to have the power for himself. Either way, the infernal power affected him."

Colt sits up straight. "Infernal power?"

Yuma nods gravely. "Yes, we later learned that the mask had been stolen from an Archdemon in Hell. And discovered which one."

Judging by the look on Colt's face, he already has an idea which one.

"It was Beelzebub," says Yuma. "The mask once belonged to him."

Colt huffs in disgust. "I've heard of these masks," he says. "They allow demons to shift shape and form without using their own demonic power. Three masks were made, two of which were stolen by a man named Dante. He found secret passageways between the dimensions and escaped to the mortal plane with his loot."

Yuma nods, looking familiar with the story. "And those masks were stolen once more by those who worship dark powers. They call themselves the Legion."

"We know of them," Gabby says, conscious of the hardening in her voice. So many loose ends are slowly being tied up, weaving a noose around the Legion's neck.

Yuma shifts, reaching out to grip his crutch as if it serves more than just a physical function. "The demonic masks were never meant to be worn by humans. And once the Nameless One wore it, the mask corrupted him. The more he shifted shape, the deeper the claws of evil pierced his soul. He haunted us. Made our lives unbearable." His gaze lands on Gabby, looking strangely happy. "We had no way forward until someone found us. Someone who reminds me of you."

"Me?" Gabby asks, confused.

"His aura was very similar. He called himself Gabriel."

Gabby's eyebrows shoot up. Turns out there are more threads to this story than they realized. "He's my father," she tells Yuma.

The old man smiles in pleasure, his walnut wrinkles deepening. "Gabriel saved us. He brought with him a friend. A witch named Celeste."

This time, it's Blaise who straightens. "Celeste is my ancestor."

"And the witch who summoned me from Hell," adds Colt. "She saved my life."

Gabby's head turns from side to side as she looks between them. More threads. More weaving of fates over hundreds of years. She returns her focus to Yuma. "And what did Celeste do?"

"By this time, the Skeleton Man was shifting often and leaving a green sludge behind. Gabriel explained that the more he did this, the more he would become like a wraith. Half in the world of living, half in the world of the dead. Celeste found him, little more than a skeleton, and buried him deep in the ground."

Lydia crosses her arms. "See, brujas can be good," she mutters quietly.

Yuma ignores her. "We had peace for a long time. Even the werewolves entered a truce with us." He glances down at the leg that's missing its bottom half. "Apart from the odd disfigurement, we were happy."

Gabby waits, as do the others. It's clear there's a great big *but*.

"Until a few years ago," Yuma continues, his voice heavy. "The spell Celeste cast was broken and the mask was stolen. The Skeleton Man woke from his sleep. We've been tracking him for some time, but he's always one step ahead, always shifting form. We did learn that he'd been resurrected by a dark bruja called Samara, who is now dead."

Lydia's back curves as she curses.

Yuma's astute eyes settle on her. "You know her." The words are a statement, not a question.

"She's my mother," Lydia spits. "The same mother who abandoned me and my sister to pursue dark magic. It's she who influenced my sister down a dark path. Now, my sister works for the Legion."

"So the Skeleton Man works for the Legion," Colt says. Everything they've learned confirms their suspicions.

Lydia sighs. "When the Skeleton Man was resurrected by my mother, Samara, she bound him with a spell. One that allows the Legion to control him. Malcolm has a penchant for experimenting and creating evolved species. The demonic weapons are also part of the plan. He'll have unbeatable supernatural beings wielding demonic weapons. He'll be unstoppable."

Gabby turns to her, trying not to frown. "You're telling us now?"

Lydia shrugs. "Without being able to locate the Skeleton Man, none of that mattered."

Blaise moves forward to sit on the edge of the sofa. "We need to track the green sludge," she says, eyes widening with realization. "Every time the Skeleton Man shifts, he leaves behind green sludge."

"Also something I knew," says Lydia. "But we don't have any to learn his unique signature. Without that, tracing it is impossible."

Gabby does frown this time. Lydia has been drip feeding them information as she sees fit.

Yuma picks up his crutch, grinning. He untwists the forearm brace from the top, then tips the length of metal over on his lap. A small vial containing something iridescent and green slips out.

It can't be...

He holds it up, pride shining in his dark eyes. "When I learned you'd be coming, daughter of Gabriel, I had my men focus on collecting this."

Blaise gravitates toward it, hyper-focused on the small vial. Yuma passes it to her without hesitation, but it's on Gabby that his gaze settles.

"The spirits told me the Skeleton Man is the key to something you want."

Gabby also rises, Colt instantly by her side. "Something like what?"

Yuma remains in his chair, once more rubbing his stump without seeming to be aware he's doing it. "Right now, you must find him." He sighs, his shoulders drooping for the first time. "Or we are all lost."

22

COLT

Away from the reservation, Blaise wastes no time in using the vial of green sludge to do a locator spell to find the Skeleton Man. Above them, the sky shifts restlessly, the blood-tainted darkness seeming thicker than it was only hours ago. Colt paces the edge of the forest they're standing on, still tense from the visit to Yuma.

He's not sure why it felt like walking into a viper's den, but it had. Keeping Gabby safe had been his only priority. Even after Yuma proved to be peaceful and willing to share information, it had been a relief to leave the reservation.

Although, even now, the edgy, prickly feeling is still stuck in his veins. And a part of him knows it's because of everything that happened in the past. Maybe it's nothing more than triggering the feeling of being trapped in Belphegor's dungeons, knowing more torture was coming. He's never liked being enclosed.

He passes Gabby and she reaches out, pressing a hand on his arm, smiling softly. He instantly unwinds, his own smile mirroring hers. Her eyes ask him if he's okay. He wishes he could kiss her, tell her that it is as long as she's by his side.

"I've found him," Blaise says, looking up from the map she's holding. "He's somewhere in this zone," she says, pointing. "But I can't get his exact location."

"It's a start," Colt says. "We'll search every last inch of it."

Gabby's hands form into fists. "And the plan is to sever the Skeleton's Man's connection to the Legion?" she asks, confirming they all understand what they're about to do.

Lydia inclines her head. "Or we transfer the connection to ourselves."

Colt spins to face her. "Is that even possible?"

"I don't see why not." She angles her head. "What do you know of golems?"

Unsure at the change of topic, Colt watches Lydia closely. "I know Klae, a friend of Gabby's, is one. What does that have to do with this?"

"Because golems usually have a master controlling them." Lydia lifts her chin. "And I control Klae."

Gabby gasps. "You're her...master?"

"She's been in the family for generations," Lydia says. "She was originally in the possession of a Jewish family who tragically died in the holocaust. The last remaining member transferred her to my mother, who then passed her onto me."

"So she's your slave?" Gabby asks, looking horrified.

Lydia scrunches her nose. "Golems are created by witches using clay and spells, they're forever linked as a result. Without us, golems couldn't function. If Klae and my connection were to be severed, she'd eventually turn to stone and die. But we also respect each golem's individuality. I try to let Klae live her life as she sees fit."

Colt realizes something. "You sent her to the Academy."

"Yes, I did," Lydia says. "I'd heard that a war between angels and demons was brewing. That would mean an apocalypse.

When I realized the Skeleton Man had risen again, I sought you two out."

"And now you want to transfer the Skeleton Man to yourself, too." Colt crosses his arms, wondering if Lydia has an ulterior motive.

"The bond that exists between Klae and I is because of a spell. If she was transferred to me, and I can transfer her to someone else, then surely we can do the same for the Skeleton Man."

"It would be risky," Blaise points out. "The witch who bound the Skeleton man to the Legion would know."

"Although, it was Samara who did that?" Gabby asks. "And she's dead?"

"She may be dead, but my mother is smart. Just like she transferred Klae to me, I'm guessing she transferred the Skeleton Man to my sister."

Gabby chews her lip, gazing at the trees. "I wonder how the Skeleton Man feels, being tied to the Legion and at their bidding."

Lydia rolls her eyes. "He's barely alive. He'd be little more than a puppet."

"And the mask has corrupted him," Blaise adds. "Evil has become a part of him."

Suddenly, lightning splits the sky, quickly followed by angry thunder. Colt frowns. They're running out of time. "This is our best course of action." Even if they have yet to be sure of Lydia's allegiance.

She nods resolutely. "The spell will take some time. I'll need to focus, and I fully expect the Legion to fight back. I'll need protection."

"We'll take care of that," Colt said. "Gabby and I will create wards."

Gabby moves closer to him. "We're stronger together."

The words warm Colt's chest, in part because they're true, in part because it's so beautiful to hear. He grasps her hand and squeezes.

Blaise folds up the map. "We need to move quickly, in case the Skeleton Man disappears and we have to track him all over again."

Colt moves so he's holding Gabby's other hand and Blaise's, acting as if it's normal. He's willing to honor his angel's possessiveness. It's born of love, and all the attempts to tear them apart. The way her eyes shine when she smiles at him makes it all worth it.

They form a circle once more and he closes his eyes.

It's time to find the Skeleton Man.

COLT OPENS his eyes to find they're outside an abandoned tenement building. Three stories high, the windows are boarded up even though there are gaping openings where the doors used to be. Graffiti colors the walls, layer upon layer scrawled on top of the other until most of it is illegible. Ahead, more lightning and thunder tear through the sky, as if it followed them from the reservation. Despite the amassing clouds, there's no rain. Not even moisture in the air.

Colt also notes that they're now not far from where the hell fires broke out a few weeks ago. In fact, the club that Gabby visited with Maya and Kalisha is only a couple of blocks away.

Gabby pulls in a breath. "Okay, let's search the place."

They enter the tenement building through the doorless entry, the smell of decay instantly filling Colt's nostrils. The graffiti has spread to the inside, becoming far more phallic and misspelled. Deciding to stick together, they comb through every decrepit apartment block, every stained, dirty story.

And even though they find nothing, tension once more climbs through Colt. It might be the fact they're enclosed again. It might be the fact he's conscious they don't even know what the Skeleton Man looks like. It might be the fact he has a feeling deep in his gut that there's still more to be learned.

They return to the ground floor and Blaise huffs. "I was so sure he was here."

"Maybe he's been here?" Colt suggests. "And you're tracing his recent presence?"

"Maybe," she concedes. "The locator spell couldn't pin his exact location."

Gabby kicks at what's left of a desk in the office they're standing in at the front of the building. It probably belonged to the manager of the apartment block. The leaning timber skids a couple of feet away before collapsing, almost looking relieved that it no longer has to continue standing.

Gabby gasps, then points. A trap door has been revealed in the cement floor, frayed carpet surrounding it. "A basement!"

Lydia pushes past them, quickly lifting it open. Creaking fills the musty room. "If he's here, then we've just found him."

Colt's muscles wind with tension once more. Since the memory of Belphegor's torture has been triggered, he's not looking forward to descending beneath this building, but there isn't a choice. They can't afford to let the Skeleton Man slip between their fingers.

And keeping Gabby safe is his sole reason for existing. This is why Colt chooses to go first. The steps groan slightly even as he treads lightly, the sound seeming to hang in the air that hasn't moved for a long time. Colt continues to descend, glad for his demon sight as it progressively becomes darker. He reaches the bottom, sniffing cautiously. But the air is stagnant and even the spiderwebs look lifeless.

He moves forward silently, registering that the concrete space is essentially empty except for a few saggy cardboard boxes in the far corner. With lightning speed, Colt approaches them, his wings ready to explode from his back if he needs to move even faster. The boxes almost disintegrate just with the rush of air, revealing old fishing magazines.

"I don't think he's here," Blaise says from behind him, sounding frustrated.

Lydia huffs, her lip curling in annoyance.

Gabby slips by Colt's side and wraps an arm around his waist. "We still have the vial. We can try again."

He's about to suggest they get out of this concrete cell when white smoke condenses at the base of the stairs, forming the shape of a man. Gabby's and Colt's hands instantly fill with magical fire, except the figure lets out a low laugh, then shoots straight for the ceiling.

He spears through it with a thunderous crack. The basement shudders at the impact as if it was just hit by an earthquake. Fractures split through the ceiling, growing and splitting as they spread out then down the walls. Gray dust sprinkles down on them, quickly becoming sharp shards of concrete.

Colt instinctively pulls Gabby to him. "Run!" he roars.

Before they can move, a large chunk of cement lands on the staircase and it disintegrates. Dust billows, coating Colt's throat as he inhales and making Lydia cough. The sound of cement fracturing echoes around them.

The basement is about to collapse.

And they're trapped.

Colt's chest heaves as it tries to contain his out of control heart. Flashes of his time in the dungeon assault him. His vision blackens around the edges, and he tries to reign in his breathing. Now isn't the time to have some sort of post traumatic response.

But the darkness keeps closing in. He loses the sensation of holding Gabby tightly against him, even as he tries to shield her from the falling ceiling. And he quickly realizes why.

His past is calling to him. Memories are determined to swallow his reality.

"No," Colt moans.

He can't afford to lose his connection to reality. Not now.

The massive doors to the meeting hall open the moment Geryon approaches them. The Kings of Hell are expecting him. He's the one tasked with trying to convince them they need to enter into a truce.

The demons of Hell need to be freed of the Sin's dark power.

Before this spills onto Earth.

The three Kings of Hell sit on three thrones, each watching him. Asmodeus looks tense, but keeps his face composed in harsh lines. Beelzebub is sneering. Belphegor's hands are wrapped around the gilded arm rests, looking as if he's holding back from murdering Geryon.

Ran's words, whispered just a few moments before he entered, rise in his mind. "Good luck. Asmodeus wants this. Beelzebub will see reason. But Belphegor will be blinded by anger. He is the one you must convince, because he will be the key to this truce."

A truce Geryon isn't convinced is possible.

"Interesting that a traitor is going to try and mediate peace," Belphegor snarls mockingly. "Where is the other little traitor, Ran? That little vermin cost me a castle and I deserve justice."

"Enough!" Asmodeus snaps. "You deserve nothing. Your petty war against me has cost us both many soldiers. Most demons are tired of your warmongering. It does nothing but feed the dark powers corrupting Hell.

Belphegor stands, replying in a bellow. "I am doing this to save Hell,"

"No, Belphegor, you're doing this to empty Hell," Asmodeus snaps back. "You believe getting out of Hell and populating Earth with demons is the solution."

"Hell's gone, Asmodeus," Belphegor says caustically. "It's been corrupted, rendered evil ever since that stone spread the darkness and turned Hell from the Paradise it once was. How can it be wrong to seek greener pastures for demons?"

"Going to Earth will only violate our already fragile truce with the archangels," Asmodeus says. "You won't be taking the demons to greener pastures. You'll be taking them to a war with the angels. Why risk an apocalyptic war when we can put an end to the darkness?"

Belphegor laughs. "Have you not felt the power thrumming through all the levels of Hell? If the corruption could be beaten, don't you think we would have done something by now?"

Geryon steps forward, conscious the peace is becoming less and less likely. If it was ever possible at all. "The dark powers are planning to open up a tear and corrupt the mortal plane. An apocalypse will be inevitable."

Belphegor finally falls silent. Seems he was unaware the darkness has bigger plans.

"The only solution is to rid us of the Sins." Asmodeus thuds his fist down on the arm of his throne.

"And what do I get in return?" Beelzebub asks, speaking for the first time, stroking his lip in thought. "If I support this, what do I get in return?"

"This is not the time to be selfish," Geryon snaps. He almost turns around and leaves. This entire exercise is a waste of time.

"I'm looking after my own, boy," Beelzebub snaps back. "If I have to shed demon blood, my forces will be weakened. I'll be vulnerable from attacks by these two." He waves a disgusted arm in the direction of Asmodeus and Belphegor.

"If we don't enter this truce," Geryon grinds out through

clenched teeth, *"we destroy each other, and the dark powers win. They're probably influencing this right now."* The Kings of Hell are more focused on their petty wars than saving their kind.

Geryon straightens, trying one more time. *"A truce will give us the strength to end the Sins. We need to be united."*

Belphegor curls his lip. *"And I should trust you?"*

"You once did," Geryon replies calmly.

Belphegor's hands clench and unclench where they rest on his throne. Emotions flit across his face too fast for Geryon to distinguish them. He has no idea what the archdemon is thinking.

But for some reason, it plants a seed of hope. That maybe a truce could be a reality.

Beelzebub nods as if he just came to a decision. *"Very well. I will unite my forces for this. We must end the Sin's influence in Hell."*

Geryon looks back at his old master. Just like Ran predicted, this all rests on Belphegor.

And whether his feelings of anger and betrayal will undermine everything.

He grunts. *"Treachery is a punishable offense. After this is over, Geryon, you shall meet justice. But for now, we will work together to drive out these dark powers."*

Geryon nods, remaining silent. He can't quite believe it. The Kings of Hell are uniting!

Today is an auspicious day, indeed.

"We shall put this in writing then," Asmodeus announces, no doubt wanting to do it before anyone changes their mind.

He produces a stone tablet and places it on the table. Slicing his hand, he squeezes a thin trickle of blood onto it. Beelzebub stands and walks over to do the same. Belphegor is next. Geryon watches, barely allowing himself to breathe, conscious the next few moments will change everything.

Belphegor raises his knife and holds it to his palm.

Suddenly, demonic smoke pours in through the doors, races past

Geryon, then forms in a figure beside Belphegor. A figure Geryon recognizes.

"Mazikeen!" he shouts.

"There shall be no truce," she growls, spinning around and throwing a knife at Belphegor. The blade impales in the archdemon's chest with enough force that he stumbles backward. "Geryon's orders," she adds gleefully.

"What are you doing?" Geryon screams.

Mazikeen turns to him, her eyes glowing crimson with hatred. "What you asked me to—ending the truce." She grins maliciously, then disappears.

Belphegor crumples, but quickly catches himself on the nearest throne. "You...you tried to have me killed, Geryon."

"No!" he shouts, even as he knows it's useless. "I did not order this."

Belphegor yanks the knife out of his chest with a groan. "There will be no truce," he snarls. "And I will have my revenge." With a curl of his lip, he disappears.

Beelzebub shakes his head. "You will pay for your treachery, Geryon. As you should." Without another glance, he also disappears.

Geryon remains where he's standing.

He failed in uniting the Kings of Hell.

And not only that. Belphegor will now hunt him until the end of time.

23

COLT

"Colt!" Gabby's voice pierces his reverie. "Colt!"

The hold the memory had on him snaps, and Colt blinks rapidly. "Gabby! I'm so sorry!"

They're trapped in a collapsing basement and he lost touch with reality!

Relief suffuses her beautiful features. "I was worried about you."

Blaise glances over her shoulder where she's holding her hands up, creating a shield above them. "We need to get out of here. I'm tiring."

Colt shakes his head, throwing off the last threads of the memory. Being trapped in this basement obviously triggered the memories of Belphegor. He can feel the claws of fear trying to gain purchase, the air feeling too thick to breathe.

Except Gabby's in danger. Nothing takes priority over that.

Above them, a new fracture appears in the ceiling, jaggedly splicing from one end to the other. "It's going to cave in any second," Lydia gasps.

Before the sentence is complete, a large piece of cement falls in the corner of the basement, crashing to the floor and spraying out rubble and dust. Colt pushes Gabby behind him, bracing himself as he acts as a shield, confused when he feels nothing.

The shards of concrete never reach them.

Suddenly, a voice calls from the door. "Gabby! Are you okay?"

Klae stands in the doorway to the basement, looking at them in confusion.

"Klae," Gabby cries out. "We're trapped. The place is collapsing and the stairs are gone."

She frowns. "What are you talking about?" She looks down and takes a step forward.

"No!" Colt calls out, breaking into a run as he prepares to catch her.

Except Klae doesn't fall. She places her foot on a step, then another on the next one down.

Colt and the other glance at each other, speechless. The staircase is back, intact and unbroken. He executes a slow spin, gaze traveling over the rest of the basement. Everything looks as it did when they first entered. "It was an illusion?" he asks in disbelief.

Klae reaches the bottom of the stairs, her brow scrunched down. "It's happened before." She glances at Lydia. "Each time someone's tried to find the Skeleton Man, they're trapped in an illusion. Usually one that draws upon a person's fear."

Lydia nods, still panting. "I'd forgotten." She glances around. "It was so real."

And it possibly fed off Colt's fears of anything that could resemble a dungeon. He grabs Gabby's hand. "Let's talk about this outside."

She doesn't argue and they all hurry out of the tenement building. It's only once they're no longer surrounded by walls that the tightness around Colt's chest eases. Not only is being caged uncomfortable, so is knowing the memories could be triggered at any moment. At least out here, that's unlikely to happen.

He turns to Blaise, wanting to get things back on track. "That decoy was magic," he says. "Which means you could track the magical imprint back to the Skeleton Man?"

Blaise frowns as she absentmindedly strokes her yellow hair. "I suppose so."

Lydia also looks thoughtful. "If the imprint is faint, it may lead us astray, but it's definitely worth a try."

Blaise's hand drops to her pocket and she pulls out her cell. "First, I'd like to call in reinforcements."

"Reinforcements?" Lydia asks.

Nodding, Blaise is already walking away so she can speak in privacy. "The Knights Templar," she explains, dialing.

Colt feels Gabby's fingers weaving through his. He looks down to find her also looking thoughtful. "Could we talk?"

"Of course," he responds, even as his stomach tightens. This will be about what happened in the basement.

And not the illusion.

With a quick smile in Lydia's direction, Gabby leads him several feet away in the opposite direction to Blaise. She stops, turning to him. "What happened back there?"

"I'm remembering things," Colt says, not wanting to hide anything from the angel who holds his heart. "From my time in Hell."

"Times you'd forgotten?" she asks, surprised.

He sighs. "I hadn't realized there were memories that were suppressed. They started when I was trapped in the stone." Even though Colt doesn't mention he was trapped there because of Gabby, she still flinches. He clasps her upper arms, wanting to reassure her. "It triggered the time I was trapped in Belphegor's dungeon."

But she flinches even more. "I'm so sorry, Colt. If I could take it back..."

He moves his hands up to clasp her face. "No, we've been over this, there's nothing to be sorry for. In fact, I wouldn't have known the memories were hidden if that didn't happen."

Gabby blinks up at him, eyes luminous with uncertainty. "What sort of memories?"

"Of Mazikeen." Her instant frown has him realizing that wasn't where he should've started. "Of facing the Shifter the first time. That's how I remembered the spell to banish him."

She chews her lip in thought. "I suppose so..."

And now he knows why Belphegor hates him so deeply. He believes Colt betrayed him and had Mazikeen try to end his life.

"It seems the past is linked far more closely to the present that I'd realized."

"There's more to remember, isn't there?"

"I suspect there is." Colt sighs again. "I just wish I had some control over when the memories came," he admits. "I can't protect you if I'm being pulled into the past when I least expect it."

That has Gabby smiling. She presses closer, her own hands coming to rest on his chest. "Good thing I'm here to protect you then, isn't it?"

His chest warms with a feeling that's fast becoming familiar. Yet one he'll never tire of. "I suppose it is."

Gabby's now grinning as she pushes up on her toes. "I won't let anything happen to you, Colt. We're in this together."

He leans down, drawn to the softness of her lips, the tenderness in her blue eyes. "Always," he murmurs a moment before his mouth brushes hers.

Her sigh tugs at something low in his gut. It stirs a completely different set of memories. Ones he not only wants to relive, but forge many more of.

"I've found him."

Blaise's voice punctures the sweet cocoon they were weaving around themselves and Colt pulls back reluctantly. Gabby seems to have trouble unclenching the fingers twisted in his shirt. She groans. "When this is all over, you're mine, Colt Grayson."

He grins, despite the situation. "I already am, Gabrielle Heartley."

Blaise walks toward them, Lydia falling into step beside her. "You've found him?"

"Yes," says Blaise. "In another abandoned building not far from here."

Gabby takes Colt's hand. "Good. Because I'm tired of this cat and mouse. I want this over and done with."

Lydia arches a brow. "We need to be careful. The Skeleton Man is a master of illusion. We don't even know what he looks like."

Colt stiffens as the witch finishes speaking. He doesn't fight it this time, even as two words drift through his mind.

Not again.

GERYON RETURNS TO HIS CHAMBERS, frustration bubbling through his veins. They'd been close to a truce, but it had been sabotaged. Now Belphegor's wrath will know no end. He'll hunt him down once this is over, and the time in the dungeon will feel like a vacation.

Geryon stops the moment he enters, closing the door with a flick of his hand. Ran stands from where she was sitting on his bed, her face somber. He watches and waits, conscious of the strange aura this little demon exudes, one that makes other demons uneasy. Yet he doesn't feel threatened by her. Maybe it's because Asmodeus trusts her. Maybe it's because she's worked as hard on stopping the darkness as he has.

"Mazikeen is under the thrall of the Sins," Ran says, her brow constricted with tension. "They've destroyed any chance of a truce and placed a target on your back. Once this is over, Belphegor will hunt you to the ends of the three dimensions."

"We need to focus on the Sins and the Tear," Geryon growls, not wanting to dwell on the obvious. He may not even survive that far.

"Asmodeus is working on something to ensure your safety. I'm just not sure he'll be able to in time."

Geryon glares at her. "Thank you for the reassurance."

Ran angles her head, her eyes suddenly twinkling. "That's why I think we should do something about it while we wait for him to return."

He frowns. "What do you mean?"

"What do you know about hell masks?" she asks, propping her hands on her hips.

Geryon frowns even deeper. Most demons know of the Hell masks forged by Beelzebub. Their power is legendary. Two were also stolen by a human named Dante and never seen again. "What of them?"

Ran smiles, a mischievous glint now sparkling in her gaze. "You find one and return it to Beelzebub and you've now got two Kings of Hell on your side. Belphegor will have to back down."

"Not possible," says Geryon, shaking his head. "No one knows where the stolen masks are."

Ran steps a little closer, looking as if she's holding a delicious secret. "I've heard stories recently. That one of the Masks was stolen by a man from a Native American tribal community after they were threatened by supernatural beings. Rumor has it that he wore it, but because these demonic masks aren't supposed to be worn by humans, it changed him. He earned himself the title of Skeleton Man."

"I don't have time to hunt down this Skeleton Man on Earth,"

says Geryon. "Especially when I don't have a way to get to the mortal plane."

Ran shakes her head. "The Skeleton Man was dealt with by an archangel and a powerful witch. He was sent to Purgatory." She shrugs. "So you visit Purgatory, find him, take the Mask, and return it to Beelzebub."

Although she makes it sound simple, Geryon knows it's far from that. But he still mulls over the possibility. Returning a mask to Beelzebub would certainly work in his favor. He won't have to spend the rest of his years on the run. "How do I get to Purgatory?" he asks cautiously, wondering if Ran's thought of that, too.

Grinning, she lifts her hand and opens it. "With this Travel Stone."

Geryon takes it, weighing his options even as he knows he doesn't have many. The small stone is his one chance at not spending the rest of his life as a fugitive.

He has to go to Purgatory. He has to try to get the mask back.

All it takes is the closing of his eyelids, a thought, and he's there.

Geryon completes a slow turn, taking in the dark replica of what looks like a dense forest that surrounds him. He suppresses a shudder. This is where spirits are sent to await their turn, to await the reapers who will take their souls to Heaven or Hell. He can see why no one would want to stay here for very long. Very little light pierces Purgatory, just enough to cast everywhere in shades of desolation.

Even the small clearing he's in is nothing but gray on gray. A thick mist shifts restlessly, obscuring everything below Geryon's knees. The dark trunks beyond look more alive than Asmodeus's forest, yet they don't move. In fact, the place is...airless. It presses on his chest like a weight, it seems to coagulate in his lungs.

Finding the Skeleton Man quickly is a priority, for more reasons than one.

Geryon takes a step then halts, shuddering at the sensation of *something slimy beneath his boot. He glances down and the mist swirls, revealing a puddle of green sludge. Curling his lip, Geryon steps around it, registering that a trail of droplets are scattered ahead.*

That they lead to a large slab of stone punching up from the ground. He approaches it carefully, registering strange letters etched on the gray surface. Ones he can't read. He grits his teeth, wondering if he'll even find this Skeleton Man.

A subtle movement of air brushes the back of Geryon's neck, making him freeze. Little moves in Purgatory, and especially not the air. He spins around, fists raised and ready to fight.

A man stands a few feet away, no more than atrophied skin on angled bones. That is, when he's not shifting through every human form Geryon's ever seen, and more. The man twitches and the cycling increases as if he's unable to stop it.

"What do you want?" he rasps.

"The Hell mask," Geryon replies. "It does not belong to you."

The cycling stops for a moment, leaving the man once more skeletal and still. "I cannot take it off," he whispers, the words almost a whimper. "It is too powerful."

Geryon narrows his eyes. "You want to take it off?" he asks, surprised.

The Skeleton Man seems to shrink into himself. "I thought... My people needed a way to defend themselves. To protect our sacred land. A group, they called themselves the Legion, promised me they could help. They gave me the mask. And once I put it on, I couldn't take it off."

"You did terrible things under its influence," Geryon states, even though he doesn't know the entire story.

The Skeleton Man flickers through more forms, male, female, old, young, then eventually slows again. "The mask whispers in my head," he says, as if it's a confession. "Terrible, terrible things. It made me do what I did, whether I wanted to or not." He looks down at his emaciated hands, the knuckles visible as if his skin is sheer. "Their blood is on my hands. I know that."

"What is your name?"

The Skeleton Man looks surprised. He thinks for a second, no longer cycling through the countless bodies he's copied. "Malan. My name is Malan."

Geryon takes a slow step closer. "Malan, I need the mask."

The Skeleton Man looks back up, his face more skull than human. "Please take it. I wish to be rid of it. I wish to die."

Relieved this is going to be easier than he anticipated, Geryon moves closer with more speed. Except the moment he's within reach, Malan explodes into a myriad of forms, one after the other.

And every one of them is defined by evil.

He shoves Geryon back, his face now twisted with hatred. "You will never have the mask," he hisses. "Never."

And then he's gone.

All that's left behind is a green pool of sludge.

24

GABBY

Gabby stands outside the second abandoned tenement building for the day, wondering if they're the Legion's go-to. According to Blaise's locator spell, this is where the Skeleton Man is.

Unless he's already moved on like last time and they're about to be trapped in another decoy.

Colt squats down, pointing at something on the ground. "He's here," he states flatly.

The pool of shimmering green goo is a testament to that.

And it turns out, Colt's seen it before.

Gabby mulls over what he told them in the car on the way here. Colt's met the Skeleton Man before. He learned the Skeleton Man hates the mask. That he's suffering because of everything he's done under its influence.

And he learned the mask has a deep, evil hold on him.

All because she trapped him in stone because she thought he betrayed her. Guilt stabs Gabby in the gut all over again. Fate sure has a twisted sense of humor. Even if it's a good thing that Colt's remembering everything that happened to him, even if he's gleaning information that can help them. Heck, even if everything that happened in the past is directly connected to what's happening now, Gabby could do without being the one to have triggered it. She'd impulsively lashed out because she was hurting. It's not a moment she's proud of.

Colt straightens, eyeing the decrepit building with its broken windows and faded brown bricks. "We'll need to be careful. We don't know what state his mind is in after all these centuries."

Hearing Colt talk of centuries reminds her exactly how old he is. Of how much he's seen.

Of how much he's endured, yet survived. No, overcome. And it never destroyed who he is at his core—strong. Determined. Good.

Actually, freaking amazing.

Gabby presses a quick kiss to his cheek, even more resolute that she wants this over and done with. The Tear will be closed. The Legion will be disbanded. Sure, humanity will be saved, but the real prize will be uninterrupted time with her demon. There's nothing she wants more.

Colt flashes her a quick smile. "Thank you."

Her heart does a little loop-de-loop behind her ribs at the sincerity in his voice. Or maybe it's the sexy sparkle deep in his chocolate eyes. Or maybe it's just because he's Colt.

And she's deeply, profoundly in love with him.

Blaise appears on Gabby's other side. "Let's be quick, before he disappears again."

They're about to walk forward when a movement at the entrance has them all freezing. A man, more like a body, appears, shuffling toward them. His clothes hang on his frame like he's little more than a wire coat hanger, his face is beyond gaunt. Gabby has no doubt who it is.

The Skeleton Man.

"I'm here," he rasps in a hoarse whisper. "And I'm not going anywhere."

Colt steps forward, his muscled frame wired to fight. To protect. "Stay where you are."

The Skeleton Man does as he's told, angling his head. Gabby quickly realizes why his face is so harsh and haggard. The skin looks stretched to the point of pain, the angles not quite matching the lines of his skull. It's the mask.

The thing that's controlling him.

That links him to the Legion and makes him their puppet.

"I come in peace," he says, his lips seeming to stretch rather than form around the words. "I need your help, angel."

Gabby doesn't respond straight away. She can feel the evil pulsing around the remains of this man. Yet, she can also sense his desperation. His soul-deep sadness. She has no idea which part of him is speaking to her.

"I tried to help you once," Colt growls. "And you ran."

The Skeleton Man turns his sunken gaze to Colt. "Ah, Geryon. It's been a long time but I'm glad we're meeting again. You can vouch that I want this infernal mask removed."

Colt curls his lip. "Your heart may want one thing, but the Legion has you under their control."

"It's true." The Skeleton Man's bony shoulders droop. "And the control has only grown with time. I've done terrible things in the name of the Legion." His gaze falls on Gabby. "Including taking the gem that can close the Tear."

She narrows her eyes, still skeptical. "You took the gem? We thought that was Pothos."

The Skeleton Man shakes his head, the motion slow and almost painful looking. "I knew that primordial shifter was trying to wreak havoc of the worst kind, so I used the mask's powers to shift into him and stole the gem." His lips pull back, revealing gray teeth in a sad parody of a smile. "I framed him in the same way he tried to frame Geryon."

Colt snorts. "You're trying to make us believe you helped us?"

Blaise and Lydia shake both their heads, clearly not believing the Skeleton Man either.

Yet...

Gabby places a hand on Colt's arm as she keeps her gaze on the Skeleton Man. "What do you want?"

"Only one thing." The Skeleton Man lifts an emaciated hand, pleading. "To be free."

The desperation in his voice is unmistakable. This man is barely living, not quite dead, and has to live with every dark thing he's ever done.

Colt shakes his head. "You said that once before, Malan. But the mask's power was too strong for you to fight it."

The Skeleton Man—Malan—draws in a sharp breath at the use of his name. "You remembered, Geryon," he whispers brokenly. "You remembered."

"I do now." Colt glances at Gabby. "And I've learned some things are worth even the greatest pain."

She holds herself still and strong even as she melts inside. Damn, she wants to kiss that amazing, delicious mouth. It says the most beautiful things.

Malan moves closer, instantly putting everyone on alert. "I know this, too. And I will prove it to you." He draws in a rattly breath. "The Legion knows of your visit to the reservation and your meeting with Yuma. Malcolm Hunsecker has many spies, including that witch of his."

Lydia shifts a little but doesn't speak, much to Gabby's relief. They need to hear what Malan has to say.

"Malcolm knows you seek me." Malan glances over his shoulder at the old tenement building. "So he's laid a trap for you here. I don't know exactly what, but it's inside, waiting for you."

"We've already discovered your traps," Colt snaps. "We were expecting the same. This could be a trap right now."

Malan doesn't take his gaze off Gabby. "If you outwit it, then you need to head to the basement. That's where the demonic weapons are, and the gem you need to close the Tear."

Colt shifts closer to Gabby. "This could all be an elaborate lie."

"There's also a knife there," Malan continues, as if Colt hasn't spoken. "It is a blade that can kill me, send me even beyond Purgatory. It will end me completely. That is what I'm asking of you, angel. To kill me with it."

"He's telling the truth," Gabby says quietly. It's there in the desperation of Malan's eyes. The trembling of his hand. The anguish that is vibrating through him with even more power than the evil of the mask.

Colt shakes his head. "He may mean it now, but when it comes to the moment to remove the mask, he will fight it."

"He's right," Malan says, and Gabby's pretty sure not even Colt expected the agreement. "The Legion controls the mask, which means the Legion controls me. The witch's spell has ensured that. When we meet next, it will be as opponents. I will be your enemy."

"All the more reason to end you now," Colt growls.

"So I can return to Purgatory? And be summoned once more by the Legion?" Malan asks, sounding sad and defeated. "Alternatively, you can get hold of the weapon and once the mask has been removed, kill me. It's the only way to ensure this is done, once and for all. That I am done. I will never be a puppet for the Legion again."

The relief in Malan's voice is evident. As is the longing.

"Okay," says Gabby, eliciting a gasp from Lydia. "I'll do it."

Colt is so still, she's not sure what he thinks, but he doesn't disagree. Instead, he remains silent and strong beside Gabby. Her protector, no matter what choices she makes.

Malan's skeletal body sags with relief. "Thank you, angel." He takes a step back, moving closer to the tenement building. "And to show my gratitude, I will tell you something."

Everyone holds still, waiting.

"Malcolm's created a weapon." Malan glances over his shoulder as if he's expecting the leader of the Legion to be there. "It's powerful enough to kill an angel or a demon."

Gabby goes still. The words ripple through Colt.

Until now, there's been no weapon that powerful.

"Luckily, there's an antidote. A cure."

Gabby's about to ask about it when Malan moves. In one blink, he's a few feet away, in the next he's in front of her, slamming Colt out of the way. Colt roars in fury, but Malan's too fast. His blurred movements are powered by the mask.

He grabs Gabby's hand, his bony fingers cold and hard. Before she can react, he disappears.

Leaving a puddle of green sludge at her feet.

And a vial of shimmering liquid in her palm.

25

COLT

Colt curses in Aramaic. Then Swahili. Then some of the words he's heard on the streets of Los Angeles which shocked even him.

Gabby looks up at him, blinking, then grinning. "Nice summary."

He points to the vial she's now holding. "That could be poison," he warns. "We can't trust Malan. He said himself the mask and the Legion control him."

"I know," she says on a sigh. "But he also escaped them long enough to talk to us. And bring us this."

Blaise shakes her head. "Which could be one of his elaborate illusions. Malcolm could be behind all of this."

"It's exactly something my sister would do," Lydia adds bitterly.

Gabby chews her lip as she debates what to do. She knows they're right. But she also saw Malan's desperation. How much he hates what he's become. If Colt knows his angel, she won't be able to turn her back on that.

"It's probably poison that will cause a slow, painful death," she agrees. "But I'm going to keep this, just in case."

She tucks the vial in her pocket, and although Colt's not surprised, he hopes she doesn't have to find out whether it's an antidote or deadly toxin. At the same time, he can't help but feel proud of her. Gabby's heart is what sets her apart from every other angel.

Blaise turns back to study the tenement building. "We'll have to be careful. There's no telling what other illusions are inside."

Colt thinks of the collapsing basement they believed they were trapped in and his fists clench just as tightly as his gut does. Going inside that building fills him with dread.

And fury.

He's had enough of the Legion and their plans. Colt doesn't have to look up to know the crimson-black sky is lower. He can feel the threat in the air. The Tear is thinning, preparing to rip open and bring Hell to Earth.

Gabby takes a step forward. "Let's find out what they have in store for us, shall we?"

Three silent, sharp nods are her answer as Colt, Blaise, and Lydia fall into step. As they approach the building, he can't help but notice how different this is to most other fights he's approached. And he'd wager even if there are ones he can't remember, they'd have the same stark difference.

He's not alone.

In fact, Gabby looks over her shoulder at him, as if she needs the physical jolt that always happens when their gazes connect. Their hands brush, cementing the connection.

Suggesting he'll never be alone again.

It's a future he never considered until now. He grabs Gabby's fingers and squeezes. One he hopes with everything he has they can explore.

They reach the entrance the Skeleton Man appeared in, finding it empty. Colt uses his demon senses to take in the peeling paint, the scent of mold, the absence of sound. "It appears empty," he says in a low voice.

He takes the lead, finding Gabby right beside him as they enter more fully, Blaise and Lydia close behind them. What used to be a foyer is gutted, the walls marked where things were once attached, and doors missing to what looks like an office and a storage cupboard.

Closed elevator doors and a set of stairs heading to the second floor are the only other things visible.

Blaise strides toward the stairs. "The elevator wouldn't be working."

Colt has no intention of stepping into that metal coffin, anyway.

The stairs creak as they walk up in pairs, the old carpet that used to be on them little more than worms of wool and threads of canvas. The second floor is much like the first. Also gutted and empty. Also smelling of mold and heavy with silence.

Blaise has taken a handful of steps when she stops. Her whole body stills.

"What is it?" Gabby asks in a whisper.

The witch slowly turns to face them. "It's a trap," she mouths.

Lydia gasps. "Yes, I can sense it, too!"

Colt's fists are instantly up, adrenaline injecting into his veins. He doesn't know how the witches can sense it, but he's not going to question it. It was likely this was a trap all along.

Before anyone can say anything else, Colt discovers how the witches sensed the illusion. He can feel it, too. A ripple in the air. The smell of mold is disappearing.

And the room is becoming brighter.

The four contract together as the walls change from gray to white. As lights appear in the ceiling. As polished tiles unveil beneath their feet.

And men appear around the room, guns held and aimed at them.

In the space of a breath, they're no longer standing in an abandoned tenement building. They're in a modern, almost lab-looking office. Surrounded by weapons.

Colt almost smiles. Bullets are futile against him and Gabby. All they need to do is protect the witches as they exterminate every one of these meshugas. They won't stand a chance.

But as Colt reaches for his magic, he frowns. There's no energy to be found. No power greater than what his physical body holds. A quick glance at Gabby reveals the same expression on her face. Blaise and Lydia also seem to be faltering.

No one can access their magic.

"Your magic won't work here," says a male voice on Colt's left.

He spins, prepared to fight every enemy and catch every bullet if he needs to. A man wearing a dark suit is walking toward them, tugging at the cuffs on his pristine white shirt, then adjusting the open collar. His dark hair is neatly combed, feathers of gray at his temples, his crow's feet deepening around his eyes as he smiles coldly.

"Magic dampeners," he explains, the smile growing. "Courtesy of Belphegor, in fact."

Colt stiffens, unwilling to believe Belphegor would stoop to aligning with the Legion.

Satisfaction glints in the man's eyes. "Did you really think that Belphegor would forgive you after what happened in Hell? Traitors are punishable by death, Colt. And Belphegor has asked me to ensure justice is served."

"We came to an understanding," Colt growls. He may not have remembered exactly how deep the betrayal went until recently, but Belphegor recognized that Colt could be useful to him.

The man chuckles as he shakes his head. "You may act as if helping Celeste never happened, but Belphegor has never forgotten, Geryon."

Colt has to suppress another wave of shock. How does Malcolm know his name from all that time ago? And what does the witch Celeste have to do with all this? Instead, he tightens his fists as he narrows his eyes. He has no intention of letting this man know he has no idea what he's talking about. Nor can he afford for the memories to assault him right now.

The man waves an elegant hand as if he's dismissing the topic. "Your foolish choices are not my business." He tugs on his cuffs again, gold cufflinks catching the bright light. "Allow me to introduce myself. Malcolm Hunsecker. The one who is about to end you all."

Colt grinds his teeth together. Not only is the Skeleton Man not here, they're now trapped, possibly in the Legion's headquarters. Surrounded by guns. Without access to their powers.

And Malcolm knows it. He straightens, pacing a few steps one way, then the other as he regards them. "A disgraced demon. An angel of a prophecy. A descendant of a powerful line of witches. And another witch, here to heroically rescue the sister who doesn't want to be rescued." he snorts. "And all as vulnerable as the pathetic humans you bother to protect."

"We'll still kick your ass," Gabby snarls.

Malcolm laughs. "I'd heard you're feisty." The smile drops from his face, his features hardening with such coldness, it's as if it never existed.

Then Malcolm is moving, far faster than a mortal can move. He leaps, spins, and kicks Gabby in the stomach. She staggers backward with a groan, clutching her middle.

"Bastard!" Colt roars, already running toward the leader of the Legion, fury thundering through him.

Two men meet him within a few steps, then two more. Colt

fights, but the butt of a gun slams into his temple and another is rammed into his chest. The other soldiers grab his arms and pull them out painfully, crucifying and trapping him.

Malcolm's already returned to where he was standing before he attacked Gabby. "Don't try any heroics, Geryon," he warns. "You're on my turf now, not roaming Hell like some vigilante."

Colt bares his teeth, once more clueless as to what Malcolm's referring to. "You will not touch her again," he growls.

Malcolm smiles coldly again. "Or you'll do what?"

"I will enjoy ending your life," Colt vows, actually looking forward to the thought.

But Malcolm simply scoffs. "Spare me the empty threats, Geryon, you have no power here." He rubs his hands together, anticipation dancing along the hard edge of his lips. "In fact, you'll never have your power again. It will be mine."

Colt glares at the man, having no doubt he's about to learn what he's talking about.

Malcolm's hungry gaze roams over the four of them. "Especially now that Heaven and Hell are no longer the only place where evolved, supernatural weapons can be manufactured."

The words send ice skating down Colt's spine.

"I'm looking forward to harnessing your powers and making them into weapons." Malcolm draws in a deep breath as if he's filling himself with anticipation. "They'll be terrifying. Some of the greatest I've created so far."

Gabby gasps. "You can't—"

"Take them to the laboratories," Malcolm orders curtly. "I'm looking forward to this."

The remaining men move in, guns raised, as Colt struggles against the two holding him. He cries out in frustration as their grip remains strong and his magic elusive. One soldier grunts while the other scrapes his boot down Colt's shin and crushes his foot. Pain scorches up Colt's leg, but it doesn't stop his struggles.

He can't let Gabby and the others be taken! Experimented on! And their powers permanently stripped from them to be used for evil!

"Don't fight them," Gabby cries out to Blaise and Lydia as the witches raise their hands.

Colt stills as he realizes she's right. Outnumbered and without their magic, they're helpless. Maybe the labs will give them an opportunity to escape.

Two men flank Gabby, gripping her arms in the same way they have hold of Colt's, then four more do the same with Blaise and Lydia. The others keep their guns pointed at their prisoners as Malcolm watches on, a satisfied smile curling his lips.

The men march them to the elevators, ready to take them further into the bowels of this den of evil. The need to fight is overwhelming. The knowledge that the further they go in, the harder it will be to get out pounds through Colt. But he goes passively. One bullet and he's dead.

Or worse. Gabby is.

Blaise is at the front and she's just reached the elevators when a deep, thundering *boom* ripples through the building. The confusion on Malcolm and his men's faces is just what Colt needs to see.

This isn't part of their plan.

The next explosion is louder. Closer. It shakes the walls and the floor shudders so hard that the men holding Colt fall down, taking him with them. A cloud of dust explodes from the stairway, triggering an echo of coughs. Colt scrabbles away from his captors, kicking one when they try to grab his leg, trying to locate Gabby through narrowed eyes.

Gray dust is all he can see, though. It stings his eyes, gets trapped in his throat. He leaps to his feet. "Gabby!"

The apparition that rises above the gray cloud has him stilling. Gabby's wings are extended, their pearl white almost seeming to radiate their own light. But how? How is she accessing her powers?

Then Colt feels it. A tingling in his fingertips. A buzz up his arms. A rush of energy infusing every inch of his body. The explosions destroyed the dampeners.

His own wings snap out, slamming into one of Malcolm's soldiers as they rush at him. Colt rises into the air, grinning.

The fury thundering through his veins is just as potent as his powers.

He's about to rain Hell down on the Legion.

26

GABBY

Colt unfurling his wings is both sexy and invigorating. It tells Gabby things just got serious.

And that war on the Legion has just been declared.

The dust settles on Malcolm's men, aging them as it turns their hair gray and their skin ashen. They don't bother shaking it off as they run at Gabby, Colt, Blaise and Lydia, their faces twisted with violence.

Just as Kenna bursts in with her Order members.

They swarm into the room like a SWAT team, deadly and focused. Gabby realizes they were the ones who must've coordinated the explosions, which not only destroyed whatever was suppressing their magic, but also served as a distraction.

One Malcolm is trying to take advantage of.

He runs toward a door a few feet away from the elevators, punches in a code, and slips through, never looking back.

"Like truck you are," Gabby mutters. There's no way she's letting the leader of the Legion get away. Especially now that she can sense the demonic weapons are close. Without the dampeners, the dark energy pulsing deep beneath them is unmistakable. And it's probable that's exactly where Malcolm is heading.

Colt's already fighting, his focus on being a battering ram as he makes his way through the Legion's men, their bodies crumbling under his assault. Gabby leaps into the fray, knowing he's trying to get to her.

A soldier runs at her, shouting a war cry. She grabs him, spins, and throws him against the wall. He crashes into it and slips to the ground, his head lolling onto his chest. The next attacker is already in front of her, but a kick to the chest sends him flying into the man behind him. With each man down, she's one step closer to Colt.

She notes another soldier focused on her demon, a knife glinting in his hand, and leaps. She lands on his shoulders, snapping his neck as he collapses under her weight. Another soldier tries to attack her, but a member of the Order makes short work of him.

"Felix!" Kenna shouts from somewhere. "Get word to Marlowe. Ask him to attack from the other side."

Gabby glances around, wondering why Kenna's dividing her forces, when she sees why. A horde of demons crash through the windows, spraying shards of glass over the soldiers fighting the Knights of the Order.

"Belphegor!" Colt roars. "Those are his demons!"

Gabby strikes another soldier as she curses internally. Of course Belphegor is working with the Legion. It's just the sort of thing the slimy archdemon would do. She glances at the door Malcolm disappeared through. The leader of the Legion would have all the answers.

Colt appears by her side, snapping out one glorious, powerful wing and hitting a soldier with such force, he slams into three demons behind him, knocking them all over. "Go find him," he says. He must've seen Malcolm escape, and has come to the same conclusion. "I'll work with Kenna and her Knights to finish these bastards off."

Gabby hesitates, but she knows he's right. Malcolm can't get away. Not with the demonic weapons here. She flashes him a glance that tries to jam as much 'I freaking love you' into it as she can, then spins and runs toward the door. She dodges any soldier or demon who tries to attack her, feeling a little like she's in a slalom race, only she's weaving her way through an enemy who wants to kill her.

Gabby reaches the door, and drawing in a deep breath, she calls on her both her magical and physical strength. One ultra-powered kick and the door shatters as if it were made of glass, revealing a well-lit staircase leading downstairs.

"Time to chat, Malcolm," she says, breaking into a run.

She's not surprised to find men coming at her within a few steps. In fact, she's glad. It means she's on the right path. Malcolm would only have these men here if there was something to protect. Gabby comes down on them like an angel with a mission, using her arms, legs, wings as the weapons they are.

One of the soldiers pulls out a semi-automatic rifle, but Gabby twists and turns as she flies, dodging the handful of shots he's fired before she's grabbed the weapon and slammed the butt into his face. He falls backward, falling onto two of his comrades, his body convulsing as the bullets from the gun held by one of them rip through him. Gabby makes short work of them, using the gun like a bat and they're her chance at a home run.

The staircase takes a sharp right, revealing more soldiers and more guns. Gabby doesn't let them slow her down. She uses every inch of the space around the wide staircase, vaulting high, darting low, twisting one way then the other. She knocks the soldiers down like they're bowling pins. The few bullets that have a chance to be fired pepper the walls and ceiling, leaving a splatter of holes where Gabby was a split-second before. Those men are even less likely to live than the others.

She finally reaches a door at the base of the stairs, finding it unlocked. Gabby bursts through it, her heart like a piston. She's in a large room, more white and light like upstairs, but this space has crates stacked to the ceiling on the right.

And the leader of the Tenth Legion standing in the center, a large gun propped on his hip. "I wouldn't come any closer," he warns coldly.

Gabby pointedly takes a step. "I just dodged every other attempt to kill me. That gun won't be stopping me."

Malcolm grins. "Overconfidence. I like it." The grin drops. "It will be your undoing."

"Spare me the attempt to psych me out," Gabby growls. "Is that really how you want to spend your last moments?"

She hasn't finished speaking before she launches into the air and spears toward Malcolm, intent on being her own deadly weapon. It's time to end this.

It's time to end *him*.

Malcolm lifts the gun and points. He fires once. Gabby's ready for it, her mind calculating the trajectory and speed without having to think about it. One shot won't stop her. Malcolm's the one who's being overconfident.

Except the bullet is faster than anything she's ever seen. One second his finger is on the trigger, then next she's falling to the ground, pain like she's never experienced wrenching a cry from her lungs.

Gabby's barely aware of hitting the ground hard enough that she tumbles like a rag doll. She can't. Agony is consuming her. Shredding her.

Devouring her.

She brings her hands to her chest, the point where the pain is exploding from, shocked to feel warm, sticky blood. It flows freely onto her palms as if her body's lost the ability to heal. Gabby groans, but even that sound is weak.

Malan said Malcolm had a weapon that could kill angels and demons...

That means she's...dying...

Gabby gasps as the pain does the impossible and grows. Increases. Flashes through her body like lightning. In fact, black veins are spearing up her arms, splitting and snaking over her skin. It's only a matter of time before whatever poison was in that bullet consumes every last cell.

Through blurred and darkening vision she watches Malcolm walk toward her, a victorious smile climbing up his cold face. He reaches down, grabs her by the hair, and drags her to the back of the basement, leaving behind a smeared trail of blood.

Gabby tries to cry out, except her lips are numb. Her throat is spasming in pain, making it hard to even breathe. It's not even the pain of being dragged by the hair that has her seeing crimson spots. The movement triggers another assault of agony, obliterating anything else that's happening to her body. It's through sheer force of will that she holds onto conscious-ness. Especially when a part of her is begging for the pain free peace of oblivion.

Malcolm heaves her, grunting in satisfaction when she hits the wall and doesn't have the strength to fight it. Her body collapses, then curls into itself, although Gabby has no idea why she's bothering. What's there to protect? The knowledge she underestimated Malcolm? The wound that won't heal because of the poison making its way through her body at an impossible speed?

Malcolm clicks his tongue as he straightens. "I've been watching you for a while now, Gabrielle. And I must say, I'm disappointed. You were supposed to be a worthy opponent."

Gabby couldn't answer even if she wanted to. She can barely think straight, the pain is so overwhelming.

"Yet, here you are, dying," Malcolm continues, disgusted. "The great seventh daughter of an archangel who defeated the Grigori. Nothing but a disappointment."

Those words hurt almost as much as the poison corroding her from the inside out. Because they're true. It should never have come to this.

Malcolm takes a step back, shaking his head. "I wanted to kill you way back when you started poking your nose into the arrival of the Grigori. But the powers ruling Hell convinced me otherwise. They said to let you forge your own doom." He laughs, the sound hard and brittle. "And that's exactly what you did."

Despite the inferno in her veins, Gabby begins shaking. Then shuddering. She feels cold, colder than she ever has before. The brightly lit room darkens further.

She's dying.

"Although I should've guessed. Rather than kill the Grigori you sent them to Heaven, which is exactly where they wanted to be." Malcolm snorts. "Stupid girl. If they can't get their hands on the obsidian, they'll search for a weapon, one that could end us all."

Even in her pain, Gabby knows this is somehow significant. Malcolm's suggesting the Grigori wanted to be sent to Heaven. That there's a weapon there they want to get their hands on.

He waves a dismissive hand as he turns away, treating her like the threat she isn't. "You'll be dead shortly. I'm off to ensure your demon boyfriend meets the same end, as will your friends. When the Tear finally implodes, Hell will become one with Earth. With my evolved demonic weapons, the Legion will rise. We will be the ones to rule them all." He bursts into harsh laughter. "Not that you'll see me in my glory. Because you'll be dead."

Malcolm's laughter follows him up the stairs, the sound almost as chilling as the touch of death worming its way through her veins. Clawing its way to her heart.

Colt.

Just thinking his name hurts as much as the poison. This can't be the end. They had too much more to experience. To feel. To create.

She can't die. She can't leave him.

The thread of defiance, the one that's clinging to life and Colt, has Gabby remembering something else Malan told her. Something he gave her.

Although it feels like her bones are shattering, Gabby reaches into her pocket and removes the vial. It sits in her blood-stained palm, the shimmering liquid a beacon of hope.

Or a guarantee of death.

The Skeleton Man said it was an antidote, a cure for the poison that's slowly killing her. But if he was lying, then it will finish what Malcolm's started. It will kill her.

But it's her only chance.

Gabby yanks off the lid and tips the contents into her mouth. The liquid slides over her tongue, down her throat, and instantly explodes through her stomach. It tears a gasp up her throat. Has her eyes opening wide with shock.

Almost has her laughing with relief.

The pain washes away as if she just swallowed an anesthetic. Gabby pushes to her feet, surprised to find she doesn't even stumble. The wound in her chest is gone, her strength is returning with every second.

The antidote worked! Malan was telling the truth.

Gabby turns to the crates stacked against the wall to her

left. There's no time to revel in coming back from the point of death. Somewhere in those crates is the gem to close the Tear.

And possibly even the weapon to kill the Skeleton Man.

Gabby strides toward it, knowing there's something she'll need to do before either of those. She needs to end the Legion, once and for all.

27

GABBY

Gabby's racing back up the stairs when the sound of clattering footsteps reach her. Although she doesn't slow, she prepares herself to power through whoever's coming at her. She needs to get back to Colt. They need to finish this.

She rounds the corner, her pulse like a freight train, ready to fight, only to drop her fists in surprise. Blaise and Lydia come to a stop, looking equally as astounded.

"Malcolm said he finished you," Blaise gasps.

The roar that echoes from behind them seems to shake the building almost as violently as the explosions did.

"Colt!" Gabby gasps, pushing past the two witches.

If he thinks she's dead, then this place won't be left standing.

Gabby bursts out into the room, instantly finding herself in a battle zone. Kenna's Knights are fighting both the Legion's soldiers and Belphegor's demons. Cries stain the air, as does the coppery scent of blood.

But the fierce fighting isn't what captures her attention.

It's the avenging demon plowing through them like they're

butter. Colt's entire being is a weapon. His fists. His wings. His ferocious fury. They all slice through the enemy in his determination to reach the door Gabby's now standing in. Yet his face is twisted with something else entirely. Agony.

Gabby leaps into the air, her own wings snapping out. "Colt!"

She means to shout the word, but it's barely above a whisper. Seeing his pain has robbed her of the ability to speak. Her demon is hurting because he thinks he's lost her.

Still, his chocolate gaze connects with hers. Widens. Then flares with a kaleidoscope of emotions.

Relief.

Joy.

The knowledge that his world is still turning.

He leaps over the fray of strikes and kicks and snarls, and lands in front of her. The hold he yanks her into is tight. Almost suffocating. And she revels in it, clasping him just as tightly.

"I'm okay," she tells him. She can mention exactly how close to not being okay she was later.

Colt pulls back. "I would've killed Malcolm if he was telling the truth. Now I'm going to kill him for lying just to scare me."

Gabby's lips hover on the edge of a smile. "Yeah, he's dead either way."

The sounds of the battle filter in again. "Gabby!" Blaise shouts, pointing across the room.

Malcolm is standing on the other side of the battle, glaring at them with his lip curled. He spins, yanks open the door he's standing beside, and disappears.

"I don't freaking think so," Gabby mutters.

She and Colt break into flight simultaneously, knocking away any demon or soldier who tries to stop them. Gabby spears one of the Legion's men into the ground, while Colt uses another to bowl over several demons, clearing a path for them.

They fly over Kenna as she yanks a blade out of the throat of another enemy. "You get Malcolm," she calls, already slashing at her next opponent. "We'll take care of these."

Gabby and Colt land a few feet from the door Malcolm escaped through and several Knights rush over, attacking any demons or soldiers who try to move in. They have an unobstructed path to go after the leader of the Tenth Legion.

The air shimmers before the door and the Skeleton Man appears. Malcolm had left him to guard.

"Move out of our way," Gabby demands, suddenly not wanting to have this showdown.

Malan shakes his head. "You know I can't do that. My orders are to stop you from getting any further." He lifts his gnarled fists. "You also know the only way forward is to kill me."

The challenge is unmistakable. As is the pleading in his dark gaze.

He draws in a sharp breath. "You have the weapon. I can sense it."

He's right. Gabby found it buried beneath strange jars of green liquid and metal twisted into shapes she thought only belonged in sci-fi movies. Malcolm wanted it found as much as the gem that can close the Tear. She withdraws the small blade, an owl etched into the hilt.

Malan visibly relaxes. "Finally."

Gabby's gut tightens. The Skeleton Man won't let them past because the Legion have tasked one of the most powerful foes to stop them. Malan has no choice but to obey the decree.

Which is exactly why he wants to escape his existence.

He wants to die.

With a cry, she launches herself at him, raising the knife high, needing this done quickly. Even a mercy killing is still a killing. The moment she's within reach, Malan's bony arm whips out and powers into her chest. Gabby's breath powers out of her lungs as she abruptly changes direction, now propelling back.

Colt catches her and she stays upright. He snarls at the Skeleton Man. "You lying bag of filth."

Malan sneers even as his eyes hold a pleading apology. "My actions are not my own. They are compelled. Malcolm's powers will be even stronger, thanks to the witch."

"He doesn't want to hurt us, Colt," Gabby tells him. Colt doesn't know that the vial Malan gave Gabby saved her life. The Skeleton Man's actions may say otherwise, but he's telling the truth. "You have to trust me on this."

"Of course I trust you," he says, not taking his gaze off Malan. "But that won't stop him from attacking you."

Malan doesn't defend himself. He can't. The truth is, he's going to fight against the death he desperately wishes for.

Gabby lifts the knife once more, glancing at Colt. "Good thing I have you to protect me, then."

She rushes at Malan a second time, Colt's promise making her heart fly higher than her angel wings ever have.

"Always."

This time when she raises the knife, Colt leaps at Malan, blocking the strike the Skeleton Man instinctively throws out. And he doesn't stop his forward momentum. Colt crashes into Malan, shoving him back into the door they're trying to get to.

Malan fights furiously, his body shifting through powerful form after powerful form. One second Colt's battling a wiry skeleton, the next he's ducking the thick fist of a man taller and wider than him, the next he's slamming his elbow into a snarling vampire. Yet he never pauses, never falters. Not when it comes to protecting Gabby.

In fact, as Malan morphs from a snapping half-wolf, half-man, Colt jams his arm across the Skeleton Man's neck and pins him to the door. Malan shifts back to his skeletal form, and Colt uses the opportunity to trap him more thoroughly. He pushes in close, snarling close to his face. "You want this, remember?"

Malan stills. His gaze yanks away from the ferocious demon pinning him to Gabby. "I do want this."

Gabby almost winces at the stark emotion in the eyes of a man who's spent centuries already half-dead. She lifts the dagger and Malan closes his eyes. "Please, angel."

Nodding, Gabby focuses her magic on her hands as she silently repeats the spell Blaise instructed her to use. Her hands lift almost of their own volition, golden strands of light curling from her palms. They twist through the air like serpents, coiling straight toward Malan.

They curve over his face. Over the mask he's been wearing for centuries. He arches his back and screams as the glittering light worms its way between the mask and his skin at his fore-head, his temple, beside his eye sockets.

Malan screeches as the mask slowly peels from his face. The battle pauses, every gaze drawn to the agonized sound shredding the air.

Gabby injects a burst of energy into the glittering threads and the mask falls away, clattering to the ground.

Malan is breathing heavily, the gray skin of his face in tatters. "Finish it," he whispers.

Gabby does it quickly, although she's not sure who she wants to make this more painless for—Malan or herself. Colt shifts at the last moment as the blade thrusts past him and straight into the Skeleton Man's chest.

There's a crackle of bones.

A flush of blood.

Malan arches his back as if he's inviting this. Welcoming it. A smile spreads across his gaunt face as a raspy breath rattles past his lips.

Then he's sliding to the ground, crumbling like a deck of cards. He disintegrates to dust before he hits the floor, the particles fading into nothing.

It's the knife that clatters to the tiles, sounding loud even though a battle still wages around them. It lands beside the mask, and Blaise appears, scooping both of them up.

Colt reaches out to squeeze Gabby's shoulder. "You gave him peace."

She nods, unsure of how she feels. Relieved? Sad?

Furious at Malcolm for torturing a soul for his own end.

Gabby spins to scan the battle, finding Lydia. "Lydia! You need to find your sister!"

Lydia nods, spins, and races away. "I'll help her," Blaise says, also breaking into a run. "A locator spell will be stronger if we do it together."

Gabby and Colt don't waste another second. She yanks open the door and they find themselves in a stairwell. They shoot up the stairs, their feet only touching every second step, intuitively sensing that Malcolm hasn't passed through any doors on the way.

He's gone to the roof.

They burst out on the flat, cement expanse, and it's not Malcolm's presence that has them both stilling. Gabby glances up as dread blooms in her gut. Although this building is only a few stories high, the sky feels almost close enough to touch. It hangs dark and low, the crimson-black clouds turbulent and oppressive.

"It will be soon," Colt says gravely.

The Tear is widening. Hell is looming.

"I have the gem," Gabby says, feeling its weight in her pocket. "But first we have to—"

Malcolm steps from behind a large industrial air-conditioning unit several yards away. "If you're going to say kill me, you'll be sorely disappointed."

Gabby's hands clench into tight fists, hating that he's right. The witch's protection will make sure of that. "That won't stop me from trying."

With a cry, she breaks into a run, Colt beside her. Their wings snap out, giving them an extra burst of speed. Malcolm simply drops his head, glaring at them from beneath his brows as they shoot toward him.

They clash, Gabby striking high while Colt strikes low, but Malcolm doesn't even flinch. He throws a wall of energy out, knocking Gabby and Colt backward with enough force to send them to the edge of the building. Gabby's feet scrape across the cement, Colt's gouging two black lines like his feet are tires. The moment they've stopped they launch forward again, wings beating the air with twice the power of the first attack.

"You're giving me an opportunity to finish what I started in the basement," Malcolm warns, bringing his arms out wide. He slams his palms closed, a sonic boom exploding from the contact.

Gabby and Colt leap high, avoiding the bulk of the energy strike, tumbling over the ripples of air as if they're little more than an obstacle course. They land a few feet from Malcolm, instantly becoming a flurry of movement, a blur of wings and fists and grunts.

Yet Malcolm blocks each and every one, proving exactly how untouchable he is. The moment Colt is close enough, Malcolm executes a spinning kick, his loafer slamming into Colt's chest. He's propelled across the rooftop, his wings spanning out to slow his momentum as his fingers gouge across the concrete roof.

Gabby's attacking before he's stopped. She lets out another cry as she launches high then comes crashing down on

Malcolm like a hammer. Grinning, he lets this strike make contact with his shoulder, letting out a grunt.

But it's almost a grunt of pleasure. Of excitement.

Malcolm grabs Gabby by a wing, spins once, twice, and with a shout of his own, releases her. Gabby's flung high into the air, tumbling and arcing through the crimson night with enough force that there's no way she's going to land on the building. Before Gabby can right herself, she crashes into Colt's arms. He steadies her as he returns them to the rooftop, breathing heavily.

Gabby squeezes his bicep in thanks as they land, once more facing Malcolm. A cold smile expands over his face. "You'll tire long before I will."

Gabby makes a show of stretching her neck and loosening her arms. Although he's right, all they need to do is keep him here long enough for Lydia to find her sister and end the protection spell giving Malcolm supernatural defenses and strength.

Please let that be soon.

"I can't think of a better way to make sure I sleep well tonight," she growls.

A single glance at Colt is all it takes. Wordlessly, they split up, coming at Malcolm from the left and right. This time, Gabby throws out a power ball of her own, the orb of light roaring through the air toward Malcolm.

Except he twists, turns, and sweeps the ball of energy straight past him.

It slams into Colt, throwing him into a tailspin. He tumbles over the rooftop, wings crumpled and limbs flailing.

"No!" Gabby gasps.

Colt tumbles over the side of the building, drawing another cry out of her. A moment later, he powers up, somersaults, and lands back on the roof. Although he seems unhurt, the distraction is all Malcolm needs.

A fist powers into Gabby's gut with enough force to propel her through the air. She slams into the air conditioning unit, the metal grate collapsing inward with the impact. A groan is wrenched out as her head's enclosed by screeching metal.

"Gabby!" Colt cries.

She wrenched herself from the wrecked unit, hissing as a sharp piece of metal scrapes over her arm. Straightening, she feels wetness trickle down and onto her fingertips. Droplets of blood splatter onto the cement.

Colt appears by her side. "You're okay?"

Gabby can already feel her angelic healing working its magic. "Mostly just pissed."

"Good," he says, relieved. "We're going to have to be more careful."

She nods, once more facing the grinning Malcolm. She'll take as many blows as necessary as they wait for Lydia to end the protection spell.

Assuming the witch does...

Gabby shakes away the thought. Above her the sky rumbles ominously, reminding her they need to end this, and it has nothing to do with the beating they may take. The Tear is widening. The veil between Hell and Earth is thinning.

If that happens, Malcolm being alive will be the least of their problems.

Malcolm walks slowly to the left, not looking like he's even broken a sweat. "The Tear will be open soon," he says with relish as they begin to circle each other. "And the Legion is ready. With our weapons, we'll subjugate every demon. Those who refuse will die. Earth will be mine to rule."

Gabby's heart stutters. Malcolm wants the Tear to open. He wants the apocalypse.

Shit.

Gabby and Colt break into a run, the realization spurring

the next attack. This time, they're faster, smarter. More focused on defense than offense.

It means they land fewer hits, but they're spared from being struck themselves. Gabby narrowly ducks a fist flying to the head. Colt leaps over a kick aimed for his gut. They become a blur of black and white around Malcolm, trying for jabs, telling themselves each strike that gets past his defenses is a victory.

Except they're tiring.

Their healing will start to take longer.

Their reflexes will slow.

When Colt blocks a strike, spins, and slams an elbow into Malcolm's face, Gabby assumes the following grunt and spray of blood is Colt's. That somehow Malcolm slipped in a punch to the face.

But Malcolm stumbles backward, bringing his hand to his face. He looks down at his fingers, eyes widening when he registers what Gabby and Colt have.

They're smeared with blood.

Malcolm slowly straightens, more crimson dripping onto his shirt. Knowledge settles on his shoulders as the edges of his lips turn down. The protection spell has been broken.

Gabby allows herself a few panting breaths as her body heals in preparation. Now the fight is far more equal.

Malcolm's lips twist. "Do you really think I'll let you kill me?"

He breaks into a run, but it's not toward Gabby and Colt. It's straight for the edge of the building. He leaps as his feet leave the cement, arching his arms out wide as if he can fly.

Except he can't.

Gravity yanks Malcolm's body down, jerking him out of sight.

Long seconds stretch out as Gabby tries to process that they just won, yet the victory feels hollow somehow.

"I wanted to do that myself," Colt growls.

Gabby understands what he means. Seems she's willing to kill if it means evil is stamped from this world.

She and Colt run toward the place Malcolm just jumped, stopping to look over the edge.

"Where..." Gabby asks, frowning.

There's no body sprawled on the hard ground several stories down. Only a pool of blood.

"I can't feel his aura anymore," Colt says, also frowning. "He must be dead."

Yet there's no physical proof.

"Gabby."

The way Colt says her name has her looking up, a heavy feeling already lodged in her throat. Her eyes narrow as she realizes the horizon is shifting. Morphing.

Then they widen as she realizes why.

An army of demons are storming toward the building, black wings a rippling background to countless crimson eyes.

And Belphegor is at the front, encased in armor.

A jagged bolt of red lightning cracks behind Gabby and Colt, making the building shudder. It also illuminates the mammoth strength of Belphegor's army. There are hundreds, probably thousands, of demons closing in.

"Belphegor always wanted the Tear," Colt says, sounding as if he's coming to the realization himself. "He's going to try and stop you."

Gabby looks up, her pulse jackknifing when she sees more crimson eyes dotted in the sky. The Tear is even thinner. It's only a matter of time before even more demons descend on Earth.

Colt grips Gabby's upper arms. "You stay here and use the gem to close the Tear. I'll keep Belphegor and his demons at bay."

"What? That's a terrible idea!"

Colt may be strong and one heck of a fighter, but he's sorely outnumbered.

He shakes his head. "I'll be fine. I've faced Belphegor's army before." His lips settle into a grim line. "I remember now. I remember everything."

28

COLT

"The apocalypse is nigh, Geryon." Ran's face is grim as she leads him to Asmodeus's library. "The Sins are close to whatever they have been trying to achieve. We can't let that happen."

Asmodeus turns as they enter, his own expression heavy with the truth. "And the truce is no more. I cannot contact Belphegor, and Beelzebub is refusing to ally with us."

"Which means we do this alone," Ran finishes. She picks up an open grimoire sitting on a table. "And we have the spell. If we can't stop the Sins, we can at least put them to sleep."

Geryon narrows his eyes. "And how do we do that?"

Ran waves her hand over the grimoire and seven vials of dark powder appear. "With these."

"I'll command my demon army to protect you, Geryon," Asmodeus adds. "You take care of the Sins."

"I cannot be in seven places at once," he replies, shaking his head. Much confidence is being placed on his abilities. Unfounded confidence.

Ran steps forward, extending the vials in her palm. "But you could project seven doppelgängers," she says, a glint in her dark eyes.

Geryon frowns. "It's not that simple. That sort of spell takes a lot of energy. And if one doppelgänger is killed, I'll lose that power."

Suddenly, a shudder rips through the castle, strong enough to make Ran stumble.

Asmodeus's face turns grim. "They've started." He strides toward Geryon, clasping his arm. "There's no more time for talk."

A flicker of the archdemon's other hand and Geryon finds they're standing in an expansive wasteland. Stepping away from Asmodeus, he executes a slow turn. In the distance, seven shimmering figures stand as if at seven points of a star. Energy rises from them, each a different color—crimson red, deep blue, coral pink, emerald green, dark purple, bright yellow, fiery carmine—yet they all progressively turn black as they twist toward each other and into the sky.

Toward the Tear.

The clouds above shift like a stormy sea, agitated and turbulent. The wisps of onyx power curl into the shifting black, creating a pulse of energy that separates the mist. Progressively thinning the veil between Hell and Earth.

Unsure whether it's even going to work, Geryon closes his eyes and summons his power. His lips moving silently, he amplifies it until it feels bigger than himself. Then he divides into seven, opening his eyes to see seven versions of himself materialize.

And they're each holding a vial of dark powder.

Simultaneously, they turn and break into a run, focusing on a Sin as they streak across the wasteland. Geryon feels like he's holding his breath. It's possible the Sins can be stopped.

"Geryon."

Asmodeus says his name in a low voice. Like a warning. Geryon turns, already sensing they're not alone. Asmodeus's soldiers surround them, but it's the demons beyond them that have Geryon's stomach turning to lead.

An army of demons clad in armor and carrying every infernal weapon possible are closing in.

With Belphegor at the helm.

ONE FIERCE, passionate kiss is all Colt allows himself before leaping off the building. His last vision is of Gabby's beautiful face pinched with worry, then she's turning away, too.

She needs to use the gem to close the Tear.

He needs to stop Belphegor and his army, just like he did centuries ago.

Colt slices through the air, the wind whipping at his hair as he registers Kenna and her Knights pouring out of the building, also intent on fighting the demons.

War has truly broken out.

Colt keeps his focus on his target, though. Belphegor is decorated in black armor, a three-horned helm on his head. Colt lands in front of him, his wings outstretched as he stalks forward. "You always wanted the apocalypse, Belphegor."

He would've refused the truce that day in Asmodeus's castle whether Mazikeen attacked him or not. Just like he tried to help the Sins open the Tear.

Just like he's trying to stop Gabby from closing it this time.

Belphegor extends his arms out wide, his demon army twitching with agitation behind him. "I sided with the Sins, why would I not use someone as power hungry as Malcolm and his Legion?"

"For what, Belphegor?" Colt roars in frustration. "For power?"

"To free Lucifer," Belphegor shouts back. "An apocalypse will break open the cage and his Lord will finally reign his fury on those who betrayed him. The angels will pay!"

"And he'll have you to thank," Colt spits.

"His second in command." Although Belphegor's face is shielded by the helmet, the smile in his voice is apparent. As is the dark anticipation. "Here we are once more, Geryon. Are you ready for a rematch?"

Colt's hands are hot fists at his side. "This time, I will finish you."

Belphegor throws his head back and laughs. "Last time you ran, Geryon, like the coward you are. There will be nowhere to hide this time."

The archdemon launches into the air. A deafening battle cry erupts from his demons as they take to the sky. More shouts of war echo around Colt as Asmodeus's soldiers and Kenna's Knights also power forward. Grunts and cries fracture the silence.

Yet Colt doesn't take his gaze off Belphegor. He lets out his own battle cry. A promise. A vow.

It's time to end this, once and for all.

GERYON WATCHES *as hordes of demons spread out, moving to the seven points the Sins are standing on. The same places his doppelgängers are running toward. Crimson lightning spears from the turbulent sky, hitting the ground around the Sins with thunderous cracks. Energy is amassing. The Tear is preparing to rupture.*

All Geryon can hope is that Asmodeus's soldiers protect his doppelgängers. There's no time to reach them.

And Belphegor won't let him.

"You think you're clever, don't you, Geryon?" the archdemon sneers, slowly circling. "But there's no stopping this."

"Siding with the Sins?" Geryon spits. "With the darkness of the obsidian?"

Belphegor yanks back his shoulders, glaring through the slit in his helmet. "I'm the only one willing to do what it takes to save Lucifer. He will reward me for that."

Geryon shakes his head. "His thirst for revenge does not run this deep. He wouldn't want the destruction of humanity."

"We're going to find out, aren't we?" Belphegor's hands open and close, his black armor catching flashes of the crimson lightning. "Because all I have to do is kill you and the doppelgängers are gone. The Sins will complete what they've started."

"You need to be alive to do that," Geryon growls, leaping as he releases a war cry that ripples across the wasteland.

He vaults high, his arms wide as he summons his magic. Heat explodes from his core, crackling down his limbs, pooling in his palms. A roar builds in his chest. He becomes an explosive preparing to detonate.

Belphegor curses, then conjures a purple shield to obscure his form.

MORE THAN WILLING for history to repeat itself, Colt powers down on the shield Belphegor is hiding behind. His fist slams into the ornate surface, his magic rippling out like a bomb blast. The shield explodes and the archdemon stumbles backward with the impact, his helmet landing several feet behind him.

The shield didn't last long the previous time, either.

Colt uses his magic to lift Belphegor into the air, preparing to slam him into the ground like a hammer.

But Belphegor laughs. "You forget I taught you everything you know, Colt."

The archdemon shoots out his own magic, shoving Colt backward and breaking his concentration. Belphegor lands nimbly on the pavement, rotating as he summons more energy, then sending more bolts of energy at Colt.

A wave of his arms and Colt redirects the deadly attack. A demon screams to his right, and although he internally winces, he doesn't drag his gaze from his enemy. He's never relished killing his own, but he also knows there's no stopping dark demons. The thirst for power that Belphegor has infused them with is unstoppable.

And if killing them means protecting Gabby and everything they're trying to achieve, so be it.

"You can't win this fight," Belphegor growls, slowly stepping sideways Colt as his dark gaze looks for an opening. "You're not as strong as I am, and you know it."

"None of that stopped me last time," Colt snaps, mirroring Belphegor's movements so they're slowly circling each other, each trying to take the title of predator rather than prey.

Belphegor throws his head back, his laughter hearty, yet ominous. "And you think you're stalling me."

Colt slowly comes around until he's facing the opposite way and Belphegor's back is to the building. It's then that he sees it.

Remembers what Belphegor's plan was all along.

It was to stall Colt.

Demons are scaling the walls of the building. Others are descending from above.

There's only one person who's their target.

Gabby.

A cold, hard smile spreads across Belphegor's face. "Here we are again, Colt. You have a choice to make. Fight me or save her?"

GERYON CONJURES A BLACK BROADSWORD, *swinging it above his head in a large arc, then slashing it through the air. Belphegor leaps high, blocking it with a burst of magic, then shoots out an offensive attack. Geryon blocks the crackling ball of fire with the powerful blade, deflecting it. A demon screams in pain, the sound quickly dissolving into garbled groans.*

Geryon doesn't take his focus from his old mentor. Nothing will distract him. He will finish this.

He's just lifted his sword once more when someone calls his name. And it's a voice that doesn't belong on this battlefield. One he can't ignore.

Mazikeen stands to his left, holding Ran against her chest, a knife to the smaller demon's throat. "Hello, Geryon."

A low chuckle ripples from Belphegor. "What will you do, Geryon? Fight me or save your little friend?"

Geryon ignores the archdemon, his hand flexing around his sword as he levels his gaze on Mazikeen. This isn't a choice he wants to make—if he attacks Mazikeen, Belphegor will be free to open the Tear. If he chooses Belphegor, Ran is dead.

Even if Mazikeen was clearly working with Belphegor all along.

"Let her go, Mazikeen," *he says, his voice low.* "This isn't you."

"You're wrong. This is exactly who I am," *the demoness growls.* "The shifter gave me what I've always wanted—power. No one will ever use me again."

"Release her," *Geryon tries again.* "Killing Ran will not prove your strength. It will be something you regret."

Mazikeen's arm tightens around Ran, digging the tip of the dagger into her neck. "No, I won't. It will be a mercy. She's as power-less as I was." *A drop of blood oozes down Ran's neck.*

"It's the hate talking," *Geryon says, his gaze flicking to Ran. The little demoness's face is impassive, even as the blade pierces deeper.* "You don't want what Belphegor and the Sins are planning."

Something flickers across Mazikeen's face, and for a brief moment, Geryon thinks he's getting through. Maybe there's a way to get past the hate consuming her.

But then she curls her lip. "Caring for this little demon makes you weak—"

Ran elbows Mazikeen in the stomach, twists, and breaks into a run. Mazikeen screeches, then throws the dagger at Ran's back. Geryon shoots a bolt of magic, intercepting it, and it clatters to the ground.

Mazikeen lets out another furious screech, her eyes flaring crimson as she glares at Geryon. Then, she disappears.

A quick scan of the area reveals Belphegor is also gone.

"Coward!" Geryon roars, spinning one way, then the other. "I do not regret my choice!"

Even if it now means that Belphegor will hunt him for as long as they both exist, Geryon would choose to help Ran. Even if he failed in helping Mazikeen, he would still choose to try.

"Asmodeus has a plan," Ran quickly assures him, although she's now looking nervous in a way she didn't when Mazikeen held a blade to her throat. "He said he did."

There's no chance for Geryon to respond because a thunderous boom rips through the wasteland, powerful enough to rock the ground.

Geryon and Ran spin around, registering that seven red glows now emanate at each of the Sin's locations. Seven shadows—Geryon's doppelgängers—are little more than shimmering figures in the piercing light, yet it's clear what each one of them are doing.

They're throwing a small object. The vials.

"The spell's complete," Ran breathes.

The Sins suddenly stretch taller and blaze brighter. Above them, the lightning intensifies.

And then they're shrinking, tumbling to the ground. The turbulent sky stops moving. The clouds lose their crimson taint.

The fight's been lost.

The Tear is closing. The portal between Hell and Earth is fusing shut.

The energy amasses in the center of the seven points, forming a bright ball of light. The sonic boom that explodes outward knocks Geryon onto his back. He gasps, blinking as his lungs seize from the impact. Blackness hovers in his periphery.

He holds onto consciousness with sheer force of will, but as the world comes back into focus, it's changed.

A thatched roof is above his head. The faint scent of smoky herbs hangs in the air.

Geryon leaps to his feet, trying to understand what's going on. Ran said Asmodeus had a plan to save him...

A woman enters the hut carrying a wooden bowl. "Hello, Geryon."

"Where...where am I?" he gasps.

She smiles, her face soft and relaxed. "My name is Celeste, and I summoned you here. There's something I need your help with."

COLT SNEERS AT BELPHEGOR. "My choice is the same. It always will be."

He will always protect. It's the only way he's able to live with honor, despite being a demon. Despite being a demon who's been hunted for centuries for something he didn't do.

Belphegor leaps over him, landing between Colt and the building. "Think about it, Geryon. Do you really want to be here again in a few centuries? Do you really want me hunting you every one of those days and nights?"

"My name is Colt," he bites out. "And my choice. Is. The. Same."

He launches into the air with a powerful stroke of his wings,

Belphegor's roar of rage as close as he expected. Yet the blow Colt expects never comes. A glance over his shoulder reveals Asmodeus grappling with Belphegor.

"Go, Colt!" he shouts. "Stop the Tear!"

Colt powers through the air, no longer glancing back. Beneath him, the battle continues between Belphegor's demons and Asmodeus's soldiers and Kenna's Knights. For every two demons they slash, one breaks past their defenses. Those are the ones now arrowing toward the top of the building.

Toward Gabby.

A demon ahead spears at Colt, his clawed fingers extended, but Colt twists, slams his clasped fists down on the demon's temple, and continues on as it falls into a death spiral. Three more try to attack him mid-air, but Colt has battled both on land and above it.

And he has every intention of reaching his angel.

He simply sweeps past one, snapping out the edge of his wing to knock it away. Then pummels the next until his unconscious body drops like a dead weight. The final one falls, his wings on fire after a bolt of magic.

Colt lands on the rooftop, instantly finding Gabby. She sits in the center, bright white surrounding her as the gem hovers before her eyes. She frowns intently as demons throw themselves at the barrier she's erected around herself, bursts of light deflecting them back. One laughs as he runs forward to do it again, even throwing an orb of fire at the shell, laughing even harder when it's absorbed into the surface.

They know they can't breach the protective bubble. But they also know that Gabby's dividing her powers with the protection spell.

She doesn't have enough energy to use the gem to close the Tear.

The sky above is now a violent red, glimpses of the Hell Colt escaped all those centuries ago now visible. Crimson lightning arcs to the building and the land surrounding it, like fingers reaching down and trying to gain purchase.

Colt lets out another battle cry as he conjures his broadsword. It appears in his hands as he's swinging, the onyx blade slicing through the air. And two of the closest demons. They screech with pain as the weapon deals swift justice.

Colt becomes a blur of slashes as he carves his way around Gabby's protective barrier. The sword becomes an extension of himself. Of his ruthless determination. Demons fall away, blood pouring from slashes to their chests, their abdomens, their throats. But he doesn't slow. He thrusts through hearts. Slices away limbs.

And with each blow, Gabby becomes stronger.

The gem glows brighter and floats higher, illuminating the bloody scene around her. Suddenly, seven shafts of light spear from its center, arcing out like a star. They come together again several feet above the gem, exploding into a ball of light.

They shoot upward, straight toward the center of the Tear. It collides with the crimson clouds and bursts, blasting outward like an ivory supernova.

Colt almost smiles. The Tear is closing.

They won.

The howls that rise from beyond the building have his eyes widening in shock. Colt runs forward a few steps, gazing out at the battlefield. Black smoke is pouring out of the demons and flying upward into the sky. The human bodies the demons possessed drop to the ground, turning to ash. Dead.

Even Belphegor's and Asmodeus are exorcized, their smoky forms dragged back to Hell.

Colt gasps as he feels a tug in his chest. He clamps his arms around his middle, as if he can stop this, his sword clattering to the ground. If every demon here, including the archdemons, is being returned to Hell, so is he.

They may have won.

But he's lost Gabby.

A mark glows on his inner arm and he gasps again, recognizing the rune.

Colt straightens, registering that the last of the demons are leaving their human shells. Yet he's still here. He brushes his fingers over the mark he didn't even know had been branded on his body, knowing who put it there.

A powerful witch named Celeste.

Bright light ripples past him, exploding out over Mercy City. Colt turns around and is running before his next thought has formed. He catches Gabby as her body crumples, carefully lowering her to the ground.

She smiles weakly up at him. "You know I love you, right?"

29

GABBY

Gabby lifts a hand to caress the handsome, concerned face peering down at her, surprised at how weak she feels. Yet nothing is going to stop her from touching her demon. Not when it's what she wants to spend the rest of her life doing.

Colt grasps her hand and presses a kiss to her palm. "Are you okay?"

She nods. "Yeah, just tired." She grins. "It was quite a spell, huh?"

He lets out a huff as he smiles, too. "It certainly was."

One that was only possible because Colt fought for her. Her avenging demon. Her sweet protector.

"Thank you," she whispers, her heart thudding against her ribs. Beating for Colt.

"I love you, Gabby," he whispers back, the words almost hoarse. "And I'll never stop loving you. Protecting you. Giving my all to you."

Her heart melts and pounds harder, all at once, but before she can tell him that she plans on loving him a whole lot harder than that, Colt scoops an arm under her shoulder. "Let's get you somewhere safe, so you can heal."

Gabby finds her legs are far more stable than she expected. In fact, the dizziness in her head is already dissipating. She squeezes Colt's bicep in thanks. "I'm already feeling better."

He looks at her dubiously. "Still, you need to rest."

To be perfectly honest, they've both earned one.

Gabby turns to gaze out over the area surrounding the building. It's the strangest mix of destruction and hope she's ever seen. Ash covers the trees, every roof, even the ground. Knights are moving around, looking a little shell-shocked. Countless lives have now ended, collateral damage because a demon possesses them.

Yet, humans are appearing, exiting from buildings or walking down the pavement, looking around in confusion. No doubt clueless to the disaster that was just averted, yet aware that something significant has happened. A few talk into their cells, wiping a tear or smiling a watery smile. Maybe they sense that lives have been lost, even if they'll never know where or how.

Gabby leans into Colt, letting out a slow breath. "We did it."

He squeezes her close. "It's over."

She looks up at him, her gaze tracing the strong lines of his face, the tousled wine-colored hair, the chiseled lips. "Actually, I think it might just be beginning."

A slow, delicious grin spreads across Colt's handsome face. It holds the promise of every tantalizing image that's rising in her mind. The two of them touching. Kissing. Free to revel in the impossible love that has grown between an angel and a demon.

"Yes, it is just beginning."

Gabby and Colt spin around in surprise. She frowns as her father lands on the rooftop, Moroni at his side.

He sweeps his gaze out over the area beyond the rooftop. "We will wipe the memory of anyone who saw something," her father states matter of factly.

Gabby nods, wincing a little. "That would be best."

In some ways, it'll be as if this never happened.

"You come here? Now?" Colt demands in a low voice. "After we ended this, you want to take credit for cleaning up?"

Moroni glances at Colt's arm, wrapped around Gabby's shoulder. He snorts in disgust. "You thought your unholy connection was the solution?"

Gabby's father slices his lieutenant a glance, but he doesn't admonish him. Instead, he settles a heavy look on her. "We came here because we have news."

"All this was nothing but a distraction," Moroni spits, throwing his arm in the direction of the destruction. "We have bigger issues at hand."

Every muscle in Gabby's body freezes. All apart from the ones in her hands, clinging to Colt. Those ones tighten. Clutch him with everything she has. "What news?"

Colt's just as still as she is as they wait for the answer. He, too, can sense this is significant.

That it's probably going to change everything.

The archangel before them lets out a sigh, one low and deep enough to drop his shoulders. "The Grigori have escaped their prison."

Ready for the next installment in the Keepers of the Light series? Check out FORBIDDEN ANGEL!

FORBIDDEN ANGEL

An old enemy has risen.
The thirst for the obsidian never died.

She's the seventh daughter of an archangel. He's a demon wanted by the Kings of Hell. Despite it all, they've fallen in love. Yet Gabby and Colt can't escape who they are.

Even with secrets in Heaven and ancient enemies in Hell waiting for them, they're going to have to face their differences. All so they can find the legendary spear with the power to end it all.

To do that, the spear's three shards must be located. The search will take them to a mysterious island with new beings long thought to be extinct. Have they just discovered a new ally? Or another enemy...

An edgy, epic new adult romance for fans of the Fallen Saga and the Hush, Hush series. Lose yourself in the paranormal heaven that is Forbidden Angel today!

GRAB YOUR COPY HERE
https://mybook.to/ForbiddenAngel

THE KEEPERS-VERSE IS ALWAYS GROWING!

The Keeper Chronicles will continue to grow, with each new addition adding to its epicness. Each interlinked series will have you falling for unforgettable characters, being swept away by captivating romance and thrilling adventure, and re-visiting old friends (you'll discover all your favorites popping up when you least expect it!).

Dive in at any series!

Keepers of Excalibur
A fated love. A cursed wolf.
A supernatural war only they can stop.
Check out Book 1, Wolf Marked, HERE

Keepers of the Chalice
A vampire. A huntress.
A cure that will change everything.
Check out Book 1, Vampire Unleashed, HERE.

Keepers of the Grail

THE KEEPERS-VERSE IS ALWAYS GROWING!

Seven Gates of Hell. Seven deadly sins.
One impossible choice.
Check out Book 1, Gates of Demons, HERE.

HAVE YOU READ THE KEEPER CHRONICLES PREQUEL?

As an exclusive for my subscribers,
you can download it for free!!

When Sierra sneaks out, determined to escape her over-protective family, she stumbles across a young man covered in blood. His last words are a plea. *Find the Grail Keepers. Warn them.*

Ryder is the young cop who was last seen with the murdered victim. Sierra doesn't trust him, no matter how drawn she is to him. Except it turns out they're both looking for the same thing—the Holy Grail.

They're quickly drawn into a dangerous hunt involving cryptic clues, a mysterious stone, and a Grail that hasn't been seen for centuries. One that leads to more questions than answers. Can Sierra trust her impulsive emotions? Should she believe Ryder's words or the truth she sees in his eyes? And ultimately, should she follow her heart?

Especially when every decision will decide the fate of countless lives.

CLICK HERE TO DOWNLOAD FOR FREE!

https://BookHip.com/TTBMTTV

ALSO BY TAMAR SLOAN

PRIME PROPHECY SERIES

He failed to shift like every one of his ancestors.

Until he met her.

KEEPERS OF THE GRAIL

The legendary Holy Grail is real.

Yet everything known about it is a lie.

KEEPERS OF THE CHALICE

A vampire. A huntress.

A cure that will change everything.

KEEPERS OF THE LIGHT

Angels and demons have battled for millennia.

Their inevitable war has begun.

KEEPERS OF EXCALIBUR

A fated love. A cursed wolf.

A supernatural war only they can stop.

DESTINED DEMIGODS

Love that defies the gods.

Powers that define destiny.

ELEMENTAL GAMES

Elemental powers. Deadly Games.

No escape.

THE SOVEREIGN CODE

Humans saved bees from extinction...and created the deadliest threat we've seen yet.

THE THAW CHRONICLES

Only the chosen shall breed.

ZODIAC GUARDIANS

Twelve teens. One task.

Save the Universe.

About the Author

Tamar hasn't decided whether she's primarily a psychologist who loves writing, or a writer with a lifelong drive to make a difference. She must have been someone pretty awesome in a previous life (past life regression indicates a Care Bear), because she gets to do both. She divides her time between helping families and writing emotion driven YA stories set in amazing imaginary worlds that surprise even her.

The driving force for all of Tamar's writing is sharing and connecting. In truth, connecting with others is why she writes. She loves to hear from readers. Find her on all the usual social media channels or her website, www.tamarsloan.com where can download one of her books for free.

(Seriously, I LOVE hearing from you guys!)